Itching Against Ignorance

A Sharp Investigations Novel

Book Eight

BY: E. N. CRANE

EDITED BY: A. O. NEAL

Dedication

Thank you to my dogs: Perry and Padfoot. Their shenanigans, antics and behavior are the model for all things Winnie.

Thank you to my husband, for keeping me in coffee and snacks. Thanks to my mom for always being there to edit at the last second because I'm a hardcore procrastinator. Y'all have no idea how close these come to never happening.

Special thanks to my boss in planning for letting me make a character based on her. She really is that badass.

Chapter One: Overwhelming Generosity

"If I move this one here... and that one there..."

My hands looped the blood red yarn around pushpins surrounded by the images of every resident of Sweet Pea, Ohio. It was like a mural of murder victims, taken while they were dripping blood-yarn in the final howls of death. None of the images were flattering, none of them taken with consent or the intent of establishing reasonable allegation. Reasonable was beyond me at this point.

We were in blind blame territory and this entire mural was just for my own sick amusement.

A cackle slipped out as I looped another piece of yarn and circled a single picture repeatedly. It was her... it had to be. No one else would have the power to orchestrate such a targeted attack of generosity.

And no one else would risk incurring my wrath... Assuming I had any.

The jury was still out.

"I'll get you my pretty..."

"Please don't tell me you've lost it."

My skin jumped away from its muscles while I whirled around, brandishing the sharpest object available to me at the source of the voice.

A thumbtack.

Against Mrs. Margot.

She was 100 when I was a child, which meant she was probably a thousand now... or a supernatural being. Vampire, werewolf, mummy... something that looked dead but wasn't.

"Will you put that damn thumbtack down and stop trying to figure out what immortal being I am? We've been over this. I'm only 85! And I can't be taken out with a thumbtack. Remember? You tried when you were six, Cynthia."

My lavender eyes flutter down at her shrunken frame.

"I don't remember... I was six. And only a vampire would know that I was trying to figure out if she was a vampire. I'm getting garlic!"

Spinning on my foot, I turned toward the rear of my office and the door to my apartment above. The entire space was about 900 sq ft, divided into two levels so I could easily get up there and back before Mrs. Margot could hobble out on her walker. Usually, I didn't have garlic cloves, but there was always garlic salt in my cabinet.

It would be perfect for taking her out if she was a vampire *or* a snail.

My first step collided with the hefty fur log half pressed against my leg.

Gravity brought me down, my body falling the almost six feet between my head and my feet. Consciously, I angled myself away from the German Shepherd Malinois mix on the floor to prevent undo trauma. With the number of times I tripped on her, you'd think she'd learn to give me some room.

She might argue that since she was always *right next to me*, I should take care to go around her.

I landed shoulder first, head tucked against my shoulder. My outstretched arm flopped down onto Winnie's tail, and she screamed. The impact sent a sharp stabbing pain down my arm with a loud *pop*, and I joined her in an agonizing howl. I was used to falling, and being injured, so it wasn't as much about pain as just a primal need to scream.

For hours, into the sky while cursing the world.

Maybe not the entire world, but cursing Florida, bigots and men sounded right... though Florida was already cursed, so maybe that was a waste of a curse.

If curses were like wishes and you only got three, someone definitely already took care of Florida.

I could use my third one to curse chickens, goats or whoever designed coffee bags with that inadequate glue on the foldy-tab so it fell off when you tried to open the bag and you were forced to rely on that clear sticker.

Where was I going with this? My brain acknowledged its own rambling even as my mouth continued screaming like an overly dramatic poltergeist. Instead of mental relief, my throat became dry and scratchy, my brain continued to hum with thoughts and curses, every part of me a contorted mass of ruminations and pain I could never piece together.

"Will the pair of you shut up? At least one of you is fine and the other screaming about it will do absolutely nothing to fix you. Honestly, Cynthia, you and the whole Sharp family are the most dramatic lot of fornicators..."

"La la la.... I am not listening," I shouted over her, refusing to hear any more allusions to my parents' sex life that was both public knowledge and public spectacle.

Absolutely nothing was private about their private lives and I, for one, knew more than enough.

They say no one wants to know how the sausage gets made, but an up-close look at how you got made is far more traumatizing.

It also, strangely, involves sausage.

Taking a few deep breaths and closing my mouth, I declared myself screamed out. My brain wasn't as easily quieted, pondering the meaning of life, the universe, and everything... I know it was supposed to be 42, but aside from that movie about baseball and my brother's age, it didn't offer any real insight.

Maybe I needed to be 42 to get it... a question for Seth if his daughter hasn't killed him.

Mrs. Margot cleared her throat with an unnecessary amount of indignation, and I put on my sweetest fake smile.

"How can I help you?"

Directing my question at the fiberglass tiles and metal supports that comprised my ceiling, I gave up the smile. Actually, it was Mrs. Margot's ceiling. She owned the building, including my office and the studio apartment above it where I lived and slept... when I wasn't slowly losing my mind and refusing to sleep. Aside from my one-woman crusade to stop the unwanted generosity of townsfolk, I was dealing with an existential crisis that followed the celebration of my twenty-ninth birthday and separation from my long-term on again off again Larry.

In one year, I would be thirty and all of my "quirks" would solidify into permanent personality traits... I wasn't ready to be permanently anything.

"Are you going to get off the floor?"

It was phrased as a question, and yet it didn't feel optional. Once, in a fit of insomnia and irrational fear, I'd tried to count the black dots in each of my ceiling tiles. After 1,989 spots, I was cross-eyed and no closer to sleep or legal insanity. That had led to trying to count Winnie furs before ending with counting coffee beans and dividing them one bean at a time into the six dozen coffee cups that had appeared in a twenty-minute period.

Which was only... I glanced at the white clock on my wall with black arms and black numbers on a white face. It looked like the clock in every schoolroom, ever. The sight brought back memories of bullying, friendship and Larry... it haunted me so stunningly.

5

I should stop looking at the clock.

Why was I looking at the clock?

"I repeat, Cynthia, get off the floor!"

Right, I was trying to figure out how long it had been since I tried to count the ceiling tile dots...

The answer was six hours.

Or 12 hours... without the AM/PM designation, I couldn't be sure what was day or night anymore since I'd given up going outside, exposure to sunlight, and human interaction as well as sleep.

Only some of those choices were mine, but all of them felt right.

Like making a cup of Keurig while waiting for the drip machine to make a full pot. Without sleep, human interaction was impossible, and sunlight was never necessary to begin with.

Except as it applied to photosynthesis for coffee plants.

"Cynthia, I will give you to the count of three. One."

"Ah, ah, ah," I mimicked The Count, and the feet of her walker crept closer, aiming for my head.

I refocused on Mrs. Margot's face. She did not appreciate my Sesame Street reference.

In fact, she looked genuinely perturbed.

"Two."

"Yes, ma'am," I sighed. Hauling my size 18 frame off the floor and stumbling back toward my desk, the canine I'd served with, Sgt. Winnifred Pupperson, ambled along beside me. My shoulder had come unseated from the ball socket, but my best furry friend looked completely fine.

Minor miracles, since her former vet was on a three-year lesbian cruise and the fill-in commercial vet was my ex-Dr. Larry Kirby.

My doctor was a revolving set of ER workers, and I was this close to filling my frequent flyer punch card.

"If you want me to take care of anything that requires a computer or paper, I can't help you."

With a sweeping gesture, I drew her attention to the completely obscured surface that used to house my business operations equipment. The second-hand monitor and CPU from a reformed porn publisher, a blotter calendar with recurring charge dates highlighted, wired keyboard, mouse and mouse pad completely obscured by coffee cups.

Several dozen coffee cups of various colors, shapes, and volumes. Each one emblazoned with dogs, a farm, or some manner of witty or snarky saying.

All of them mysteriously materializing in or around my office, apartment, car and one on a cow at the dairy while I was checking her over.

It was creepy and impressive since I hadn't seen a soul.

Maybe it came from the cow herself?

Mrs. Margot, however, did not seem dissuaded by the new collection.

"Why don't you put them away, Cynthia? As I understand it, your previous collection was destroyed. Just place them where those once lived... honestly..."

She tutted at me, and I narrowed my eyes at her, glancing between her and my string art conspiracy theory board.

Could it be...

I watched her hobble on the walker and dismissed it. While she could get around reasonably well, I couldn't conceive of her having the motivation to hunt down townsfolk and collect coffee mugs. No... Carla had all the leverage to do this to me.

Her glaring image judged me from the wall where it sat framed by red yarn.

"Will your partner be joining you or has Sgt. Winnifred forgotten her manners?"

The dog in question, retired from the Army alongside me, had flopped onto the floor again and was now doing a sideways wiggle on her back. Rear paws kicking out, front tucked against her chest, the dog could have been scratching her back or jazzercising. Whichever it was, she managed it in perfect time to the music coming in from the public library next door.

"*Baby, I'm just gonna shake, shake, shake, shake it off,*" her tail thumped in time to the beat with each foot kicking out to punctuate the claps before the bridge.

"Considering she wrecked your BINGO hall and tried to blow up Florida, I don't know where you got the idea she had manners." Scoffing, I tried not to roll my eyes even though I had resting sarcasm face.

It was like RBF for people who used dark humor to process their trauma.

Jiggling my dislocated shoulder, I stifled a scream and decided it was well and truly out of place, but I would need coffee to get it back in. Picking up one of the coffee cups and putting it next to the coffeemaker, I tried to choose what to put inside the cup with my magic bean water. "It's like you've never met us and think we somehow developed social skills and competence."

A sharp side eye from Mrs. Margot attempted to maim me, but I elected to take TayTay's advice and... well, ignore it.

Only Winnie could work a tail shake like that in our dynamic duo.

I'd probably un-seat another ball joint if I tried.

"And I can't put the damn coffee cups away because when the old ones went down, the shelf broke and I don't own any tools! I tried to buy some tools, but I ended up in the grocery store buying cheese and coffee creamer... and then I went to... somewhere. Probably work? Definitely not bed because it smells like Larry, and he's gone..."

I blinked at her, wondering when she'd lost focus.

"When did you last sleep, Cynthia?"

"Do you want some coffee?" I replaced her question with one of my own, gesturing the cup in my hand out to her. Beside the coffee maker was another full cup, one I'd apparently poured and forgotten about at some point. I poked the side and discovered it was still lukewarm.

Like the inside of a Tauntaun.

Snickering at my own joke, I waited for Mrs. Margot to answer while I chugged the tepid liquid.

"I do not want coffee. I want to know why you aren't sleeping," she scowled at me. Ambling slowly over to the front window, she ripped back the heavy drapes and let in the morning light.

A sharp hiss at the brightness passed through my lips as I looked through the front window. It was adorned with our names in vinyl letters:

SHARP INVESTIGATIONS, CYNTHIA SHARP AND SGT. WINNIFRED PUPPERSON, K9.

Only Winnie had earned rank and title.

My name looked like what my mother would call me when I was in trouble, and she couldn't remember my middle name was Natasha.

Outside the glass, people ambled up and down Main St in the not-so-sleepy town of Sweet Pea, OH. I'd been born and raised here, but it had never felt like home. In a search of a sense of belonging, I'd gone to school in Colorado, joined the Army and started my career in Texas with no luck. After seeing a few parts of the world and some other parts of the country, I wasn't sure anywhere would ever feel like home.

Winnie's tail bumped my leg, and I amended myself, the only place that felt like home was beside her.

Through my window, I watched the average citizens of my average town continue on with their mediocre lives and wondered at the key to their happiness. Nothing about their movements was hurried or motivated... It was unclear if they had places to be or were simply enjoying the cooling temperatures of early fall. Either way, I was mildly envious of them as they enjoyed the trees' early-stage death drop of foliage. September had barely arrived, but pumpkin spice everything had already made its way into Mo's bakery, the Coffee Cabin, the lube section of the adult stores, including Phil's Curious Courtship, and my coffee maker.

Mankind's greatest invention and the only love in my life, besides Winnie, I could trust not to let me down. The little orange light on the maker was off... the coffee maker should never be off... though the carafe was getting darker.

Except it was getting darker from the top and not the bottom... strange.

"Cynthia!"

My head jerked up, and I shook off the cobwebs.

"Hmm?"

"Why don't you ask one of your male... friends... to fix your shelf? Would you be able to sleep then?"

I shook my head slowly, looking into the empty coffee cup still in my hand.

"I don't have any man friends. Cruz went away and Larry.. .. Is dumb. His whole family is dumb... and my bed smells like him. I want to wash the smell away, but I can't because then it's gone, and I can't have it back because he's a little mama's boy and I have some pride! Somewhere..." I stared down at my desk. There was just enough space to use as leverage to push my shoulder back into place. Bracing my forearm, I chomped down on my lip and pushed.

The wet *pop* was unnerving, but I'd managed it without crying... more than I already was. I looked out the window again, waiting for the mist in my eyes to clear before addressing the vampire in the room. I'd read once that I wasn't supposed to show weakness to vampires, or maybe it was predatory men.

Potentially, it was both.

"What about your intern, Stella?" She tried again, and I pointed to a pile of confetti in the corner.

"She quit and brought me a pile of resumes for potential new people. Winnie ate them."

The mist in my eyes was clearing and I could once again see the blissful town with its cheerful people and its happy coffee that they could make because everyone they cared about hadn't jumped ship and abandoned them to their own inner thoughts.

"No one has abandoned you, Cynthia!"

Almost inner thoughts... I clarified, wondering if that too would escape my lips. A shadow momentarily blocked out the sun, and I darted out the door like a drunken troll.

"You!" I shouted, an accusatory finger leveled at the rather expansive chest of my brother's wife and the town's sheriff... or chief.

"You did this..." I tripped over a collection of coffee mugs on the sidewalk. They fell over, and I toppled after barely angling myself away from the shattered ceramic. I landed on the shoulder I'd just popped back in and felt it threaten to slide out again. Frustrated, I blinked up at the sun and the outline of my curvy in all the right places, sister-in-law. The shorter version of Jessica Rabbit, with an equally sexy voice and lethal hands. My squinting eyes marred my attempt to glare as I fought to keep them trained on her for signs of guilt.

She just stared down at me.

"This sidewalk is unclean. You should get up," she advised, and I waited for the horror to fill me. I'd seen things on this sidewalk. Horrible things and yet...

Horizontal on the sidewalk was actually kind of comfortable, a weird discovery since my bed had felt possessed by fire ants recently. I closed my eyes against the sun and the second I did, everything else faded and I fell asleep.

Chapter Two:
Country Music
Catastrophes

"I don't think now is the time to ask her for help with anything..." a sultry voice whisper-hissed, and I rolled over to get away from it.

"Well, you said it was out of your jurisdiction. What choice do I have?" An ancient voice creaked in response, and I tried to growl them into silence, but the sound wasn't very threatening and might have been a snore.

"You *can* ask her, but she's a wreck and you *shouldn't*. She can't take on anything important. I think this is more ridiculous than anything, she also can't handle ridiculous. You'd be lucky if she could find soap on a rope in her own damn hand." The sultry voice came back at her, and I gave up on whatever version of sleep I was nearly enjoying. "You don't even know for a fact anything is actually wrong."

"Trudy said..."

"Said what? Stop claiming I'm dead?"

"You know she's..."

My eyelids slid open, expecting to see the sidewalk and sunshine of Main Street.

Instead, I was on a bed... my bed...

Beside me, Winnie was snoozing with a paw draped over her snoot. Blackout curtains covered the square window behind the couch, and I'd obscured the rectangle one that looked out on the alley with the metal rod I used as a closet. Based on the slivers of light peeping between my clothes, it was no longer morning, but it wasn't too far past. If I was asleep, it wasn't for long.

Mrs. Magot and Carla were whisper-fighting near my fridge in the kitchen. They had to have known arguing six-ish feet away from my bed would wake me up. The genuine mystery was which one of them had managed to get me up the stairs.

It's rude to ask another woman her weight, but I knew mine. It was easily twice their combined total... as was my height.

Now *that* was a hard task to accomplish.

Carla's Latin descent kept her height in the five foot even range, while Mrs. Margot's slowly hunching shoulders and narrowing vertebral discs spaces meant she would be lucky to meet the height minimum for a merry-go-round in a few years.

Searching my room, I tried to decide if I wanted them to leave so I could sleep or I wanted to find an object to lob their way.

Nothing heavy. I didn't want to cause permanent damage, but I did want them to be annoyed and uncomfortable. To my left was the angled wall that ended the A-framed roof of my apartment with a small plastic chest of drawers Larry had bought me when I accidentally threw away all of my underwear.

Stupid Larry Kirby.

There was nothing on that side of the bed to throw.

Searching toward the right side of my bed, I gave up on projectile objects. The room held a wooden nightstand that also doubled as an end table for the couch beside it. In front of the couch was a low coffee table that sat in-line with an armchair pushed against the wall beside the stairwell up, an entry point with zero security between my living quarters and the fire door off the alley below. My kitchen began on the other side of the opening, a long counter with a single barstool dividing it from the living area. The counter also had a sink and enough space for a coffee maker and a handful of cabinets, one of which was currently useless until I purchased... probably a hammer? Maybe some dowels...

What the hell holds up shelving units?

The kitchen alcove had a fridge, a microwave and two women arguing over my competency. There was nothing on my visual that didn't remind me of Larry, so I was better off getting back to work.

"What do you need me to investigate?" I asked, clearing my throat when a small amount of spittle dribbled back into it.

"You should sleep!" Carla scolded me, and I rolled my eyes at her.

"If you want me to sleep, don't fight with someone in my kitchen. How did I get upstairs?" I moved to sit up and felt my left arm protest. The sharp pains reminded me of the abuse it had suffered earlier that I still hadn't recovered from. Nothing felt broken, and I didn't have any new bruises, reconfirming my belief that no one in this room who'd been awake had dragged me upstairs.

The women might be strong, but there wasn't enough space between them and the floor to keep my arms and legs off it. I had A LOT of arms and legs to keep track of.

"Umm..." Carla sucked her lower lip into her mouth, guilt marring her otherwise flawless complexion. Her eyes were darting between my eyes and my cheek, a clear indicator of where I might find my answer. Swiping my hand across my face, it came away smeared in neon yellow highlighter and what looked like either dried blood or ketchup.

"Seth? And he brought the alien spawn?" I asked, wondering if my brother had moved me before or after my eight-year-old hell-raising niece had graffitied my face.

"Yeah... and Erich. He helped carry your legs above Sylvia's head when she started trying to cut..."

I lifted my pant leg and saw the scratched-out marks spelling out her name. Looked like Sylvia was planning to become some sort of tattoo artist, cattle brander or a serial mutilator.

"She was trying to tattoo me... with..." I studied the light scratches, wondering if I could call being scarred a tattoo. Both were permanent, but only one was art. The other was a fast track to the fancy hug coats with all the buckles if you tried to DIY it.

"What did she use? And why would anyone give that kid a sharp object?"

"Thumbtack. It was on the sidewalk beside you when they arrived," Carla sighed, and Mrs. Margot gave me a dirty look that suggested I better not go looking for my self-defense thumbtack.

It was also a not-so-subtle reminder that most, if not all, of this was my fault.

"That tracks," I huffed, scrubbing my hands over my face. More yellow highlighter ink and something sticky rubbed off onto my hands. My niece was the smallest, cutest ball of big "future felon energy" to walk the Earth. She'd been a handful before her mom passed away, but now that my brother moved her out here and she'd met up with Daniel Kirby's litany of delinquents, it was worse. Her behavior was about the same, but with them backing her up, I was positive I'd be visiting her in prison as soon as she was old enough to be tried and convicted as an adult.

But we all still loved her, a testament to familial obligation and pretty privilege.

"Not to interrupt another round of *why Cynthia looks weird*, but as she is awake and appears mentally competent, may I proceed with my request?" Mrs. Margot huffed, dragging her minuscule frame out of the kitchen under the aid of her walker and shuffling toward the armchair. Winnie tracked the motion, eyeing the tennis balls on their feet for any sign they may one day be hers.

She'd stolen one before and she was plotting to do it again.

"Leave it," I warned my partner. She let out a wide yawn, showing me *all* of her teeth before flopping over onto the far side of the bed. "Let's get this over with. What do you need, and do I have time to shower before I do it?"

Mrs. Margot narrowed her eyes. Another not-so-subtle hint that I was being both petulant and ornery. Since I could still define both words despite their generational irrelevance, I decided I was awake enough to have earned more coffee.

I also decided that Mrs. Margot had a really expressive and accusatory face, and I should go find the garlic salt.

Only a vampire could reach such an advanced age and still have enough fine motor skills in her face muscles to insult me in silence.

"No!" Carla held out a finger before my feet even touched the floor beside my bed. "I know that look. Mrs. Margot is not a vampire! And you can't have any more coffee until you drink the water beside your bed. And if you mimic a brat and try to dump it in a coffee maker, I will find a Dom to punish you for it."

"If... you... what?" I asked, strangling the skin between my eyebrows in confusion. "Are you..." I dropped my voice another octave. "Talking about BDSM culture in front of Mrs. Margot *and* telling me I can't have coffee???"

Carla took another step toward me, doubling down on her threat.

"Don't give me that. You know why and how I know about this nonsense?"

"Because you were a military spy honey trap who seduced boring vanilla money men into doing her bidding?" I asked, grabbing the cup of water and chugging. Small rivulets dribbled from the corner of my mouth, streaking icy water down my chin and into my shirt where it left a neon yellow stain on the white fabric.

"No," Carla snapped, and I set down the empty cup. "I know this because I married into your family and my in-laws have no boundaries! And both of your sisters are ALSO over-sharers with no boundaries. And now I know about subs, brats, doms, dommes, and a whole bunch of other nonsense that I did NOT sign up for, Cyn."

I nodded and started in on the second cup of water before responding.

"So, you're here to tell me you're divorcing Seth? You should know, if you hurt those kids..." I started plotting murder scenarios. They'd never find her body if she took another mother from Erich and Sylvia. The latter might be a damn monster, but she didn't deserve to be mother-less... again. "I know people, Carla."

"Stop plotting my death! I'm not leaving your brother or those little gremlins. But I am telling you, I'm not in the mood for dramatics and nonsense. You can have coffee after you finish the water, you can listen to Mrs. Margot, though I don't think you should get involved, but you can't do it with garlic. Not the least of which because you don't own any."

"I have garlic salt!" I challenged her, but she just kept going through her list of dos and don'ts.

"I will accept a reasonable discussion on the topic at hand, but you shouldn't decide on anything until you stop looking like a *Walking Dead* extra. And most importantly, you will start going to therapy again in addition to your community service because

I think you are losing it based on the string art downstairs. Do I make myself clear?"

Carla's eyes were nearly popping out of her skull, and I wanted to give her something to help with the madness of joining my family, but all I had was coffee and dog hair. The impending mental breakdown on such a strong woman was nearly enough to shove aside my melancholy for a higher purpose.

Almost.

Carla's life choices before joining my family had gotten her framed for murder, so it wasn't like she was living a life of sanity before joining this circus.

"I'm sorry. I won't be going back to therapy because that is way too much talking and very little fixing, but I will take the rest of your conditions under consideration."

My sister-in-law made a face but remained quiet, gesturing for me to talk to the old woman.

"Please, what do you need?" I asked, standing up and ambling toward the kitchen with my empty water cups. Instead of dealing with my trauma, I started mentally preparing myself for the gymnastics I'd need to get from the fridge to the coffee maker amid all the homeless coffee cups.

"Have you heard the song *Night the Lights Went Out in Georgia*?" Mrs. Margot asked, and I stopped on my mission to look at her.

"That country song by the red-haired woman?" I asked, blanking on the name of a country star who had her own sitcom in the 90s... or 2000s...

Country music was all the rage in the early 2000s, but I think her show preceded it.

"Reba, yes. She covered it. The song is from the 1970s. But yes," Mrs. Margot nodded at her own train of thought, and I continued walking into the kitchen. "I think I'm amidst something similar."

I froze, hardly hearing her at the sight of my perfectly empty countertops.

There were no coffee mugs.

Not on the counter or in the sink.

Not in a box or with a fox.

There were no shards or remnants on the floor.

A sob slipped out, and I clutched at my chest.

"How? Why?"

"Larry came with Seth. Your brother does not own tools. .. protractors, pencils, a dozen graphing calculators... but not tools." Carla passed me an envelope bearing my name. "He asked me to give this to you in exchange for his handy services in your cabinet."

I stared at my name in Larry's neat all caps handwriting, an anomaly in the medical field, and dropped the envelope beside the sink. While I was feeling grateful, I was not feeling forgiving. It also irked me to no end that he refused to accept my thoughts and feelings, continuously trying to force himself back into my life.

Like a creepy stalker, but worse because everyone acted like I should just forgive him.

My feelings be damned.

"So, you think someone's sister murdered her brother's cheating wife and her main squeeze of a long list of... squeezes?" I asked, pulling out the glass carafe and filling it with tap water. A few errant drops splashed on the envelope, dotting the surface to showcase the security blue lining beneath.

I wanted to drown the letter in my sink.

And then set it on fire.

"No... I don't believe there is a sister involved... I suppose it's more like Goodbye Earl," she tried again, choosing a Chicks song. It was strange how many songs involved murder... and worthless men who were cheaters, abusers or willing to sentence men without a fair trial.

"So, you think an abused wife and her best friend murdered a man?" I asked. Pouring the water into my coffee maker, I pulled out paper filter and placed it in the basket before searching my counter for the coffee tin.

"No... that's not right. What's that song by that little blonde girl? The famous one who started Country but is now everywh ere.... Swift something?" Mrs. Margot looked to Carla for help, and I choked on my spit, gasping for air around my horrified realization.

"You mean Taylor Swift? The billionaire poet, lyrical genius, who can take a simple melody with complex words and create a work of..."

"Yes, yes. That one, breathe Cynthia," Mrs. Margot scolded me while I fought for air alongside any manner of understanding how a human anywhere could refer to the powerhouse that is Taylor as "that little blonde girl".

It was too much for my overtaxed brain, and I let Carla handle the next leading statement.

"I believe she's referring to *No Body, No Crime* but-"

"Yes! That one," Mrs. Margot cut off Carla's attempt at bringing reason into the conversation as I gave up on the coffee tin and pulled a bag of fresh coffee grounds out of my freezer.

"You think a husband killed his wife and then got killed by her friend in revenge?"

I was used to thinking people in this town watched too many True Crime specials, but apparently Mrs. Margot needed to step away from her radio.

Also, musicians might need to be placed under investigation for their catchy murder ballads.

"Not quite. My niece's man has a best friend who was working construction with him. Then one day, the man stopped coming to work. Turns out he was also performing at the male review as... a construction worker, though I heard he did a few sketches with a hose..."

"Male Review?" I asked Carla, and she snickered.

"Pickles."

We shared a look of disbelief before going back to the pensive senior.

Her considering expression was amusing once you knew the "male review performance" was stripping. Not that it was disgraceful to be a stripper. Sex work is probably WAY harder than construction. But considering her niece was dating a man she'd essentially kidnapped from Canada to act in her self-starring porn with the other seniors on hormone replacement therapy, it was definitely a reminder that Mrs. Margot was squarely in pot and kettle territory when she trash-talked my parents.

Every senior in this town was more promiscuous than the dirtiest sailor in the Navy.

Mrs. Margot's vision glazed over and I snapped my fingers twice to bring her back to the land of... my apartment. So... coffee and dog hair.

Living felt optional in my current state.

And definitely no male genitals, so she could continue her story without drooling out her dentures.

"OK, so.... He's dead but there's no body? And you think his... spouse was involved?"

Carla let out a long-suffering sigh, and I chose not to look at her. Internalizing her thoughts and feelings wouldn't help me work through this situation. It was more than obvious they'd had this little chat before, but it was my first time, and I wanted to go in with a positive attitude.

May that positivity not be as big a letdown as some of my other major first times.

Like deep fried Oreos... what a waste of an Oreo.

"Well, his wife was cheating on him, kind of. And shortly after he went missing, she moved her girlfriend in. Then she went missing too, and the girlfriend was incredibly worried and confused..."

"She who? I need names and not pronouns... Which is missing and which is confused?"

My hands drifted toward the coffee machine, slowly dripping my life juice, an IV that I forgot to insert into my veins and now I had to wait and get it the traditional way. I'd never had issues drinking my coffee before, but now it just seemed slow and boring and...

The growing silence prickled my neck hairs, and I switched from watching the drip of coffee to the tapping of Mrs. Margot's fingers against her arms. The steady rise and fall of her chest seemed more pronounced, and I wondered if it was the story or annoyance that I'd interrupted her.

Probably annoyance.

I annoy everyone.

Cuts down on banal jibber jabber.

"The wife, Ferrah, is missing. Her girlfriend was worried and confused... she'd told me it was looking weirder and weirder, but... She was known for dramatizing commonplace occurrences, so we all got superb at dismissing her hysterics over the years."

"Accusing women of being hysterical is how you get kicked out of the sisterhood, Mrs. Margot. Next, you'll tell me you suggested she get a lobotomy to 'be more normal'," I hooked air quotes around my accusation. "Maybe next you can send her to the insane asylum for getting abused and wanting to do something about it."

"Would you stop being a sassy pain in the ass for once, Cynthia?"

She spat my name like it was a curse before returning to her faraway reverie of "the good old days" when women were only docile little sheep for herding into the kitchen or bedroom.

It's not an act of love if you make her, you make me do too much labor. The Paris Paloma song popped into my head and the swell of the chorus brought out my urge to fight.

Take a chill pill, you're bitter, tired and projecting.

My inner reasonable person came out, despite no one asking for her opinion.

Being reasonable was *so* overrated.

Mrs. Margot was still working her mouth, suctioning her dentures away from her gums and allowing them to snap back with a slurping sound that slid down my spine in a slimy crawl, and I shuddered. Instead of informing her of the obvious, that I was always a pain in the ass, I went back to her original statement. *Known for being dramatic... ignored over the years...*

"You know the girlfriend?" I prompted, and her eyes slithered toward me, a sharp warning sparkling at the edges. "You said over the years... how many of them were you ignoring her for? Could some of her 'hysterics' have resulted from being a filthy murderer everyone underestimated?"

"She has nothing to do with Leonard's disappearance."

"Who's Leonard?" I asked, looking at the people in the room for answers. Carla appeared to be chewing off a hangnail on her middle finger and almost completely checked out of this conversation.

Lucky duck.

"The man who's missing! Have you been listening?" Mrs. Margot snapped at me, and I narrowed my eyes.

"I haven't slept in days, Mrs. Margot. Forgive me for not knowing the owner of a name the first time you say it. I'm get-

27

ting tired of your sarcasm and attitude, since I'm the one you're asking for a favor. So, you think the girlfriend, whose name you also neglected to share, did it?"

"I told you; Trudy has nothing to do with it!"

Solved half my problem, and I silently cursed whoever taught her English back in school. Clearly, she forgot to mention you needed to have a proper noun before you replaced it with a pronoun when telling a story.

"How do you know that?" I asked, practically jumping for joy when the coffee maker beeped, and I could pour some into the waiting mug I'd already added milk to. "Couldn't you have just been underestimating the woman for years?"

Mrs. Margot slurped her dentures again and Carla punctuated it with another sigh around the fingertip in her mouth. She was just shaking her head, a gesture that said she found this entire conversation unbelievable.

"Gertrude, Trudy, is my sister. She goes by Gertie, but she's always been my Trudy." Her eyes misted and Carla looked annoyed.

"OK... where's Gertie?" I asked, taking a long drink of coffee and considering who would name their child Gertie, Gertrude, or Trudy. The name was probably older than the woman in front of me and if you're going to have a later in life child, why not give them a later in life name? Like... Chelsea or Sarah? "And how much younger than you is she?"

"Trudy was my older sister... until she died tragically two days ago."

Chapter Three:
Cucumber Savior

There wasn't much to the concrete block outside of Dayton that served as the all-male review. It wasn't the most logical place to start, but I knew where it was. By the time I'd talked Carla and Mrs. Margot out of my apartment, it was nearly time for the strip club to open and there was little to no chance I'd run into Larry here.

He wasn't a fan of looking at man meat and high-quality dance costumes.

Pickles had once been owned by a Coast Guard mafioso who also owned a funeral home and a faux Italian restaurant that promised acid reflux and cardiac attacks in the same bite. It had a weird name that sounded like grocery store cheese sauce but was more creatively named than Vincenzo's Mortuary.

Especially since there was no Vincenzo and very few dead people passed through the supposed mortuary.

Lots of money though... and maybe drugs.

Of the three, only Pickles had remained the same before and after his incarceration. The Italian restaurant had become a Taco Bell, sans drive through, so one could still get acid reflux in an imitation of food from another culture. The cosmetician who used to put make-up on the dead bodies purchased the funeral parlor. She then turned around and opened a corpse make-up beauty school as part of a prison work release program. Henrietta Harkness, aka Retta, was a total badass, and while I'd love to go visit her and chat, I had no interest in visiting her workplace.

Putting make-up on dead bodies was far creepier than making dead bodies, which I suspected at least some of her students had.

I hadn't concerned myself with who had purchased Pickles. There were news articles about the bidding war over the right to purchase the establishment, retain the current business model, and its employees, but I hadn't followed the story. I'd only been here once, and it wasn't as a customer, but the torn-up parking lot and barrage of workmen assembling scaffolding showed a substantial financial investment.

And they were definitely real construction workers, because even the most hard-up woman wouldn't pay to see them take their pants off. I assumed it was still going to be a gentleman's review, but part of me hoped it was transitioning into a place that served coffee and they needed taste testers.

Trying to flag someone down, I hit a wall of invisibility my excessively tall and curvy self hadn't encountered before. Prior to leaving my apartment, I'd taken a quick shower and put on clean clothes, removing most of Sylvia's highlighter and ketchup decorations. Since I was still tired, I'd chugged more than the recommended ounce volume of coffee, but I hadn't spilled any. I was clean and caffeinated, but still the workmen seemed off put by my khaki cargos and olive t-shirt.

And not a single wolf whistle when I dropped my keys and bent over in slightly too-tight cargos... accidentally, of course.

I'd be insulted if I wasn't so damn tired... and on an "all men are useless asshats" kick.

Probably time to adopt another dog... and maybe a cat or six.
At what age can I throw in the towel and become a spinster?
"Cyn?"

The voice nearly jolted me out of my flesh suit and into the afterlife.

Turning, I watched the man exiting a red Ford Mustang, noting his fluid movements and wondering if he was worth dying for. He was minutely taller than me, a lot slimmer and built like an athlete, thick muscles that were toned for function over showing off, but not so bulky they'd intimidate a lesser mortal. In his basketball shorts and plain T-shirt, he could have passed for a pro-dancer or a basketball player between sportball seasons. Aviator glasses covered his green eyes, his dark tousled hair styled by running his fingers through it. The man had a perpetual bedroom-ready look that made you want to see him *in* your bed or his... without clothes on. And when he took off his clothes...

All thoughts would probably turn into goop.

Because I'd seen it all and boy howdy. While lying on the ground looking up at his junk wasn't a superb view, the upright sight of his cut and gorgeous abs would haunt any straight wo man... or gay woman if she was a fan of art and willing to forgive a turgid penis.

"Hey, Jake... what's going on?" I asked, stepping out of the way when a man threatened to crush my toes with a wheelbarrow. He was one of about seven, all giving Jacob Weissman dark looks when a passing woman wolf-whistled at my old schoolmate and he offered her a wink.

A few more men joined the glowering session.

Given how studiously the construction workers were ignoring me, I was equal parts jealous and resigned to play second fiddle to Jacob. I wasn't of the school that women should compete for men, but if I competed against Jacob in anything except most objects tripped over in a thirty-minute period, I'd lose every time. As would all these workers trying to flex their biceps beneath sweat stained shirts. There were a few with adequate physiques, but flexing only drew attention to the softness of their beer bellies.

And the clearly sour expressions of bitter men with their panties in a bunch.

It was the familiar look of men who thought they were dog's gift to humanity confronted with a man who was nicer and better looking.

"Renaming and rebranding," he shrugged, pulling a duffle bag from the trunk of his car. "This is the fifth day of actual construction, but we'd been warned it was coming for three weeks. Last weekend was the final show under the old moniker. There's a week of rehearsals and then we launch with the new material under the fresh signage."

"Why? Who owns this place now?"

"No idea but.... Geez, what happened to your face?"

He lowered the sunglasses perched on his nose and studied my face. While I hadn't been sleeping, I also hadn't been punched recently, and the shower had taken care of Sylvia's "art". Nothing had exploded and singed off my eyebrows... and I was fairly certain that I had cleared out my eye crusties before leaving the house.

Honestly, I was pretty sure this was the best I'd looked in at least three days.

"Do you want me to call a bellhop to help you check the bags under your eyes?" He chuckled at his own joke, and I considered punching him.

Maybe he's only better looking than them and the nice was a lie.

"Do you practice being catty or does it come naturally to... you... performer type humans?" I stumbled to come up with a crude nickname for him and those in his profession. "Thong jockeys" seemed a little too on the nose and "hip gyrators" wasn't really insulting, so I just glared at the man four years my junior and attempted to scare him into a puddle of flesh and muscles. "Or is that just a side effect of all those salami sword fights in the dressing room? Did you lose the last dick measuring contest?"

"Keep glaring like that and your face will freeze that way. Then you'll have to go as a bitter old lady every Halloween for forever. Worse, you'll probably have to start paying for your salami," he started toward the front door, and I followed. Beside us, a worker was attaching mounting brackets to the sides of a metal base sporting a series of neon tubes. Three interlinked kidney beans beneath three impaled star anise herbs at varying angles. "Where's Winnie?"

"In the Jeep. Construction sights are notorious for having sharp objects lying around and arbitrary snacks," I answered, skirting a bucket that smelled like an impromptu urinal and holding my breath. "Can't have her bloody or eating cheese."

"It's weird that you consider those two disasters equal."

"I'll let her fart in your face and then we'll revisit your tone, young man," I sniped, wondering if I needed my scowl to become permanent before I could really sell the bitter old lady angle.

"Yes ma'am. If I'm a good boy, will you give me a hard candy from your Mary Poppins bag?"

"Bite me, Weissman. If there was candy in my pockets, I'd have already eaten it."

He stopped in his tracks to lean in close and whisper, "Biting costs extra, cinnamon bun, and you don't have the cash." Before nipping my ear and sauntering away.

My whole body flushed, and I shuddered in horror as I followed him.

Cradle robber! We'd be a cradle robber! Think sanctimonious thoughts!

I followed Jake into the building through a side door. Though the workers had propped it open with a can of nails, there was hardly any daylight penetrating the inky black paint of the hallway. Instead of light going in, a cacophony of noise poured from the belly of the building, an omen of what lay on the other side of the tunnel.

Nudity and sensory hell.

A mash-up that promised to assail me with slowly exposed butt cracks, pickle brine smells, loud noises and men in G-strings.

Or worse, no strings.

I glanced behind me out into the parking lot and saw butt cracks, sweat and sunshine.

Heads or tails... Heads or tails...

"Get a move on, Cyn," Jacob called over his shoulder, and I made the reluctant choice to drag my body toward the thumping beat of bass and hammers. Following the former scrawny kid, we turned left into a changing room with a wall of lit-up mirrors. Between each vanity along the counter was a box of tissues, spray bottles, baby oil and what I could only guess was chafe cream for unsupported testicles.

"What fresh drama club hell is this place?" I asked, not daring to stray too close to the furniture. It was all littered with sequins, glitter, and smelled like Hollister had a baby with dirty gym shorts. If anything in this room touched my clothing, I'd have to burn it and get a tetanus shot.

"Dancer prep room. The guys are all coming in to learn a new number to... *intro* the new name," he gestured toward a dark purple kidney bean on the wall dressed like a Planters nut lifting a green stem from his head. Instead of a black and white cane, though, the purple bean was stuffing green rectangles into a line of paint transecting the lower portion.

"What the hell is that?" I asked, looking away before it could imprint onto my brain and join the other intrusive thoughts. It was bad enough I wanted to scream before a dramatic climax in a movie, and shout *is that dog poop* when the line at the coffee shop was too long. But it can't be too late to forget that... thing.

"Eggplant."

"What?" I asked, looking between him and the impressionist painting.

"It's an eggplant," he repeated and opened a social media app to show me the redesigned logo. The anthropomorphized vegetable drawn into an image of the building. Swiping through the post, I looked at concept art with the whole rebranding schematic, a cascade of colors that made my eyes water.

People who hated the arts suddenly made perfect sense. Because a kindergartner with a fingerpainting set could have done better.

The new, drawn-in, neon sign was of an eggplant removing his stem like a top hat and dancing. It's possible that was the tube thing being built outside, but I questioned the sanity of anyone willing to bring this horror to life.

"Why? Just... why? What was wrong with Pickles? They're already gross. Why ruin another veggie?"

Despite the atrocity, I couldn't stop staring. The graphic just kept dancing, doing a can-can that might include decapitating himself... while thrusting. It was a fatal car accident before EMS covered the mangled corpses. All I could do was stare and panic, trying to figure out what not to look at first.

"I guess there's a network TV show with a strip club named Pickles and the new owner was worried about lawsuits." He shrugged and removed his shirt. The rippling muscles in the single fluid movement of pulling it over his head from the back were the stuff of eReader smut dreams.

Then he dropped his shorts.

"Eeep!" I slapped my hands over my eyes. "Give a woman some warning before you just... disrobe!"

"Literally my job, Cyn. You're such an odd mix of pervert and prude. I've heard stories..."

My hands fell from my face, and I gaped.

"What stories? From whom? I'll kill them..." his undies hit the floor, and I screamed. Slapping my hands back over my eyes, I decided to live and let live. Forgive and forget, take the miracle move on drug and get on with this fortnight... or early evening. "Never mind. What do you know about Leonard?"

"Who?" Jake asked, sounding like he was moving around the dressing room... or undressing room. I'd learned in the Army not to just follow men to whatever room they asked you to, but apparently the lesson hadn't stuck. Normally, you get caught making out.

Catching some guys' one-eyed snake hanging out was way worse.

Especially since, as he said, it was his job, and I didn't have any tipping money.

"Leonard? He works here and does construction? Sounds like he was friends with one of the Canadians trafficked here to have sex with old ladies on camera and had a cheating wife."

I cocked my head to the side, still not daring to take my hands away from my eyes. I didn't have a picture, a physical description, or anything other than who he was friends with, his wife's affinity for... vintage seniors, and song lyrics.

Now I had to wonder if I was losing my edge or my mind.

Probably both, though I don't remember *having* a mind. I dropped my hands, letting my eyes lose focus while Jake talked. Blurry outlines of furniture and fans echoed around the room, the safest I was going to get being here with my eyes open.

"Hmmm... Might be the guy we call Construction Carl? He's a smaller dude, older than the rest, but a kind of silver fox appealing to a certain crowd. We try to keep a diverse portfolio in our dancers to keep the audience interested and lusty. Never would have pegged his actual name as Leonard. Leonard sounds like a short, asthmatic physicist and Carl was only one of those things... at least by the standards we set here. In the real world, his height is probably average. Carl had more of a hard labor muscle than an eight hours a day in the gym body, but he was definitely not soft and doughy like the dudes out front. Hard to picture him being allowed to work with that bunch without some serious backstabbing and sabotage."

"You make them sound like 'on Wednesdays we wear pink' style mean girls," I laughed. He gave me a knowing look, and I glanced back toward the door. "Ouch, someone has mean dude trauma. Did he work with any of the 'dudes out front'?"

"Couldn't tell you. We aren't big on real names or outside personal details here, so I don't know if the dude was really in construction married, straight, or anything else. He never acted married or gay. Those types of dudes are easy to spot, but he also wasn't as flirty as some of the other guys. More of a middle of the road type, but I don't ask a lot of questions of the guys here. Keeps the separation between persona and person. You wouldn't catch any of us hanging out after hours," he concluded.

"Well, that's good, since hanging out outside is indecent exposure," I joked, but Jake didn't laugh. Shorter and muscled silver fox wasn't a lot to go on, but it was more than I had before. "So, when did you last see Construction Carl?"

"Shoot..." he sprayed something, and I clenched my jaw to avoid inhaling.

Unfortunately, the smell burned my nostrils, and I couldn't breathe through there either.

Gasping and drooling, I folded in half and choked into a cloud of overly fragrant deodorant.

What's worse? Winnie farts or Axe body spray?

"You're so dramatic... it's been a while since he's been in, but you'll want to talk to Larry if you need more details. He has a better memory than a lot of the other guys," he shrugged into a vest with a faux tie Velcro-ed between the two sides. "He's a little less heavy handed with the drinks and I doubt he's taken as many head shots as the other bartenders."

"Larry? Why the hell would Larry know about..." I gestured to Jake's barely contained... Eggplant.

"Because he works here part time now," Jake threw over his shoulder, striding past me with a full moon sporting a dimple in the left butt cheek. "Thought you knew."

Chapter Four:
Ghosts and
Boyfriends Past

I t was a slow, labored walk to my car.

The thumping beat trailed behind me, punctuated with shouts from a dance coach... or Nazi commander. Whoever it was, they were putting the dancers through their paces down the hall and beads of sweat dripped down my back just thinking about it. There was nothing more terrifying to the uncoordinated than the sound of an 8 count. Couple that with the promise of full moons and squirrel food, and I was out the door faster than Jake had ditched his clothes.

Man-parts were not attractive.

"Running away from the show?" A male voice purred into my ear when I was nearly back to my Jeep. Instinctively, I threw out an elbow and followed it up with a back kick to my estimation of where I would find... "Crap, Cyn, chill! It's just me!"

Glancing over my shoulder, I looked down at a bent over Dr. Lawrence Kirby. His arms were cradling his abdomen. He was gasping for breath, red-faced and slightly purple lipped, but not in a way that suggested his life was in jeopardy.

His survival erased any inkling of guilt I had and replaced them with annoyance and a smidgeon of regret.

"I knew who it was when I started throwing hands," I said, using slang I'd heard the last time I passed a middle school. Though the comment wasn't directed at me, the collection of mostly naked girls in impractical shoes gave me hardcore childhood bullying flashbacks and I crossed four lanes of traffic to get away from them.

Kind of like what I wanted to do right now, but we were in a parking lot. And on one side was a building full of men practicing choreography in outfits that would probably make my perfectly healthy heart give out. On the other was a group of workmen with exposed cracks, rotten teeth and unfortunately placed body hair.

The hands I didn't actually throw were deep in my pockets to avoid reaching for Larry and checking if he was OK. I'd given the man enough of my affection and emotions. The hurt and anger I had left were mine alone to dole out to whoever would take up the mantle of the cat villain in Wonder Woman.

They weren't helping me, and I was all about supporting other women.

"No, you didn't," he laughed, righting himself to show off his crooked smile. His dark hair was less kempt than it had been, bright eyes dulled from our reacquaintance almost a year ago. His jeans and T-shirt were a little looser than they'd been, his ever-present lab coat missing from an otherwise ordinary outfit. "You've been avoiding me."

"Obviously," I snorted, turning away to unlock the Jeep. "Take a hint and go away."

A few months ago, there had been a secret from the Gulf War that came to be unburied. Several veterans had nearly lost their lives, many more wearing the scars of conflict that kept them from re-joining the regular population, preferring to live on the fringes of the un-housed community. Working with Sgt. Ian Cruz, a member of Army Criminal Investigation Command and my former canine training sergeant in the Army, we'd tried to right the wrongs of history. This time, he'd been hanging around Sweet Pea waiting for the decree of how he could repay the Army for his participation in one of my hare-brained schemes that saved lives but cost them a coveted weapon. After spending months deciding the best way to punish him, the powers that be in the Army sent him on a super deadly mission overseas.

As far as I knew, he was still over there… Whether or not he was still breathing was a bigger mystery than the one that landed him there.

We had fun, but Cruz wasn't exactly a forever kind of dude. After Larry and I had ended our months-long relationship, I needed fun. Cruz and I had gotten closer, a comfortable friend with benefits that had a lot of potential to become love... heart stopping, burn the world down for him sort of love.

And then he was gone.

Gone and recommending I get back together with Larry despite his mom shoving him with Amber Carter-my mortal enemy who tormented me from kindergarten through high school. Larry's mom acted subversive, sneaky, and manipulative, making what she'd done far worse than anything Amber had put me through.

She had never wanted me to date her son, and she'd made sure I knew it.

He'd sworn she would back off, that she understood my value in his life and the community and was done with playing mind games. We'd gone on a real first date. Reconnected and rekindled the love that was so easy to fall back into.

Until my birthday.

My stupid birthday that he'd promised to spend with me, playing paintball and drinking margaritas. It wasn't a huge ask, but it was the party I'd wanted when I turned twenty-one that no one in my college wanted in on. Apparently, paintball was "too violent" and I had an "unfair advantage" because I "played all the time", even though I really only played Duck Hunt on Nintendo. But it was finally going to happen.

I waited, dressed and ready to live out a dream, but he never showed.

Didn't answer my texts, didn't call... nothing. My best friend, Mary O'Connor aka Mo, came over and we got wasted before I stomped indignantly over to Larry's house. She cheered me on and led the way, only for us to arrive and see his mom crying. She'd come over, distraught about losing a family member, and I joined him in attempting to console her over the loss of Peter Darling.

Except, when I first came home, I'd shaken every branch of the Kirby family tree, and that particular branch wasn't ringing a bell. So, I made a call and... yup, she'd made the bastard up. The whole thing was just an unbelievably elaborate plot to wedge herself between us... again.

The woman should switch from being retired to writing thriller novels, since she loved murdering imaginary people and toying with their emotions.

Because she was done using me as the villain in her son's story.

Pulling my phone from my back pocket, I texted Carla. I told her I needed a picture of my missing man, the woman he was married to, and Mrs. Margot's sister. It also occurred to me I would need the address of their once residence and any other occupational and demographic specific information. Because now that I was slightly more awake, it seemed like a good idea to actually know something about the people I was being asked to find.

"Who are you texting?" Larry asked, loping behind me like a newborn calf. His movements lacked grace and any semblance of rhythm. There was no way a place like Pickles... or Eggplants should have hired him. "Is it Cruz? Is he back? Are you together again, or is he still MIA?"

"Go away and stop using acronyms that have nothing to do with you!" I said, wrenching open my door. Winnie shoved herself into the opening, rubbing her head against Larry. Though he was stroking her silky ears, they were both facing me with pleading looks that would have tugged at my heart, but that was shattered on the floor back in Sweet Pea.

Where his whole damn family had taken turns stomping the pieces into dust.

"We need to talk, Cyn," Larry declared, and I snapped.

"No. We don't need to talk. Why does everyone always want to talk? How come no one ever chases after me to raid a puppy mill, liberate all the dogs and throw all the bad guys into the Fire Swamp?" I nudged Winnie back into the car with my shoulder. She resisted briefly, but I stuck my hand in my pocket and grabbed a handful of crushed dog treats mixed with cheese crackers.

"Because the Fire Swamp isn't real and *The Princess Bride* is old enough that if it had been real, some developer would have flattened it and put-up condos," Larry retorted, Winnie retreating with her muzzle in my hand and coating it in slobber. "Why won't you hear me out? Didn't you read the letter? I think you owe me..."

"I don't owe you anything, you entitled, misogynistic..."

"I'm sorry, that was a terrible choice of words. Just... can we please talk?"

"Why doesn't anyone ever want me to take out a bunch of rapists by putting a coffee can of thermite through their engine block then caging them in their disabled vehicle with hallucinogenic sex drugs until they ravage each other to death," I rattled off the most disturbing visual that was both vindicating and made me want to puke.

"That was dark. Did you quit sleeping to stay up and watch *Burn Notice*?"

Larry knew me too well and I hated him for it. Because that level of familiarity meant he should know better than to force the issue. I deserved to be listened to and have my wishes respected.

"Or Taylor Swift started traveling by tour bus and she's parked on the side of the highway giving a free concert. And whoever can sing All Too Well, Taylor's Version, from the Vault, Ten-minute Version, with her, gets to board the bus and be her new best friend?"

"Pretty sure that sentence doesn't even make sense. You need to sleep, Cyn. And we need to have a conversation where you try listening instead of yelling."

I ripped the door out of Larry's hand and pulled it closed. Winnie finished her snack crumbs and was back to sprawling across the back seat of my Jeep Wrangler. Beside her was my box of random rubber ducks people kept leaving on or around my car.

I'd meant to Google it, but I kept forgetting whenever I was near an internet capable device and not driving. But I held onto them and put them on other Jeeps, just so I wouldn't seem uncool. Hopefully, it wasn't drug related or a weird sex thing.

"No, you need to try listening to what I'm yelling! I said I was done. You don't get to decide when I'm done. You don't get to wear me down until I do what you want. No is no, and you need to move on! Keep this up and I'm filing a report. It's harassment."

"Come on, Cyn," Larry's plea was shouted over the engine. "I'm doing the best I can. I work here to get out from under the Carters. I cut off my mom... I don't want to be without you!"

My Jeep slid easily into reverse, and I started backing out. Larry's words swirled around me, but I couldn't hear them.

Not again.

A woman could only give a man so many chances to rip out her heart and stomp on it before she was a cliché.

Punching a button on the radio, the device switched to disc and Taylor's female rage filled the car.

So, I leap from the gallows, and I levitate down your street. Who's afraid of little ole me?

My voice joined Taylor's as I eyed Larry in the rearview mirror.

"You should be."

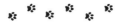

The address Carla sent me for Leonard and his wife... and then his wife and her girlfriend, was in the middle of Dayton's Fairborn suburb. The area would be called quaint by history buffs. The look catered to people who wanted to pretend they were in the country while still keeping one eye on the city, but ended up housing college kids and military families. The designs were practical for a college town touching an Air Force base in the middle of tornado country, but not necessarily appreciated.

Brick storefronts lined wide two-lane roads. Every colorless Lego inspired building sporting neon signs and just the right amount of dust to convince you it was there on purpose. Wooden rails ran along the storefronts, and the opposite posts gave it an old-town saloon feel.

Though the advertised fare of vegan patties with avocado burgers was a fair indicator I hadn't time traveled, the place was eerily familiar. Like every pass-through town in the Midwest had hired the same architect and city designer. My brain was certain it had been here a million times without ever having stepped foot here before.

Despite being near Wright Patterson and a college town, the tract housing was a standard fare of single-family dwellings and wide front porches. The yards were oddly un-fenced, and I was pretty sure there was an inappropriate number of American Flags, but it looked like any other suburb in the rural Midwest. All that was missing were pies cooling in every window and Detroit steel cars to make me feel like I had wandered into a Norman Rockwell painting.

Or time traveled to the 1950s.

Carla had texted me an address and a promise to get me a picture of Trudy / Gertie / Gertrude as soon as Mrs. Margot forked one over. Apparently pulling up DMV photos was only for "real cases". But she'd managed to get me the basics: Leonard Hollbrook, born May 29th, 1952. Married to Ferrah Lovelace, born September 19, 1958, in the late 1970s. They had only lived at their current residence for a few years and before that... well, Carla wouldn't tell me where they lived before that because it was "illegal" and "unethical" to get someone's address history.

But it was fine to let me ask about a man slightly younger than my dad at a strip club.

"What the hell?" I asked Winnie, but she let out a long snore. I studied her prostrate form with mild irritation and significant jealousy. The dog was my only sounding board for the current visual atrocity, and she was literally sleeping on the job.

After I spent three days not sleeping so not only was she failing to do her job-she was mocking my exhaustion.

I need to research places better before I go to them.

In front of us was a vivid lavender house with pea-green shutters. The manicured lawn held an army of gnomes, two of which were mooning passing motorists, and an over-sized, oddly shaped bird bath with an old woman lounging in the basin. The base was six feet high; the bowl adding another four feet, putting the woman's butt at my eye level. Her pointed toes kicking in time to the brass-heavy music seeming to come from all around us.

"Excuse me?" I said, climbing out of the car and approaching the pedestal bird bath that might also be a Lucite rainwater collector or the martini glass from the Taylor Swift *Bejeweled* video.

None of which seemed an appropriate ornament for the front lawn, since birds probably wanted to bathe in privacy.

Especially if you planned to swim in it with them in full view of the world with minimal clothing.

"Excuse me!"

A spotted arm swiped at her left ear and removed an earbud while she kept crooning, kicking her feet in the air. Around us, the music paused, though I wasn't certain how or who had done it.

"You make me feel like I'm living a... Hi dear! Care for a swim?" Martini Woman asked, humming the Katie Perry song that I could clearly hear from her ear buds now that the other music had ceased. In the air, her legs kept moving in perfect time to the music, a cabaret performer in a geriatric review.

Unfortunately for me and the residents of this street, our water sprite was not a cabaret dancer. Cabaret dancers wore lingerie at the very least, and as more of the bubbles faded, I was looking at... not lingerie.

"You're naked!" I shouted, waiting for my brain to catch up with my mouth. The gravity tarnished body parts took a minute to view correctly and the sight before me was an unwelcome glimpse into the future.

"Of course I'm naked, dear. What else would I be?" she cackled as a few neighbors poked their heads out. "It might be a senior community, but we know how to have a good time."

"What?"

"Who is she?"

"Should we call the cops?"

"My neck hurts!"

The chorus of complaints and questions came from the silver-haired women and bald men, all at least a decade into social security. Winnie chose that moment to lift her head, peering out the open window with a wide yawn that showed off her teeth.

"Whose dog is that?"

"Do you think she bites?"

"Someone cook me some bacon!"

The last word had Winnie catapulting herself from the car, ears and tail locked in on a small man with glasses. He looked like a ninja turtle from the old 90s Teenage Mutant Ninja Turtle movies, the version that starred people in cushioned turtle suits. The very tip of Winnie's tail flickered from side to side, her eyebrows wiggling in thought while keeping a laser focus on Turtle Man.

"Winnie, leave it!" I commanded, and her gaze flicked back to me for a second. "I'm serious."

Her tail lowered slightly, and she spared me a second glance.

"No one has snackies for you," I explained, but another resident chose that moment to amble out on a tennis ball footed cane. The brown coat and thick glasses were the spitting image of Carl from the movie *Up*. He stumbled, and one ball came loose, rolling gradually toward the grass on the edge of his front walkway. "No! No! No no no no..."

Winnie lunged toward the man, zeroing in on the ball as he shuffled after it, and she picked up speed. Carl the second lifted the cane off the ground like a sword, prepped to defend himself from the dragon who wanted the stray ball. I took off across the street, steering toward the hunter green colored house four to the left.

"Winnie!" I shouted again, watching her teeth clamp down on a ball, the airborne siblings of the stray suddenly more interesting than the one laying on the grass. The man pulled on his cane until the ball came loose, floundering backward off balance toward his front door frame. Carl the second caught himself, slowly lowering himself down to the stoop to catch his breath. My former military canine chewed on the ball, head held high, as she pranced around, showing off her prize. The man on the stoop was not amused, shaking his remaining balls at my dog.

"Out! Spit it out," I ordered her, squaring off and giving it my best growly voice. Winnie's tail twitched, and she lowered her head. "No, it's not play time. Out!"

Her head lowered all the way to the ground and placed the ball.

"Good girl."

I walked closer, maintaining eye contact. My knees bent so we were at eye level and my hand closed in on the ball.

Which is when her tail twitched.

My fingers had barely grazed the fuzzy green surface when Winnie's teeth clamped down on it and she took off barreling up the street. She made a sharp turn toward the Martini Lady's house. The naked occupant had just crested the rim when my partner barreled toward the glass.

"No!" I shouted, running again and wishing I owned rocket shoes. "Winnie! Stop!"

The dog side swiped the glass, and it quivered, water sloshing over the sides and splashing my partner. It was slow motion, watching her nose and ears connect the concept of her sudden bath with pink water hovering overhead. She released the ball and bounded toward the glass, the dancing occupant sliding down the pole beneath the spot Winnie planted her paws.

"No!" I grabbed her collar, pulling her away from the glass and the naked woman, but it was too late.

Another shuddering wobble sloshed more scented water, and the glass careened toward the lawn, crashing with a wet thud and covering all of us in a soapy, strawberry water shower. Winnie circled twice in joy, flopped to the ground and added mud to the carnage already coating my clothes.

It was like being showered with the leftovers at a bachelorette party.

Except instead of stripper sweat, it was naked old lady skin cells.

"Are you OK, lady?" I asked the woman, wondering if I should be more concerned about her or the rogue canine now sliding on her back through the soapy water. She swished this way and that, belly up to the sun with paws crossed on her chest. With her tongue hanging out, she looked both half-dead and happier than a pig in mud.

Winnie, not the old lady.

The latter was standing naked as the day she was born, showing absolutely zero interest in clothing, robes or... not being naked.

Maybe I am a prude...

Disturbing thought, that. Maybe I needed to revisit my early twenties where I occasionally hooked up with random guys in bar parking lots... those encounters were awkward, but I couldn't stomach the idea of being less adventurous than a naked old lady in a martini glass.

I wasn't even thirty yet, for fluff's sake.

"I'm fine. Don't call me lady... ick. Name's Gertie," she said, offering me a wrinkly hand. "And you are?"

My brain short-circuited as I stared at the very solid, very pruney, hand before me.

"Gertie? Mrs. Margot's sister, Gertie or Trudy or Gertrude-y?"

"The one and only," she curtsied. "Hate being called Trudy, though."

"But... you're dead?"

Chapter Five:
The Melodramatic Margots

There's something to be said about coming face to... not quite face, with a dead woman. She wasn't exactly the picture of health, but her lungs appeared to be more than functional as she belly-laughed in front of me.

Or at least I hoped she was laughing.

When the woman folded in half and mooned the roadway, I took up a serious interest in my shoes.

"Winnie, place!" I ordered her and waited as she unfurled her body and rose. Trotting the two steps toward me, I nearly passed out with surprise that she'd listened on the first try. "Good-"

My partner shook her coat, showering me with mud, foamy strawberry water, and wet dog fur that stuck to my clothes and skin. From the tippy tips of her pointed ears to the black tipped fur of her tail, the dog released a tidal wave of water and mud that soaked me to the bone and had Gertie laughing even harder.

"You both suck," I grumbled, swiping at the rivulets of water streaking down my cheeks. A streak of water went rogue and dripped into my eye, immediately irritating the delicate organ. "Crap!"

Squeezing my eye shut, I swiped at it with the back of my hand.

My wet, soapy, muddy hands, dripping water harvested from my hair and face.

"Ahh!"

The dual burn sent my eyes watering and boogers dripped out of my nose. Around me, I could hear Winnie's tags jingling and Gertie moving through the wet grass with a *squish*. Bouncing on the balls of my feet, I danced and swiped at my eyes-trying in vain to make the burning stop while only making it worse.

"Ow ow ow," I started spinning in a small circle until...

Whoosh!

A jet of water connected with my chest, drenching my olive tee before traveling upward. The stream pummeled my neck, my chin and then doused my entire face in freezing water that mingled with the mucus, tears and soap.

"Why aren't you dead?" I shouted around the stream, but it only got an extra helping of snot water sliding down my throat. Like any woman who didn't want to vomit, I swallowed.

Not for the first time in my life, but it was the least gross.

"What?" Gertie shouted, shutting off the water.

She waited until I had to swallow on purpose.

Giving my best stink eye, I tried to convey my hostile assessment. Instead of cowering in terror, she gave me the same look white women give puppies who fall in mud puddles.

Probably has cataracts... I lied to myself.

I didn't need a mirror to know I didn't look like an adorable puppy. The hair sticking to my face was squarely in drowned rat territory, and I was fairly certain there was still mucus dripping from my nose alongside the mud flecks that were probably now permanently staining this shirt.

Even with my eyes closed, I knew Winnie was rolling on her back in the wet grass... again. But I admitted defeat and peeled them open just enough to see... yup.

Soaking wet, mud encrusted dog.

A long sigh escaped.

"Why aren't you dead?" I asked again, flinching when she approached me. Clutched between the fingers of one hand, she held a sheer gauze robe, feathers trimming the hem and sleeves. In the other was a large angora rabbit trying to swallow her.

Gertie thrust the rabbit toward me, and I lurched backward, tripping over Winnie, who howled as I once again found myself sprawled out on the ground beside her.

Her wagging tail splattering mud over every soaked inch.

"I think you'll need more than a towel, dear," Gertie spoke, holding up the rabbit that might conceivably be a towel when placed in context. "Get up and you can use my shower. Just try not to touch anything."

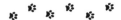

"What is this place?" I asked, trying in vain to cover my top and bottom with the old lady sized towel she handed me. Once I'd found the will to continue living, I hauled all size 18 of me up from the ground. Sadly, the will was fleeting and my reflection in the tinted windows of the purple house was a stark reminder that blonde hair and mud were not ideal.

And I'd picked the wrong day to wear my khaki cargo pants.

Mrs. Margot's sister had led me past the lavender monstrosity and into a small building to the rear. The color scheme matched the house, but size alone meant it was cute instead of an eyesore. Though I was strongly encouraged to disrobe on the porch, I declined the invitation to remove more than my shoes, citing outdated purity culture and the potential for my nipples to cut the glass windows of the tiny home in someone else's backyard.

"It's a house, dear." She rolled her eyes at my stupidity, and I felt slightly less bad about the pile of dirt I'd left behind in her shower.

"Why is it behind another house?"

Just through the front door was a sitting area with two cream-colored leather couches and a glass coffee table. Immediately to the right of the door was a series of hooks for keys and life alert buttons, and to the left was the rest of the house with a half wall separating the kitchen from the couches. Alongside it was the bathroom I'd covered in mud and filth.

A bathroom that only contained towels made for short people.

Winnie laid out on another towel in front of the couch. Somehow, the older woman had managed to get the wet, muddy, disobedient little fluff monster to lie in a designated location without violating the cleanliness of anything else.

It was an act of betrayal on par with asking Larry for pets.

"Oh, that. It's an accessory doohickey. Where the homeowners request permission to build a separate living quarter for family or to rent..." She was bustling about her kitchen, and I realized that her "accessory doohickey" was not only bigger than my apartment, but it also had its own full kitchen with an oven. The shower I had used was part of a full bath and there was still another door.... Meaning she had a bedroom.

A real one.

With a door.

Not just an open door frame to a stairwell that led into an alley.

"How do you take your tea?" Gertie asked, and I shifted from staring at Winnie to looking at the woman in the kitchen. Her hand was wrapped around the handle of an electric kettle, the device held slightly aloft in my direction.

"I don't drink leaf soup, but thanks for offering." I tried not to sound bitter that my dog listened to her, she had a bedroom door, and was short enough to use these towels. But half of my ass was exposed, and I was tired, so when her eyebrow spiked dramatically, I knew I'd failed.

"Leaf soup? You kids these days try so hard to be unique," her statement came with another eye roll. After doing them for so many decades, it was impressive she wasn't cross-eyed or blind. "Do you want coffee, then?"

"Only with my oxygen. Where are my pants?" I asked, not enjoying the airflow to my undercarriage. There are a few things of my mother's I endeavored to emulate, but having my nether regions naked in a strange place was not on that list. My life philosophy had always leaned toward "out for sun, out for fun" and there would be no fun here... and hopefully no sun.

Application of sunscreen to my butt cheeks was not part of my beauty regimen... *Is highlighter on my face a beauty regimen?*

I might not even have a beauty regimen.

"In the laundry. You can sit down, the furniture here is no stranger to a naked ass," she declared, dropping a filter in her coffee maker. I decided at that moment I would not be sitting on a single surface in this dwelling until I was once again wearing a cloth barrier against crabs, herpes and anything else you can get from shared surface contact with a diseased bottom.

"So... why did Mrs. Margot say you were dead Ms..."

"Mrs., It's Mrs. Margot."

"You also married a man named Margot?"

She had stopped making coffee and was staring at me.

"Why are you just standing there like a statue? I told you to sit."

I waited in silence, but she refused to address my question.

"I don't do naked. Until I have clothes on again, I can't sit on anything," I paused, waiting to see if it would prompt her to answer my question.

"Until you sit down and behave like a proper guest, you will not receive coffee," her abrasive tone was meant to quell further argument, and I was finally starting to see the family resemblance. If she and her sister were involved in a creepy polygamist thing, I was going to need to move. What I wasn't going to do was follow orders.

Just ask the army.

"Fine," I crossed my arms over my chest, death gripping my towel. "Then don't give me any coffee. Don't answer my questions, don't give me back my clothes, don't do any damn thing you please. But my bare ass isn't touching that couch."

My chest constricted. Telling someone they could deny me coffee was like telling the world to deny me air. Cruel and unfair... but I had a point to make.

Maybe Jake's right, I am dramatic.

"Why you aren't dead?" I narrowed my eyes, giving the older woman my best estimation of an *I'll fight you* face.

"Don't sass me, child," she threatened, holding up a giant knife and pointing it my direction. "You'll sit and drink your coffee like a civilized person. If you don't want your naked skin on my sofa, grab another towel."

The shiny knife had a black handle and despite her advanced age, she kept it up without a single quiver.

"What's the knife for?" I asked, admitting defeat and ducking back into the bathroom for more towels. I draped one on the leather couch and sat, then put another on my lap like a table-cloth. Mrs. Margot #2 lowered her knife back onto the counter and resumed making coffee.

"Making points to dense house guests. I can't believe you are related to Lynn and Monty," she grumbled, name checking my parents. "I've seen where you came from, child, and it is by far more trafficked than my couch."

"Who hasn't? Also, ew. That is not the old lady Yoda wisdom I need," I grumbled, shifting to get comfortable. Sitting on a towel on a leather couch was like riding down the giant slide at the county fair on a burlap sack. "Now, why does Mrs. Margot think you're dead? And if you're not dead, does that mean your girl-friend Ferrah isn't missing and she also didn't off her husband, Leonard? Leonard who works construction and also performs at Eggplants?"

Mrs. Margot #2... or number one if chronology of birth was the source of numbering, walked around the counter with two mugs. One cup had a paper tag hanging from a string laying over the edge, and the other smelled like the best thing in the world: coffee. Winnie twitched and I raised my finger in warning, needing her to stay down and not trip the old woman bringing me the only other reason to live.

Her tail thumped gently, and I smiled.

Dogs were a girl's best friend... even if sometimes this one was an asshole.

"Leonard and Ferrah have gone missing..." Gertie answered, her jaw working the dentures in her mouth. "And he doesn't work construction, as she said, but owns a company. The Pickles nonsense was just the fall-out from the lack of available construction materials. I wasn't 'moved-in' when Leonard went missing. I've rented this house for about a year and spent a great deal of time socializing with both of them. The Hollbrooks have an open marriage, but by all accounts, they were very much in love. When her husband went missing two weeks ago, I was spending more time with Ferrah, providing her consolation and investigative assistance. It wasn't anything sinister and she wasn't inclined to my particular brand of affection though I personally enjoy the diversity of a woman's touch, Ferrah was pretty dedicated to male companions."

She took a long drink of her tea, and I mirrored the movement with my coffee. It felt like the description of a soap opera and Leonard would be found wandering down Main St., naked, with a head injury and no recollection of how he came to be near death on the side of a highway. Then a man in an eyepatch would appear and try to kill him while he was making love with his wife. Leonard's memory would return just in time for him to remember he knew jiu jitsu and save them both.

"She said he was working on a project, and it had become more strenuous and time intensive than anticipated. He was spending more and more time out of the house, citing how they'd dug for the base months before the project was approved and far too deep for a foundation. Ferrah did the books for Leonard's construction business and when he was gone for a week, she went out to the site he told her about. There was a crew out there to lay the foundation, only now the ground was level at a normal height. When she asked the construction foreman, the man said he was hired after the hole was filled and no one in the area had any knowledge of what company had dug the hole. I think they were trying to convince her she was senile, but she had an invoice for the work. Two days later, she was gone too. I personally thought they'd taken a weekend in Vegas, until Monday rolled around."

"I mean... when I was little, I dug a hole in my backyard and filled it with water and called it a swimming pool. People dig holes sometimes," I suggested, taking another drink to hide my flattened lips and furrowed brows. "The *trying to convince her she'd never seen the hole or been paid for it and then going missing* is suspect."

"Just suspect? Construction isn't a small industry, but the tools needed to do the job are in limited supply... as are the number of certified operators. If no one knows, it's crossed suspicious into criminal."

"Like they weren't licensed or like they... were paid to keep the mouths shut?" I asked, wondering if I should be writing down notes or if this was a dream conversation with a ghost and my feet were going to become lime Jell-o.

"That's what we were working on... Ferrah had a lead on an excavator, the thing that digs precision holes, and a shady looking guy of some sort on her husband's payroll... IDK, she took off her bra and I was appreciating the view," Mrs. Margot's eyes went a little glassy and I shifted on my towels. She'd said Ferrah wasn't interested in what she had to offer, but it doesn't sound like the feeling was mutual.

Ahh... unrequited love, I knew thee well.

"Do you... need some alone time with those memories? Cuz..."

"Don't get smart, Cynthia. I may not be as uptight as my twin, but I will not tolerate insolence..."

"Your twin??" I interrupted. "She said you were her *older* sister!"

"She's always been sore that I beat her out of the birth canal by two minutes. Now she acts like I'm somehow one foot in the grave while she's some spring chicken and not hobbling along on a walker..."

Her tirade faded into the background as I started trying to superimpose the features of Mrs. Margot the First on this Mrs. Margot and see if they fit or made a Picasso painting.

Which...

"Why are you both named Mrs. Margot?" I cut her off mid-rant about boobs or bras... maybe Buicks.

"Because we're married to twins," she answered with an imperious hand wave.

"I mean, yeah, but being a twin and married doesn't give you the same last name... unless you were sister wives? Which is gross and weird, but I bet that asshole was super pat on the back high-fivey about it because men are stupid and gross and only think with the head that lacks ears and..."

"No, we are twins who married twins. Technically twice, but the first was another life," her clarification interrupted my running tirade about the virgin whore Madonna nonsense, and it took me a moment to comprehend.

"You... both married a Mr. Margot twice? And they were twins? Identical?"

"Fraternal the second time... Technically, my wife and I were both Mrs. Margot... Though it wasn't legal until she was nearing the end. For a country that considers itself great, they certainly don't believe in equality," she took a sharp slurp of her tea. "But we had a very large and ostentatious celebration when we were finally allowed to be ourselves."

Her celebration probably stood as a declaration and a protest. That no one controls love and they had no right or power to invalidate hers. But it was too short a time to be allowed what her sister had been given without question.

"Why did she claim Leonard's a friend of one of the Canadians you trafficked? Why not just tell me it was you? She knew you were involved, why didn't... just why?"

Mrs. Margot just shook her head.

"Glen likes to make everything so complicated. Didn't she not so long ago steal Bingo money and ask you to find the cash resting with her knickers? You should stop being surprised when she lies to you to get what she wants."

I stared at the bottom of my empty coffee cup wondering why I hadn't questioned her further. It was a sad commentary on my current mental state that none of this raised the ten dozen red flags that are clearly obvious now.

"So... is that why she said you died two days ago? She was mad you were.... Dallying with Leonard's wife? Or wanted to before they ran off to Vegas?"

Her fire alarm laughter nearly startled the skin from my bones.

"Gracious, no. She claims I died because I stopped sharing my Netflix password with her. She wouldn't stop watching Cobra Kai and it was ruining my algorithm."

Chapter Six:
Zombie Squirrels

It was a long drive back to Sweet Pea, my damp clothing clinging awkwardly to every crease in my flesh. Since the alternative was to stay and hear more about what shows Mrs. Glen Margot had watched on Gertie Margot's Netflix account, I'd elected damp driving over sibling gripes.

I had three siblings; I knew how these things ended.

Gertie hadn't been able to find her copy of Leonard and Ferrah's key but had promised to get in touch if she did. She gave me their phone numbers for program searches and possible tracking, if Carla would stop questioning their disappearance, and addresses for all the construction projects she'd thought he mentioned working on, but nothing could be confirmed without the invoices from the house. She'd also handed me a basket full of mail she'd collected from them and invited me to commit a federal crime by opening it.

I declined.

Orange was not my color.

We split the difference between misdemeanor B&E and federal felony by taking pictures of all of the envelopes and peeking through the windows. Though I hadn't gotten to look at everything I'd taken a picture of, the house had looked unmolested from the parts I could see from the backyard while wearing a towel.

The doors and their locks were intact with no tool marks. Window frames didn't have any broken locks or signs of tampering, and though most of them wore curtains- the view through the openings showed an undisturbed interior. Aside from the soggy grass and spots of mud, even the lawn had remained pristine, even beneath the weight of Gertie's giant plastic martini glass.

She claimed it was because of good base soil.

I was pretty sure it was because the owners wisely chose to only water the grass when Gertie decided to perform burlesque on the lawn.

Which, if the numbers of visible curtains were any indicator-happened often.

"Do you think Carla knew Gertie wasn't really dead?" I asked Winnie. The dog had mostly dried on her towel and was now one step down from roughed up cotton ball with small amounts of grass poking out of her mud-caked dewclaws. Unlike me, she hadn't lied and claimed to have to leave for work moments after her clothes were in the dryer.

Pulling on damp cargo pants was a new level of hell only matched in unpleasantness by having the bulky seams of said pants digging into my underwear-free butt.

"Do you think that's why she was all eye-rolly about it, or do you think she was concerned Mrs. Margot wanted to involve us in another 'missing person' deal? Do you think her sister also pretends stuff is missing to get out of admitting she made a mistake?"

Winie let out a sneeze that shook her ears and released a fart that startled her awake. She looked around, letting out a small growl and then seemed to notice her butt and the enticing smell it had made. Ignoring my questions, she stretched out her ribs to stuff her muzzle under the weapon of mass destruction known as a tail and went to town.

Since the only town I was visiting was the one I lived in, I decided she could take the vacation to Fart Town solo and rolled down the windows.

Just as we passed the "Welcome to Sweet Pea, OH" sign, my phone chimed with an incoming image message. I slowed to the town's twenty mile per hour speed limit and opened the message, studying Leonard and Ferrah's images as I crawled past a gas station, a movie theatre and a public restroom.

Ferrah had dark hair and a smooth complexion, very minimal grey at her temples. The generic photo that may have come from any number of social media sites, showed a woman with curves wearing a dress and an easy smile. Sunglasses covered her eyes, but

I could still see some of the smile lines at her eyes and the edges of her mouth. The woman was just my side of my parent's age but she had a striking grace that couldn't be learned.

Leonard was beautiful like Jeff Goldblum with a George Clooney smile and a build like Channing Tatum. Though in this picture he was wearing a pair of jeans and a flannel shirt, his physique was unmistakable. Silver Fox wasn't my breed, but I had a moment of regret that I hadn't gone to see him at Pickles before it became Eggplants to see if the package matched the wrapper... well, before it became Eggplants *and* he disappeared.

Hopefully the two weren't related.

"Do you..." I started, but a woman ran full speed into the road. I slammed the brakes, trying to keep the wheel in check so it wouldn't skid into her. We'd only been going twenty miles an hour, but the used Jeep didn't stop on a dime. Inertia flung us back against the seats as the woman draped herself on my car hood, screaming.

"Help! Please! You have to help! There's been an uprising and I cannot fight this alone!"

"A what?" I asked, not needing to raise my voice through the open window. Through the high dried-out grass beside us, a tan and white barrel-chested husky trotted toward my new hood ornament, tail and hackles in the air. I expected an alligator to follow, a gnashing and snarling monstrosity threatening to eat them all.

But nothing else emerged, and both the dog and human were still in hysterics. I'd made it past the initial crop of shops, and the only thing out this way before I hit Main St was a couple of farms and a vacation rental.

"You need to stop the uprising of the zombie squirrels!"

At the word "squirrel", the husky tucked their fluffy tail between hind legs and let out a small whimper. Winnie's ears perked up, and she searched the horizon for her favorite chew toy.

"Could you... get off the hood of my car and I'll park?"

It wasn't my first thought to ask her to move before I floored the Jeep away from her, but once the words left my mouth, it felt like the right call. The woman's hair was a mess, spread out in a matted mass of dirt and sweat caked reddish-brown waves. The car obscured her clothing, but what I could see of her arms showed no signs of injectable drug use, so she was probably either very good at deadpan humor, completely serious, or recreationally smoking reefer.

Compared to my usual clientele, none of those options were too dangerous.

"If I move, you won't drive off, right? You'll come help? I won't move unless you pinkie swear you'll help! I can't sleep, I can't eat... it's just... squirrels! You do not know how annoying and terrible squirrels are until they're ruining your life!"

A pinkie rose from my car bonnet, and I wondered how she expected me to shake without running her over. Unless this was an insurance scam plot, in which case she was in for a rude awakening, because I had no idea where my insurance card was or if I'd paid my bill.

"Can't pinkie swear from here, but Winnie will...." The dog jumped out of the back window and went to offer the husky comfort... and probably some judgment, since that was how Winnie rolls. "Stand by until I park, I guess."

My new hood ornament glanced at the two dogs, assessing.

"I'd never leave without Winnie... I mean I did once, but my best friend was taking risque pictures with a knife partially naked and..." I trailed off and Winnie flopped over on the side of the road.

Satisfied, the woman slid off my engine cover, letting her skin streak along in a loud shriek. Staying in front of the vehicle, she walked toward the edge of the road, looking prepared to re-insert herself into my pathway if I decided to leave my best friend behind and make a run for it. She didn't know about the bees/crocodile/giant spider incident I'd stuck with Winnie through, so I had to forgive the skepticism.

Maybe this was the worst thing *she'd* ever been through, but I'd lived in Florida.

Once I was safely on the shoulder, I put the Jeep in park and climbed out. Winnie trotted over and I leashed her to be safe, not sure if the bigger threat was zombie squirrels or the woman threatening me with them. In the event we needed to run, I wanted to have some level of control over her and I didn't keep cheese in my pocket.

"OK... Ms.?" I prompted.

"Doctor. Bridgette. Doctor Bridgette Ampersand, but you can call me Bridgette. And don't look at me like that. I know that look, and I'm not crazy. I shouldn't even be here. This is a vacation rental from hell and Caleb is going down for dragging me out here. After all that I've seen, I did not think that naked yoga for seniors would be up there with young women who've had their eyelids cut off to force them to watch the sexual assault of their friends. Or the ultrasonic torture device implanted in my leg... or watching my best friend die. But let me tell you, I could do something about some of those, but this is a whole new level of hell, and I am helpless. There is no bad guy."

So maybe this squirrel isn't the worst thing she'd seen.

"Alright... and who is that?" I pointed to the dog beside her. Upon closer look, it was a pit bull / husky mix with a longish coat and white toes. Winnie was sitting beside her, and the two dogs were waiting for us to do something.

"Heihei... like the dumb chicken in that animated movie? I didn't name her. I rescued her from the police when her owner experienced a brutal murder and the killer locked her in the bathroom for days, dehydrated and starving. She is far from dumb, though. Lockhart is running around somewhere. We named him, and I don't know if it was a self-fulfilling prophecy or just bad luck, but he is dumb. This whole thing is his damn fault," she was talking rapidly and taking fast strides toward a small ranch house. The bright red door stood out against the beige stucco walls and brown trim. It was one of the few houses in the area available to rent online and I wondered at the sanity of a woman who'd allow someone to take her on vacation to our town. It wasn't very big, but we'd made national news at least twice.

Both times because of me, but that was beside the point because nationwide, people should know better. It was like vacationing in Florida after all the hurricanes and alligator stories, sure they had Disney, but if you weren't at the Airport or Disney, you were just asking for trouble.

"Who's Lockhart?" I asked, half running and barely keeping up. Bridgette was about my size, maybe a little bigger and just a hair shorter, but she moved like a woman trying to outrun the past and stay just beyond the reach of whatever demons stalked her mind... probably those eyelid cutter-offers and the killer locking her sweet baby in a bathroom. Still, Bridgette had an authority that sent me trotting after her despite common sense. The common sense that dictated I should not get out of my car for strangers and then follow them into a strange house.

"Golden retriever. Like the character Lockhart in *Chamber of Secrets*, he's beautiful but dumb. The asshole brought a dead squirrel into the house and while we were getting them fed, I went to dispose of the squirrel, only it was gone." She'd arrived at the front door and threw open the screen and then the red door to show a living space stuffed with mis-matched furniture. "Gone and never to be seen again, but oh, do we hear it."

"You're a doctor. Have you considered... prescribing yourself something?"

"I'm not that kind of doctor. You don't believe there's a squirrel, do you?"

"I believe... you believe there is a squirrel and that you're a doctor. So... you think it... rose from the dead?" I asked Heihei, and she let out a snort that mirrored my thoughts, but I thought it best to keep my snot to myself. "Or it's staging a coupe?"

"Wow, now I know how Caleb feels when I sarcastically validate his feelings. Of course, I don't believe the squirrel was ever dead. I'm an optometrist, you can't have a doctorate and believe in zombies or vengeful squirrels with an axe to grind. But this whole incident feels personal. It's irrational... except..."

"They don't have a literal axe, do they? It... I thought there was only one squirrel."

She held up her hand, and I exchanged a look with the two dogs beside me.

None of them displayed any sign of knowledge about the possibility of there being an actual axe. Winnie because we just got here and Heihei because she probably hadn't seen it.

Despite the need to scream, we kept quiet, waiting with shallow breaths for whatever we were supposed to...

The chittering began somewhere to the left. It echoed around the room, coming from everywhere and nowhere at the same time. Following the first wave of chitters, a squeak joined the chorus, and then a subtle scratching.

"Sweet Anubis on the River Styx! What the hell is that?" I asked, backing toward the door and praying Winnie would follow me when we made a break for it. I felt guilty for doubting her and using the therapist doublespeak, but I wasn't inclined to stick around and apologize.

Squirrels were annoying on their own, but zombie squirrels were above my pay grade.

"It's the squirrel... or squirrels," she sighed, gazing toward the tapping claws of a lumbering Golden Retriever who appeared in a darkened corridor. He moved without haste toward a squishy bed in the corner and lowered his head toward the sherpa surface. Carefully, the massive dog followed his head down and curled into a semi ball, licking the area beside his paw.

"See, we found the squirrel after the first day and it was a little pudgy. It started pilfering cotton and a washcloth..." she was walking and talking, listening at the walls but I couldn't take my eyes away from the Golden. "When I tried to corner the damn thing, Lockhart got in the way, and it disappeared when I went to get a... I don't know what I was going to get. You can't trap it under a cup, but I don't own a net. Not that it matters. Before I could figure out how to get rid of it, that beautiful dumdum had helped it escape."

I crept closer to the "beautiful dumdum", thinking he was pretty smart if he could aid and abet a squirrel prison break, transfixed by whatever had his attention.

"And then I didn't see it for a day... but that's when the sounds started..."

Glancing over my shoulder, I checked on Bridgette and Heihei. Winnie might be attached to me, but she wasn't all that interested in helping on this one. As I got closer, the dog adjusted his paw, and I saw a cute, little pink toe bean.

"What do you..." the toe bean twitched and then... rolled over.

"Oh, my dog, what the hell!" I shouted, stumbling backward. Winnie was right there, and I tumbled over her, not questioning the fact she wasn't screaming while I crab-walked away from the bed and the miniscule pink pimple with eyes and ears and...

"You're being haunted by baby squirrels?" I shouted at Bridgette. She was wide-eyed, statue still and enraptured by a sight just above my head. Sucking in air, I glanced up just as a brown ball of fluff flew from a shelf and scurried around the living room toward the Golden Lockhart.

Winnie, sensing a game was afoot, took off after the squirrel and dragged me a few inches closer. For her part, mama squirrel showed no fear. Smacking Lockhart on the nose, she took back her baby and darted up a drape.

Like that squirrel in the *Animaniacs* cartoon.

My partner gave chase, ripping at the floral fabric and rattling the curtain rod in its bracket. The brown puff tail twitched, but she kept her balance to leap off the rod and scuttle into a tiny alcove above the cabinets, forming a small barrier between the kitchen and the rest of the house. Winnie stood on her rear legs, ready to get in there, when a streak of gold cut in and blocked her path.

With a low growl, Winnie took a step back from the bared teeth of Lockhart.

"Apparently, he considers himself their second mama," Dr. Ampersand surmised, and I hauled Winnie away from him before she did something stupid. "First time I've actually seen a baby, though, so that's a relief."

"How is that a relief?" I panted, putting all my strength into holding Winnie back until either she lost interest, or my arms ripped out and I no longer had a say in this.

Dropping to a crouch, I put all my weight into it and just as she decided she didn't want to meet a baby squirrel that bad, a loud rip cut through the chaos. I finally got the right flexibility to sink into the crouch and... felt cold air on my backside.

"Because I still wasn't sure there were baby squirrels and not just a battalion of mystery squirrels that all somehow lived in the walls," she answered, grabbing her phone and making a call. "There are baby squirrels in the walls. Whatever you're doing, stop and get help or not only will I change my mind about marrying you, but I will also whack you in the nuts with a tennis racket... again. This time to crush your nuts instead of protecting them from squirrels!"

Shoving her phone back in her pocket, she turned to me and Winnie. Her entire demeanor changed, like knowing somehow made her world OK.

"Now that that's handled... you want some coffee?" she asked me, moving toward the kitchen with a wary eye on the squirrel hiding hole. "And I have peanut butter pumpkin treats?"

Winnie stopped fighting me and sat down, paw extended.

"You suck, Winnie," I muttered, and I heard Bridgette laugh while I hauled myself up.

"Lucky they're cute, right?"

With a long exhale, I pulled out my own phone and sent off a text message to Larry. My heart hammered in my chest at the idea of doing anything that might give him hope and encourage his relentless assault on my boundaries.

"So are those damn squirrels. I'd love a cup, because coffee is life. And when my ex, who's a vet, shows up, if he does, since he might be learning a new stripper routine, I'd love to borrow your tennis racket. His nuts haven't suffered enough, and I don't own any sporting goods."

Bridgette raised the whole coffee carafe in a salute.

"They belong to the rental. But if you're feeling super vindictive, I think I saw some golf clubs in the garage if you want to lie in wait for him after he looks over the babies. In the interest of full disclosure, my future husband is a detective, but I'm willing to flash him to cause a distraction if you do it outside where I have plausible deniability," she finished with a wink. "But... and you might know this, your pants ripped, and I can see... well..."

I curved around to check and... yup.

Butt cheeks.

"I wish this was the most embarrassing thing to happen to me today."

"Oddly, this might be my favorite part of today," a deep male voice said from behind me.

I said a silent prayer to Anubis that he was ready to let me board the ferry before I had to turn around.

"I'd be careful about talking about women like that in this house if you don't want to leave with your testicles in a jar like a set of Rocky Mountain oysters," another man spoke, softer and with a wisp of another region I'd never seen.

Bridgette held up a kitchen knife, emphasizing his point. I followed the... well, point of the knife to the open door and saw a man with a russet complexion and shaggy dark hair standing beside an equally appealing Larry, holding his medical backpack.

"Hey, Cyn. Make a new friend?" He asked as Bridgette brought me a large cup of coffee.

"I think I met my twin separated at birth. It feels like we were practically made by the same person."

Chapter Seven: Familial Fascination

B ridgette kindly allowed me to pull my undies on in her rental bathroom while Larry got to work checking on and rescuing the baby squirrels. Since said undies were hot pink with a rainbow unicorn flipping everyone off, I elected to keep them a secret from the rest of the house and opened the bathroom window to climb out.

Except bathroom windows are not sized for adult escapes and only my head made it through.

I needed a new plan.

Leaving the bathroom, I tiptoed to the neighboring bedroom and found a set of French doors. A quick peek through the sheer white curtains showed a sprawling yard that had more dirt than grass. Unlocking the doors, I quietly pushed one open, hoping it wouldn't squeak or creak. The early evening breeze ruffled my hair, and I smiled at the minor triumph.

Once outside, I took a deep breath and plotted how to get Winnie from the house and back to my car without having to see Larry. His view of my naked butt is all he'd be getting from me today and every day in the foreseeable future.

"We really are basically the same person," Bridgette said, and I practically jumped out of my skin. She had appeared beside me with a travel coffee cup and Winnie at the end of her leash.

"How?" I stammered, staring at her.

"If my ex had shown up and seen my naked ass in front of strangers, I also would have tried to sneak out a window... You know, if I had an ex. Step one is always get outside, then make a plan to get what you need, like furry best friends and coffee. Finally, escape without encountering the object of your ire." She tried to smile reassuringly, but it looked a little too self-aware to be comforting. Whatever this woman had been through, she was no stranger to sneaking out the back door and coveting coffee.

Unlike me, she appeared to have figured out a system for such things, and I wondered if she'd teach me her ways.

"Thank you," I said, while accepting the leash and the coffee. "Sounds crazy when you say it out loud."

"Doesn't mean it won't work. You heading out?"

"Yeah, I'm really sorry to duck out, but maybe we can hang sometime?"

"We're headed home tomorrow. But I'm really glad to have met you and we should text maybe... Just... can I offer some unsolicited advice?" She tapped her fingers against her thigh in patterns of three. Three taps of each of the three middle fingers, index to ring and back again.

"If it's unsolicited, I think asking ruins some of the 'interfering in your life' vibe. But since you've seen my naked butt, rescued my dog and brought me coffee, I think you get a free pass on offering life advice. Also, I hope one day you'll email me the template for your tried-and-true method of sneaking out of awkward situations."

Taking a long drink of coffee, I watched her shift over the rim. In her eyes, I saw the weight of knowledge and experience. There was something else, something more, that I didn't think she often shared with strangers.

You're probably imagining things.

"You take on a lot and avoid intimacy," she shifted uncomfortably. "You try to act like nothing bothers you, but I can see the toll it's taken. I think... well, that man in there has a lot of guilt when it comes to you. If you decide to let him back in, wait until he works through it. Right now, you both might be a little toxic for one another."

The eye doctor stopped making eye contact, her hands moving uncomfortably beside her. She definitely saw more than just what was visible and while I had questions, I wasn't ready to dive into another mystery.

"I sound like a fortune teller, but I promise I'm not trying to sell you anything."

"Thank you. Really. I think I knew that, but it's nice to hear something besides 'he's a good guy, just hear him out'. Because really... I think I've heard it all, and all of it is... well..." I sighed and drank coffee, because it was there. With my other hand, I stroked the soft fur on Winnie's cheek, using three fingers that tapped three times. "Dismissive of what I need so he can have what he wants. I feel like his excuse and maybe his prize..."

"An excuse to avoid dealing with his own demons that also validates his self-worth?"

I nodded at her words, not sure what to say.

"Well, thank you for stopping and helping."

"Sorry your vacation is turning out so chaotic. This town is more than a little nuts, pun intended," I said, offering her a hand.

"My whole life is chaotic, I expect nothing less," she sighed as something crashed inside and two dogs started barking in tandem. Her left eye twitched, and I contemplated offering her my coffee. She handed me a business card with her cell number on it. "Excuse me, duty calls."

With a last wave, the optometrist left us to exit the side gate and head back out to the road where I'd left my Jeep.

What demons does Larry have?

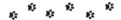

My apartment didn't have a laundry machine.

When I was with Larry, I used his washer and dryer. When Cruz was here, the place he had... owned? Rented? However he had it, the place also had laundry and I could use that too. But since both were out for the foreseeable future, I was unfortunately forced to use my parent's laundry machines.

Which came with strings.

At the end of those strings were family dinners with my parents, Seth and Carla, the terror and her brother, and my sisters. One sister, Heidi, lived near enough that she sometimes attended in person and helped my mom host personal pleasure device parties. Heidi was the oldest, and a doctor of some sort. Technically, having once been professors, my parents were probably also doctors, though no one called them Dr. Sharp in my presence. Our other sister, Molly, usually videoed in from whatever country she and her wife were in. I had no idea what she did, but it was for the betterment of mankind... and the acquisition of novelty sex toys, which she then shipped to my parents, who put it in their "playroom".

Also known as my childhood bedroom, that now looked like the set of a very well-funded porno.

Winnie and I had stopped at my apartment so I could change pants only to find I was out of clean pants. I was also out of clean socks, clean bras, clean underwear, and patience with the universe.

"I can't do dinner tonight, Winnie," I told her, and she just wagged her tail.

Winnie loved family dinner because Sylvia was an agent of chaos who snuck Winnie various foods to see if she could make her farts stinky enough to kill me. It was unlikely my niece would succeed, but her willingness to try was another reminder she'd be on a post office wanted poster in ten years.

Since my underwear and shirt were technically clean, I fished out a pair of jeans from under my bed that were a half-size too small. Squeezing into them, I glanced at myself in the mirror.

"If I don't eat or breathe, I can probably wear these..." I told my best furry friend. She didn't look embarrassed by me, so I packed up my bag of laundry and all the courage I could muster to head back down the stairs, up the alley and into my not-yet cooled waiting vehicle.

With the promise of a long night, we set out to the house of my childhood. The light blue paint and white trim hadn't changed much. The American flag waving proudly above the front door had been joined by a LGBTQIA2-S flag that would have made my parents a target in our small town if it wasn't full of adventurous seniors who ran the town. We had more sex shops and bookstores than churches and I took that as a reassuring sign that the Jesuits weren't going to be charging down the block with torches and pitchforks any time soon.

This left the Carters and the Kirbys as the only people who would really have a problem with it, and I couldn't see either working up much of a fuss. Amber was a wannabe actress not averse to adult film roles and Larry's parents were Pony Play fetishists.

Information I wish I did not possess, but was not above leveraging.

"They're here!" Sylvia screamed, and I had to force my shoulders away from my ears. Her voice was coming from everywhere and nowhere at once. It burrowed into my ears and tormented every one of my auditory receptors. She was the superhero whose screech murdered bad guys... which made me the least effective super villain ever.

Erich opened the door and Winnie walked in like the queen of the house. I followed behind her, lugging my giant laundry bag like her valet.

"Hey kid."

I held my hand out for Erich to fist bump. He wasn't big on touching and, based on the noise canceling headphones he was sporting, Sylvia had already pushed him past the point of sensory overload. With his dishwater blonde hair and light brown eyes, he favored my side of his gene pool. Sylvia was the spitting image of their mother. I hadn't met the woman who'd brought these kids into the world, too wrapped up in being a bitter teen to go to the wedding, but the Peony's were patient, open, and loving. They supported Seth getting these kids a new mom, still actively participating in their lives despite having lost their only child and were always on standby to babysit or replant a burning shrub when Sylvia learned about matches.

They were the gift these kids deserved, but I suspected they would also be Sylvia's first call for bail money.

Erich fist bumped me back and then motioned for me to come closer, eyes darting around.

"Grandma brought a date for you and was planning on blackmailing you into coming over if you didn't come over on your own. I think she stole the rest of your clean clothes," he whispered, then ran off like a skittish rabbit at the thunderous footfalls of his nemesis.

"Auntie Cyn!" Sylvia shouted, taking a flying leap four steps from the bottom. Like the athlete I never was and would never be, I slid along the runner and collapsed in front of her. As though it was her plan all along, Sylvia crash landed on my belly and rolled off with a cackle.

"You're like a bounce house!"

Then she took off toward the kitchen where I hoped equally that she didn't catch on fire and also that she'd sustain some sort of injury to instill caution, if not fear, into her. Nothing life threatening, but the girl needed at least two trips to the ER to curtail some of her diabolical tendencies.

"Cyn!" Seth appeared from either the living room or the formal dining room. He leaned in and gave me a quick hug before stepping back and checking me over. "You look tired. I thought you might sleep after I walked you upstairs."

"I thought I would too, but your wife wouldn't stop arguing with an old lady in my kitchen," I snapped, looking at the woman herself. "And you! You knew Mrs. Margot #2 wasn't actually dead, didn't you? And that most of the story she was telling me was a lie?"

Carla rolled her eyes and also gave me a hug, despite my best death glare.

"I had a feeling. Not to cast aspersions, but she's been dead before..."

"And still you let me go ask questions at an all-male review. Does Leonard even know her niece's illegally smuggled lumberjack?" I stared down at her bombshell figure and classy dress with strappy sandals. Next to her, *I* looked like a lumberjack trafficked out of the Canadian wilderness... I'd consider changing if it wouldn't potentially make my date like me.

"No idea... But we can ask her at lunch on Thursday." I gave her a *hell no* look. "It's not optional if you want to keep Sharp Investigations open. I think she's lonely and wants leverage to make us spend time with her. I promise there will be coffee. What was Gertie's cause of death this time?"

"She changed her Netflix password. What do you really know about Leonard and Ferrah? Because Mrs. Margot's portrait of murderous country-ish songs seems far, far off," I continued as I followed her into the kitchen. "Cheese down, Sylvia!"

My order froze the child midway to her destination of handing Winnie a piece of cheese. The little girl squealed, dropped it, and I dove to the floor. Winnie was faster, and before I could acknowledge the jarring of my joints, the cheese disappeared into her schnozzle, swallowed whole and never to be seen again.

But oh, would I smell it.

"Damn-it, kid!"

My niece just laughed, skipping out of the kitchen while my dad announced.

"Dinner will be ready in a few. Go wash your hands!"

No way was that hell spawn washing her hands, but it was cute that he tried. Walking toward my dad, I gave him a side hug while he was mid-sauté of something green and chicken-y.

"You need to wash your hands too, Cyn," he warned, and I walked to the kitchen sink and did as he asked... why, I don't know. Listening wasn't my strong suit, but the man was holding food and it smelled good. Since I'd had my dad's cooking before, I knew it would taste even better.

Soap and water was a small price to pay to get that food in my mouth.

"Is that your sister, dude?"

Soap, water and... being set up by my mother... again.

I needed to buy Erich a burner phone so he could send me messages *before* I walked into a trap.

Grabbing the towel, I turned while drying my hands and plastered the fakest smile I could manage on my face. It might look more like a deranged snarl, but I wasn't exactly in a meeting company mood and the sooner he ran away, the better.

"Yup, hi. I'm Cyn," I declared, holding out my hand to a man with wire-rimmed glasses in a henley tee with jeans and work boots. His wavy light brown hair flopped over one pale brown eye; squared jaw graced with a smattering of scruff.

Sweet cheese and crackers...

The man took my hand while I prayed to all that was holey—like Swiss cheese and saltine crackers—that drool wasn't dripping out of the corner of my mouth.

I owe my mom an apology. Her taste was improving...

"Levi Lovelace," he answered, and my brain pinged with an incoming message that I should be alert and weary, but I could not figure out why. "I work with Seth."

"Engineer?" I asked, trying to check my mental messages for the source of my concern. I was coming up with nothing but rodeo images. I'd never wished to own a saddle more than right now.

"Architect."

"A real architect? Or a... performance architect?" I clarified, narrowing my eyes. I wasn't sure what the muscle situation under Seth's perpetual button downs and Dickies was, but I was pretty sure he didn't look like that... and honestly, if he did, I would rather burn my eyes out with a hot spoon than ever know or remember such facts because... ew.

"A real architect... what's a performance architect? Do you guys have a community theater here?"

Chewing my lip, I made eye contact with Seth and tried to ask if this man was new here. My brother shrugged, daring me to explain that I thought his coworker could make a killing as a stripper.

"Never mind. What are you working on?"

"I'm designing a new multi-family housing project out near Dayton. It's pretty cool... Assuming the developer doesn't low ball the contract and we end up with a boxy grey box of sadness," he laughed at his own joke. None of those words tracked in my over-tired brain, but I decided he was talking about apartments, maybe.

"Designed? I thought you weren't an engineer... Seth designs buildings," I accused, falling back to my assumption the man was actually a dancer in nerds clothing. While I wasn't confident enough to date a man all the girls wanted, I'd be down for a lifetime pass to whatever establishment he worked at.

"Architects design layouts and planning, dumdum. I do safety and feasibility," my brother chimed in with an eye roll. All he needed was to ruffle my hair and the *look at my idiot kid sister* act would be complete. "He tells them how to position everything to maximum benefit, and I tell them whether or not it will stand up."

"Sounds like a scam, but whatever. How did you end up here? Lose a bet?" I asked Levi, still feeling uncomfortable at the notion of a man being invited here for me. No matter how hot and how seemingly smart he was, there had to be something wrong with him.

This family doesn't attract normies.

"Seth invited me? He said he thought we might... holy smokes, what is that?"

I turned quickly, terrified my dad had set dinner on fire and I would die of starvation only to see Winnie. She was wearing a tutu, a tiara and fairy wings, all of which were fairly normal for her, but the horror was probably from the marker drawn cheek circles, blue pencil eyebrows and pink nail polish on her toes.

"What the..." I whipped back to Seth and glared. "You! Fix!"

"It's water based. We don't have non-water based markers in our house, butthead. It'll wash off," he chuckled, but Levi was still wide-eyed focused on Winnie.

"This isn't your house, Sethanie. This is mom's house, and we don't know what manner of..."

Levi went pale, grabbing Seth's arm, who joined him in looking like the crypt keeper's henchman.

"It's just Winnie. My canine partner and reminder that no matter what she does, she's way better than his crotch fruit..." Seth shook his head and urged me to turn. Beside Winnie, wearing a chauffeur's hat, black leather straps strategically covering her naughty bits, and holding a riding crop... was my mother.

"Cyn! Glad you've met Levi. Levi, this is my youngest daughter. She's a bit of a prude, but... Don't stop stirring, Monty!" my mom ordered, slapping my dad on his butt with the riding crop while we all watched. "Don't make me tell you again, or you won't be allowed release tonight."

"Yes, ma'am," he answered, and my cheeks flamed while bile rose in my throat. None of those words and sights would be leaving me and for that, I needed a coping mechanism that didn't involve scooping out my brain with a melon baller. Searching the immediate area, I found a bottle of tequila to the left of my mom.

I grabbed it without another word. From the cabinet to my left, I grabbed three cups and poured about a shot in each and passed them around.

"If we remember this night tomorrow, we will need to find a Groupon for therapy," I hissed. Seth and Levi nodded before we all threw the shot back and heard another slap of the crop against my dad.

I poured us another round.

Chapter Eight: Phishing for Pants

B right sun pierced my room, the taste of sandpaper and nightmares clinging to my dry mouth. One of my arms was asleep, completely numb under the weight of either my torso or my Winnie.

"Errgh," I muttered, rolling to the side and hoping to dislodge my arm and hide from the sun in the same movement. My roll didn't free my arm, but it did put me face to fur with my best friend... on the opposite side of the numb arm.

"No, no, no," I whispered, scrunching my face to open as little of my eyes as possible to look under my blanket.

Wearing PJs and underwear, thank dog!

Having established that whatever happened hadn't ended in naked times, I felt prepared to look toward my other arm.

Brown hair mussed from sleep was an adonis who did not belong in my bed, hugging my arm to his chest like a security blanket. His *bare* chest with rippled muscle and smooth skin that gave off heat like the metal coils in an electric oven.

Levi.

I adjusted the blanket and confirmed he was wearing pants, but no boots. A sure sign that sexy times had been averted, but the manners of not wearing shoes to bed had held up in the world of Jose Cuervo.

Jose Cuervo...

Last night came back in flashes of black leather, tequila and too much food. Levi had leaned as heavily into drinking as I had while Seth had cited heartburn and old age as an adequate reason to give up the gambit. Carla must have driven us here, but why?

Why would I need to harbor Levi...

My eyes landed on my phone, and I swiped it open to search for clues as to who or what might have inspired the current sleeping arrangements. Taking it with me into the kitchen, I started my daily ritual of adding water and coffee grounds to the coffeemaker while I flipped through the hand-held computer that was... mostly functional.

There were a few messages from Larry asking me to call him. A missed call from my mom that informed me I'd forgotten all of my clean clothes at her house, and I had twenty-four hours to come get them or they would be donated and I would need to walk around naked.

As though this town needed more naked Sharps...

And nothing. No notes from Carla or missed calls from Mrs. Margot... first or second. Nothing from PETA about the testing of markers on non-consenting canines. There was, unfortunately, an e-advertisement for the newly refurbished Eggplants with a rehearsal video I wouldn't watch while there was a man I didn't know in my bed.

Or a man I knew.

Or an actual eggplant.

"Alexa," I started, wondering what explanation the robot assistant could offer, but nothing came to mind, and eventually, the blue lights shut off. The click clacks of claws on linoleum announced the arrival of company, and I looked down at the reddish head and pointy ears of Sgt. Winnie. Most of the marker had come off her face, but I think we gave her two pounds of treats to get her to let us remove it. She let out a soft whine and glanced toward the staircase.

Yup, dog mom time... I glanced at the man asleep in my bed and then down at my sleep shorts and tee. Both were fine for a short outdoor excursion, and I led Winnie to the top of the stairs. Stuffing my feet into silicone clogs and leashing her up, I took a last glance at the sleeping man and grabbed my pepper spray.

He probably wasn't dangerous, but it was never a good idea to leave weapons lying around after your mom gave a sneak peek into your origin story. It was still unclear to me what architects did, or if he was an architect, but I was pretty sure blinding himself with pepper spray would hurt his prospects in either career.

And his eyes.

The downside of living above my business, aside from trash day in the alley, an unknown number of people with keys, the noise from the street and the absence of an oven, was that I didn't have a yard. No front yard, no backyard... not even a strip of green space between my front door and the curb. When Winnie wanted to do her business, we had to walk up the alley, dodging questionable puddles and potentially sharp trash, to the community micro-park at the end of the street.

Cars lined both sides of the connector street. Though every house on the streets branching off of downtown had a garage of some sort, no one put their cars in them. A car occupied almost every inch of curb space, a barricade of cars between me and the green space with a best friend who needed to tinkle.

Guiding my partner between a Buick and a red... thing, we made it across safely and she flung herself to the ground. Rolling on her back in the damp grass, Winnie showed me her belly, her toofers, and all of her toe beans.

"Keep it up. You're only making bath day come faster," I warned.

She sneezed at me, and I shrugged.

"You'll see."

Hopping up, she started sniffing while I looked at all the cars. Many of them I knew the owners of, like the Casey's bar owner—Gloria. Her pointless husband. The weird old dude who likes to hang out near my parent's house to ask if his junk "looks normal". But mixed in with those were newer, shinier, more expensive cars.

The town wasn't a hot spot for the wealthy, so tourism leaned heavily toward families on road trips passing through, campers who realized inside is the best place to sleep, and social media "influencers" who saw Sweet Pea videos on YouTube and thought it would be a great place to get content.

Since I lived here and most of the videos involved me, it wasn't a longshot bet.

Unfortunately, it also usually paid off, so I was two stooges short of my own physical comedy show.

Winnie's head butted up against my leg and I looked down at her and then at the steaming pile of poo she'd left for me. Tucking away my car related thoughts, I pulled out a bag, scooped up the poop, and Frogger-ed across the empty street into another small gap to head back into the alley, reverse the path of hazard avoidance, and into my building.

We paused at the bottom, listening for signs of life from above, but only the quiet gurgling of my coffee maker could be heard. Hazarding the trip, we climbed the steps to the landing and saw Levi where I had left him. My partner scented the air and gave me a raised brow. She also wanted to know why a man was in our space.

"No idea," I whispered to her and led the way back into the kitchen, where I poured food into her dish and served it. My coffee maker beeped, and I pulled out a cup, pouring in liquid until it looked and smelled like a reason to live, and took a long drink.

My phone stared up at me from the counter and I opened it again, swiping left and right through the apps I could see on the slightly cracked screen. I slid my finger up along the bottom of the screen, looking at the open applications, and started closing them.

Email, messages, BlitzMoji, Chrome with an active search for "can I give myself a lobotomy..."

"That doesn't look like a good idea," a warm voice said from beside me and I screamed, dropping my phone in the sink.

"What the hell?" I demanded, turning into Levi. "Give a woman some warning!"

"Sorry. You looked deep in thought, and I was trying not to disturb you... it's just... I smelled coffee and..." he gestured at the pot, and I nodded. "Seth warned me to never get between you and coffee, so please don't murder me."

Before I could move, he rested a hand on my hip and slid in behind me to reach up and get his own cup. Heat flooded my southern hemisphere, and I froze. Nearly everything besides my heartbeat stopped as confusion warred with lust.

Is this man magic?

I checked out his fingers where they rested along the outside of the mug, long and slightly callused. Following the curve of his arm to the bare expanse of his chest, full lips... His hair flopped over one eye and my heart thumped louder to the beat of a 90s boy band song.

Yup... magic.

"Did you..." he stared into his empty mug before setting it down and reaching for the pot. His hand was still on my hip, his bare chest warming the exposed skin of my shoulders. "Did you kick over a collection of coffee mugs in front of your office and shout about Godzilla and Tokyo?"

I lost most of his words to the low hum of my brain short-circuiting at his touch.

"Hmm?" I asked, openly staring. Lance Bass, my boy band mega crush, had turned out to be gay. But I was pretty sure Levi wasn't... or maybe I was just hoping. It was one thing to wake up naked in bed with a stranger and no pants, but a completely different unfamiliar situation to wake up hungover and mostly clothed beside a man. "Role playing?"

"You... destroyed... but not all of the... Never mind. I don't think you've had enough coffee for questions..." Something moved lower on his body, and I bit the inside of my cheek to keep from letting out a moan.

Magic, magic man.

His hand slid down slightly, a caress that ended when he rudely took back his hand and walked around to the barstool facing me across the sink. The temperature dropped a few degrees without him, but I was fairly sure he adjusted his pants before taking his seat. On the counter beside him was the slightly water damaged letter Carla had left here yesterday.

"Love letter?" He asked, and I glared at it.

"Pitiful attempt to make amends. I don't want to talk about it. New topic?"

He nodded, taking a drink of coffee and searching for safe topics of conversation.

"What were you looking at?" he asked instead, gesturing toward my phone in the sink. Words stuck in my suddenly dry mouth and reached for the mug beside me, chugging the scalding coffee to buy myself a few seconds until the mug was empty.

"I was trying to figure out how you ended up in my bed," I answered, grabbing my phone and wiping it with the dish towel hanging off the door handle to the fridge. "I remember leather, tequila, food, more swatting, more tequila..."

"I uhh..." His bare arm reached behind his head, flexing his right biceps and forearm in a way that should not be sexy but... "I was too drunk to drive home, and Seth was already giving you a ride. He was going to let me stay in their guest room at his house, but your niece started speaking in a demon voice and insisted if I entered their house, she would eat my soul?"

Nodding, I opened the freezer and put an ice cube in my mouth, then poured another cup of coffee. Trying not to drool, I drank a reasonable sip and let the ice cool it down.

"Sounds like her. Pretty sure she can't actually eat your soul, but she can draw on you with a marker and carve her name into your leg with a thumbtack."

He gaped at me, and I bent my leg to put my foot on the counter and show him the scratch marks on my ankle. They'd faded since the initial encounter, a good sign I wasn't permanently branded, but I could still make out the general shape of her name. Instead of reading my ankle, Levi's gaze fell on the exposed sections of my upper thigh and flashes of neon orange underwear.

He licked his lips, and I dropped my leg to the floor before I got any more terrible ideas. I didn't need to be psychic to know where his mind had gone, and it wouldn't take much effort to get us prepped to do the horizontal dance with no pants.

Especially since I wasn't wearing pants.

He seemed to shake out of the lust-induced trance enough to form words.

"So... Why does your mom think you're an uptight prude who can't get her own date? Cuz outside of who you have as parents, you seem pretty normal."

His gaze lingered where my leg had been, shifting uncomfortably in his seat.

Maybe he has hemorrhoids.

"I live in a tiny apartment above an investigation office with a dog. I work at a farm and usually have some manner of something disgusting on me. Also... sometimes things explode near me. Usually it's Winnie's fault, but I'm responsible for all crimes committed by her." I paused to drink more coffee and let my words sink in. When he didn't run away or ask about Roger's chicken farm, I decided he must not have heard all the juicy gossip yet. While I could fill him in, my lack of embellishment would ruin the entertainment value. "What member of your family hates you enough to ask my mom to help find you a date?"

Winnie clanged her metal bowl against the underside of the sink. I picked it up and put it in said sink, running the tap with hot water to clear the drool residue and food particles. My partner head butted me in the leg, and I gave her my standard *one breakfast per day kid* face.

She yawned widely and showed me all of her teeth.

I showed her all of mine back and she huffed out hot doggy breath against my calf.

Levi cleared his throat, and I refocused, noting that the look of intense concentration hadn't faded. Apparently, determining who hated him enough to ask my mom for help was more mentally taxing than I'd thought.

"I don't think anyone... My mom moved to this area maybe ten years ago, but I didn't come east until six months ago while still working over in Idaho doing the remote commuter thing. I started at Seth's design firm three weeks ago. Your brother just came over to me at a job site one day. Asked if I wanted to come to dinner and meet..."

I watched his face and could pinpoint the exact syllable where realization dawned on him.

"Damn... I'm only thirty!"

"Yup... meddling family has a stench, and you reek, buddy." I tapped my coffee mug against his and quickly put it to my lips to stop more stupid words from falling out.

You reek? Smooth, Sharp. Real smooth.

Staring at the phone in my non-coffee hand, I unlocked it again. Shutting the Chrome window, the next app was photos, the preview showing a bunch of envelopes. Tapping the thumbnail, I opened the app and enlarged one picture.

It was Leonard and Ferrah's mail. This piece addressed to Mr. and Mrs. Leonard Hollbrook.

Gross.

Another addressed the same way, set my teeth on edge. The idea that getting married stole your autonomy, forcing a person to be reduced to a three-letter addition to her husband's name...

"You OK?" Levi asked, and I glared at him over the phone.

"Why don't women get to keep their name when they get married? How come they get reduced to 'Mrs. Husband's Name'? It's..." My arms flailed, but I couldn't find the right words to express my anger. Though it had probably been standard practice since the times of Jane Austen, I struggled to imagine being nothing more than someone's Mrs. someday .

"Insulting?" He offered, and I nodded.

"My mom has similar thoughts... and my aunt. Though Aunt Ferrah has a lot of non-conventional ideas..."

"Aunt Ferrah?" I interrupted, looking away from my phone and studying his eyes.

"Yeah, my dad's sister. She's polyamorous, which is cool, but she tends to over share... I actually think she's the one who asked your mom to get me a date. They have this live-in friend and I think..." I tuned him out and closed my photos. Launching the messenger app again, I loaded Carla's thread to confirm.

Ferrah Lovelace, Leonard's wife.

"Were you going to ask me to find your aunt?" I asked, a sinking feeling hollowing my gut. He wasn't interested in me, he needed help. "Because Mrs. Margots the First and Second beat you to it. There's no need to flirt if you want my help..."

"Find my aunt? Why would I need you to find her? She lives in a huge purple house in a senior community." He pulled out his phone, and I shifted from foot to foot. Refilling his coffee to stop the trembling in my hands, I waited for him to show me something that disproved what I'd learned yesterday. "It's pretty huge and obvious. Let me show you a picture."

Telling him he stinks is about to be the least awkward part of this conversation.

"Levi, she... I was at the house yesterday. She's missing, I heard from Gertie Margot."

I put the coffee carafe back and then grabbed a towel while he blinked at me. Winnie made a small sound, and I spared her a look that said *help me!*

I wasn't good with other people's emotions.

Or mine.

I just ignored them until they exploded out of me at inappropriate times.

"Oh! No, she's not missing. She just went out of town for a while. She sent me an email, see?"

It took him a moment to navigate the device, searching for the message while I counted my heartbeats, hoping it was authentic.

He handed me his phone with an open email, and I knew in a second I was about to break his heart. The sender was Ferrah Lovelace and the body of the message said she was going on an adventure with Leonard so he wouldn't be around for a while, but she'd be back. It was pretty formal, with too many periods and commas for casual correspondence.

"Does your aunt normally email you?" I asked, closing the email and pushing the search icon at the top of the app, entered Ferrah.

Just one message.

Crap.

"No, she'd usually call and tell me something like that. Or maybe tell my mom to tell me, since I don't really answer the phone." He stopped to drink his coffee, and I swiped up, minimizing the app and going to his contacts. Using the search again, I found his aunt and viewed the contact details he had listed under Aunt Ferrah... which included her email address, s3xktn @gmail.com, as well as her phone number and a picture of her and Leonard in front of the purple house. I switched back to the email app, trying not to pry while expanding the sender and recipient info.

"Is this a work email address?" I asked, noting it was an @PD PArchitects.com domain. I never knew the name of Seth's firm and I wondered what the acronym stood for. I made a mental note to ask him while I waited for the man in my house to cotton on to the truth.

Levi carried his coffee into my kitchen, looking at his phone over my shoulder with only a hair's breadth between us.

"Huh... yeah," he answered, steadying himself with a hand on my hip. I tried not to lean into his touch or inhale him like a creeper. Beneath his work email was a 123FLH@gmail address as the sender, and I wondered if architects knew about phishing and cyber security.

"Hang on a second," I breathed, dialing Mrs. Margot the first, or the first one I knew.

"Cynthia-" she started, but I cut her off.

"I need your sister's phone number."

"I can't just..."

"It's important. Please? I'll forgive you for telling me she was dead," I responded. She sucked in a breath and gave me the numbers. I scribbled the digits onto a coffee filter because I was out of post-its and wondered if I could still make coffee in it. "Thanks. Stop lying to me about crap."

I hung up on Mrs. Margot the first and called the second one.

"Gertie," I interrupted when she answered. "Do you have an email address?"

"A what?"

"An email address. Did you get an email from Leonard or Ferrah a few days ago?" I clarified, still looking at the one on Levi's phone. He was still behind me, fingers moving in small circles that massaged my hip flexors. He was attempting to distract me, or I had a magnetic field he could not resist.

Unfortunately, neither possibility lessened the waves of desire radiating from his fingers down to my toes.

"I showed you all their mail yesterday, Cynthia. Don't you think if I had mail from them, I would have shown you?"

"Not mail, email. Like do you have a virtual inbox on your phone or computer where people send messages and advertisements?" Levi's fingers wavered, Gertie's words sinking in more effectively than mine had.

"If you're talking about the internets, I don't mess with those things."

I nodded at nothing and bid her goodbye. Setting my own phone down, I collected my thoughts before saying to Levi, "Your aunt didn't send this."

I pointed to the email address and then, swiping over to his contacts, showed him his aunt's email. "The name and email don't match your contacts; the language is super formal and... she sent it to your work account."

He leaned in closer, my sweaty palms threatening to drop his phone.

"Maybe she has more than one address?" His voice was an odd mix of denial and hope. "I mean... I have more than one?"

"Do you really believe that?" I asked.

"Not really." He exhaled deeply, ruffling my hair before resting his forehead on my shoulder. "What should we do?"

My lady parts said to ride him like a cowgirl, but my brain said people were missing and it wasn't the time for shenanigans.

"I think we need to call the police... and maybe put on clothes," I answered, stepping away and toward my bed to pull cargos off the metal rod I used as a closet... except it was empty. Taking in the room, I realized all my clothes storage places were empty, and I knew why Levi had slept in jeans.

"Damn."

"What?" he asked, zooming in and out of the email on his phone.

"We need to go back to my parent's house," I sighed, grabbing my Crocs. Levi looked up from his phone, real panic replacing the abstract worry that had just been there.

"Why?" Adam's apple bobbing. He shifted and swallowed.

"My mom stole all of my clothes."

Chapter Nine: No Body, No Crime

I 'd never reported an actual crime before, and I was pretty sure after this I never would again.

"Look at the email, Duncan," I said again, but the doughy man in front of me just rolled his eyes and sucked on a toothpick. Clyde Duncan, if the business card he'd stuffed in my hand was really his and not a scrap of paper that he'd fished out of a claw machine game in a cheap arcade. If he had, it probably also came with the badge, mostly obscured by his ample waist and untucked shirt. "This is classic phishing."

"Phishing is a ploy to steal data from you. Lying in an email is just a prank," he shoved the phone back into Levi's hand and I considered my options.

Option One: Keep trying to convince him this was not a case of overreacting.

Option Two: Let him leave and handle this myself.

Option Three: Punch him in the face, spend a few hours in jail, and then handle this myself.

Option three was my favorite, but I had been punching men in the face a lot since I got out of the Army... and before I got out of the Army... and in college. Also possibly in high school, but did it really count if you were trying to save their lives?

It might be nice to try something new.

Not as nice as punching a jerk in the face, but really, what was?

When Levi and I had finished the pot of coffee and donned last night's clothing, we took the walk of shame to my parent's house. His Forester was parked neatly behind my Jeep, neither appearing worse for their night parked in front of the house of horrors. Inside my parent's house was almost completely silent. We managed to make it to the basement, the usual place where my mom hid my clothes, before she snapped on the lights and caught me red-handed.

Stealing back my own stuff.

It was followed by fifteen minutes of "What happened with Levi?" and "Why are you so repressed? Did we not give you enough freedom to experiment?" that ended with a slide show presentation on an honest to goodness slide projector. Photos of naked and contorted bodies, both in history and not so history, had been enlarged on the blank white wall so she could point and wave to the "areas of interest".

By the time we'd made it out of the house and driven his car to my office, I was confident there was no chance in hell I was ever seeing Levi's southern borders. It was disappointing, but more disappointing was that it turned out to come in second for the worst conversation I would have today.

"Clyde," I tried again, summoning the patience and tact that I was certain I had somewhere.

"Detective Duncan," he snapped. I pressed my tongue against the blister in my mouth, using the pain to keep in my sarcasm. It popped and the salty liquid coated my tongue.

Patience and tact.

"Detective Duncan," I managed through clenched teeth. "I know that it's not much to go on, but Leonard has not been seen at either of his jobs in over a week. Ferrah hasn't been seen in four days, and whatever that type of email is called, it's meant to mislead and misdirect. It couldn't hurt to..."

"Do you know what this neighborhood is?" He interrupted me, moving the chewed toothpick from one side of his mouth to the other. "It's a senior neighborhood. 55+, and we're out here every other week for noise complaints. Not the same ones as the college kids, at least that has drunk chicks with their tits and cheeks hanging out. Sometimes you can catch them doing the deed and get a free show."

"You can get that here, too. But none of that means..."

"It ain't the same. I'm not into watching wrinkled, saggy flesh slap against..."

"Look here, you sick disgusting POS. You clearly are a piece of nasty work that treats women like crap and gets your jollies flexing your non-existent power because no woman wants to be with you as evidenced by your divorce," I gestured to the tan line on his ring finger. "Bitter, pencil-dick personality, but someone is missing and..."

"What did you say, girl?" He advanced one step toward me, and Winnie poked her head up from the back of my Jeep, letting out a soft growl.

"I said you're a useless piece of garbage!" I shouted, my fist clenched as I cocked my arm back. Levi grabbed me around the waist and hauled me backward while a uniformed officer stepped into Duncan's airspace.

"Why don't you head back to the station, and I'll finish up here?" She offered, as I struggled against the vise grip Levi was using to trap my arms. He'd managed to get my feet off the ground, a feat in and of itself because we were the same height and I easily had forty pounds on him.

"Yeah, you do that, Kate," he sniffed, hiking up the basket weave belt under his over abundance of belly and patting the gun resting there. It was a blatant threat, one I wasn't convinced he had the cajónes to follow through on, but I'd let him try. Then we'd see who had the bigger balls when he was picking his teeth up off the sidewalk.

He turned his back on all of us, strutting awkwardly back to his car.

The uniform stayed put as I stopped struggling against my brother's coworker and watched the over-sized man child heave himself into the unmarked Crown Vic, and drive off with a stiff middle finger aimed our way.

"Hate that man," Officer Kate muttered and took a few steadying breaths before turning to us with a forced professionalism. "Sir, I think you can put your girlfriend down now. Even if the fight hasn't gone out of her, I doubt she can hit him from here."

"He's not..."

"We just met..."

We said at the same time, but he placed my feet on the ground.

"You just met?" she asked, a single eyebrow arched with a dimple in one cheek. Her entire demeanor transformed under the anticipation of juicy gossip.

"Yeah, though we did sleep together and look at a bunch of naked people, so I guess not complete strangers," I stammered, sweating under the arms Levi had left banded around my waist. "Either way, it's new and by sleep I mean sleep, not slept together..."

"Get it, girl," she smirked, and I felt my cheeks burn.

"No, not... I meant..."

"You can tell people we slept together if next time I get to take off my pants," he whispered, and my hands went clammy while my throat dried up.

"Water," I wheezed and removed his arms to stick my head into the Jeep and grab the metal bottle off the floorboard and chug its contents. Without Detective Doughboy raising my blood pressure, I opened the door and let Winnie out. "Could you get Mrs. Margot?"

The dog wagged her tail and trotted off toward the "accessory thing" Gertie lived in. After a few more steadying breaths, I faced the officer and architect, who were both watching me with very different expressions. Hers was an interested curiosity while his was... pure lust.

Dog, help me.

"Officer..." I read her nameplate. "Stead?"

She nodded, and I cleared my throat.

"Do you think we should be concerned?"

The woman gave serious consideration to the question, looking between us and then toward the house. Her hands were resting on the many pouches attached to her duty belt, not fidgeting while she worked and assessed the facts she'd overheard.

"Maybe... but I'm not sure what I can do without the detective's buy-in. Have you looked inside the house?"

Gertie came around the house in a hot pink negligee, being led by Winnie and pulling a man on a leash behind her. He was wearing nothing more than a black banana hammock while Mrs. Margot #2 sank into the grass as she crossed, aerating the yard in four-inch stilettos.

"Is that poop stain gone?" She called, her voice echoing off the surrounding houses. "Winnie said it was safe, but that skid mark has been a blowhard for far more years than his mama lived to see. When I see him coming, I find a place to lie low. Which is pretty easy. I'm far nimbler than he is, and everyone on this block will let me in their house to hide. Clyde couldn't get laid in a women's prison with a fistful of pardons... hell, most women would rather shank him and get life than let him touch them."

I nodded in agreement, on behalf of all women everywhere. Pretending Gertie wasn't mostly naked and didn't have a man on a leash. I looked back at the officer.

"We haven't been in the house. Mrs. Margot number... Gertie can't find her key. Any chance you recognize a hide a key anywhere?"

Officer Stead glanced at the front yard, seeming to share my thought that ignoring the eccentricities was the best option out of all the really terrible ones available to us.

"No, but is that canine scent trained?"

I nodded and then called Winnie over to make an introduction.

"This is Sgt. Winnifred Pupperson, Winnie for short. She's explosives detection and bite work trained, but without a scent for her to match, I don't know how she'd find it," I concluded, watching as the officer accepted Winnie's paw.

"Do you have anything of the missing persons?" She asked Gertie, letting her eyes go unfocused on their trip to the woman's face. "Clothing would be preferable, but furniture or tissues might work too?"

Kate checked with me, and I made a "kind of gesture" with my hand.

"Nothing like that. Keep a pretty clean house and they usually invite me to the main house when we spend time together. Who's that handsome man?"

Gertie eyed Levi, letting her eyes rake up and down his frame with hunger. I wanted to be offended, but some things were just worthy of appreciation.

"That's Levi. He's Ferrah's nephew," I answered, noting the daggers leash man was shooting from his eyes. "So... what're the other options? If we can't find a hidden key, what else can we do? Warrant?"

Kate shook her head, "Not enough to get a warrant... and I don't know what judge will sign it if Duncan says no."

"Can anyone pick a lock?" Everyone shook their heads no. "Anyone willing to break a window?"

"Or... we can just ask my mom," Levi piped up, and we all turned to him. He held up his phone, the display showing text message bubbles as he waggled it in the air. "She has a key and only lives about ten minutes away?"

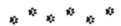

Levi's mom didn't ask a lot of questions.

Within fifteen minutes, she was there, handing over the key with a hug for him and a casual howdy for the rest of us before she drove off again in a dust-covered pickup. Gertie and her man didn't warrant so much as a second look, and I had to wonder what the dark-haired woman had seen in her lifetime at this house. It was a good sign she'd be cool with my parents if Levi and I got married.

Married? What the fluff... Shoving that intrusive thought deep, deep down, I looked between everyone present and came up with a plan of entry that would minimize risk and safety concerns.

After a quick discussion, it was decided that I would go in first with Officer Stead and Winnie. Together, we'd check the rooms immediately inside and if nothing looked amiss, she'd leave us to check out the rest of the house.

"Does your mom not get along with her sister-in-law?" I asked into the settling dust cloud of her departing vehicle.

"They like each other OK. I think she's just needed back at the farm. At this hour there's still a lot of animals to feed," he walked and talked, leading us to the front door and putting the key in. "I'm also not sure Gertie's friend is something she is... comfortable with. But she'd never say anything."

Everyone nodded except Gertie, who gave us a pout. Even the man she had leashed was more self-aware than she was, and I felt that was both telling and a little sad. Watching Levi's arm muscles flex beneath his rolled-up sleeve, I felt another pang of longing for a man I barely knew.

Gertie gave a knowing smirk, and I sighed.

Pot meet kettle.

At the threshold, Kate and I took up our positions, Winnie between us with her nose working. Gripping the doorknob with one hand and Winnie's collar in the other, I turned the handle and pushed in the door, letting it bounce off the wall while Kate shined her flashlight into the room.

A couple of sharp sniffs and Winnie let out a pair of sneezes that jerked my arm.

Just inside was a grey corduroy couch, capped by two end tables in front of a glass topped coffee table. A few AARP magazines sat on the transparent surface, lamps on the end tables, and a thin layer of dust on all of it. Everything angled just so, a sitting room no one sat in.

Winnie and I went left while Officer Stead peaked into the coat closet before continuing off to the right. Behind the couch was a dining table, the faux wood flooring continuing through both rooms before changing to linoleum at an open frame entryway. The table had six chairs, a placemat and metal ringed cloth napkin at each place setting. Sunlight slid in through small cracks in the curtains, catching the glass doors of a China hutch and tower shelves of fragile looking crystal statues. All of them were upright, nothing out of place or missing based on the perfect symmetry.

A dining room no one dined in.

Creeping past the table, I spotted seams along the drywall, a sign the next room had been intentionally walled off from this formal area and I pressed on, listening and pausing before moving on to that room. Back flat against the wall, I let Winnie scent the air and waited for any of her alerts.

She let out a wide yawn but didn't sit.

Rounding the corner, I came up short in a mostly white and yellow kitchen with tiled backsplash and a large table off a pass through to the other side. Off white cabinetry, also sporting a layer of dust, stood closed beside white appliances.

And in the center of the room, a massive red stain that tainted the air in the metallic taste of blood.

Chapter Ten:
Heme-No-Globin

"Any chance it's pasta sauce?" I asked Officer Kate. Beside me, she had gone a little pale, with beads of sweat forming at her hairline. Instead of immediately sounding the alarm, I'd finished searching my side of the house before announcing my find.

It was the only disturbance in a house that was disturbingly normal.

At Gertie's insistence, I'd gone back through while the officer called it in. There were no invoices or records of Leonard's business. The office had two monitors and a docking station, but no laptop, CPU or paper copies.

Even his work truck was gone from the garage.

"You OK? Do you need... water or like a..." She bolted from the house, and I heard the rasped heaves of vomiting. "Yeah... That's probably what normal people do."

Winnie flopped over, apparently bored with the evidence of possible murder before us.

A low whistle came from my elbow, and I startled at the shock of grey hair beside me.

"That's enough blood for a lifetime of menstrual cycles," Gertie decreed, and I shuddered. "There's nothing shameful about periods, Cynthia."

"No, but menstrual blood in a kitchen reminds me of this joke about oral in a pizza parlor..."

Gertie snickered.

"Eating pizza."

I shuddered again. It wasn't really the time for jokes, but humor was my most effective trauma response. If you can't fix the problem, say something dumb and make it awkward.

Awkward humor would always win out over fear and tears in my book.

"There weren't any files or a work truck. Do you know what his business is recorded under? Maybe I can try to find the tax filings... or..." I wanted to bring up Mrs. Margot's cracker niece who was really a hacker, but there were too many cops around. Mrs. Margot the Second just shook her head, eyes on the massive congealed stain.

"When the officer is done tossing her cookies, think she'll call Detective Dumdum back? Or can he only move forward if there's a crew nearby to check his blind spots?"

Apparently, Mrs. Margot was in the same trauma response club.

"Is it weird to insult a man's size when I, myself, am excellently padded? I'm fine being fat, but there's something about the way he throws his weight around that makes me want to throw said weight in his face... usually with my fist, but I probably need to stop punching people."

"Probably. I've known Dumdum Duncan a long time. He's vain and self-conscious about his appearance. If you call him a misogynistic pencil dick, he'd just be glad people wanted to talk about his dick. Assuming he's seen it this decade."

We cackled cruelly as the sounds of people arriving on the scene drifted in through the open door.

"Should we talk about who all this blood might have come from?"

I shrugged, looking at the small woman beside me. Her face was the same color it had been, but she was sucking at her dentures. Though she didn't need a walking aid, her hand was white knuckled on the wall while her elbow was shaking.

"You OK?" I place a hand on her shoulder, the vibration of nerves traveling up my arm. "Do you want to sit?"

"I'm not some fragile piece of parchment, Cynthia. I've seen blood before," she snapped. Her words were at odds with the subtle shuffle she took closer to me. "You think childbirth is neat and tidy? You think my wife's death in our bed was the first body I ever saw?"

Instead of responding, I brought the slight woman closer and gave her an awkward hug. Using humor and aggression to mask

121

fear and hurt was as familiar to me as Winnie's farts. I didn't need her to admit her emotions to know she needed a hug. My partner got up and leaned against both of us, weighing down our feet.

"We'll find them," I assured her. "I'm really good at finding people."

"Alive?"

I studied the amount of blood in the kitchen and felt her do the same. In the Army, field dressing a wound was a normal part of basic training. You learned to shoot the baddies, and then you learned to patch yourself and others up when they shot back. There was a little less than a gallon and a half of blood in the average human body, and losing forty percent wasn't survivable.

"Did Leonard and Ferrah go to the doctor often?" I asked, not willing to answer her question just yet.

"Yeah," she accepted the subject change, taking a step back from me. "Ferrah had some joint issues and Leonard was diabetic. They were healthier than most, but not without medical help. What are you thinking?"

"That the fastest way to identify the blood is by typing it, and it would be best to know their blood type. Depending on how common it is, that could rule them out or..." I left the sentence unfinished, kicking myself for starting it, but needing to say something to sound like this might eventually get sorted out.

The woman beside me nodded. She knew the score and didn't need me to lay it out.

"Get the hell away from my crime scene!"

Gertie and I turned toward the dough-tective, Winnie's hackles doubling her size above the pearly white tooth show she was offering. He looked angry, and a little scared. His eyes were darting around, like he thought the victim would pop out and shout, *gotcha*!

"Get your dog under control and get her off the premises before I have animal control come muzzle her and put her down," he roared, peacocking for the crime scene techs and uniformed officers standing around awkwardly. "Now!"

Rolling my eyes, I put an arm under her abdomen and scooped her onto my shoulder in a show of muscle meant to emasculate the jerk detective. I moved toward the door with Winnie grumping on my shoulder, scene personnel moving out of our way.

The front yard was covered in red and blue emergency lights, dimmed in drama by the mid-morning sunlight. An ambulance sat at the curb, the medical team leaning casually against the bumper waiting to be cleared.

"Are you going to be OK?" I asked Gertie, looking down at her beside me.

"Yeah... can you take me to my sister's house?"

Nodding, I escorted her to the Jeep with Levi leading the leashed man, bringing up the rear. I let Winnie in first, setting her in the backseat. The rest piled into the car, Gertie taking command of my radio and somehow located a big band channel that filled the silence as I got the car pointed back toward Sweet Pea. Winnie was lying between the men in the backseat, keeping her body as far from the naked-ish man as possible.

"Is Mrs. Margot going to be OK with you bringing a friend over? Can we drop you off somewhere?" I asked him in the rearview mirror, but he kept his gaze downcast.

"He's a sub in training. I took over his training for an out of commission dominatrix recovering from hip surgery. I'm in charge of keeping him... compliant," a smile played at the corners of her mouth. "Glen should get a kick out of him. She always wanted a slave..."

When no one could think of a response to that, I just turned up the radio and hoped like hell I didn't get pulled over.

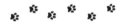

Mrs. Margot the First looked very pleased to see her sister... and her sister's charge. While Levi and I watched from the car, the original Mrs. Margot pinched the man's butt and stuck her finger in his mouth like a vet checking the gum health of a pet. Whatever she found, it pleased her and allowed him access into her house.

"That was creepy."

"We've seen a lot these past few hours. I'm not sure that even registered on my traumatizing and or creepy scale."

My passenger leaned into his new seat beside me, letting his eyelids droop closed.

"You OK?" I really needed something new to ask people, but since I knew he wasn't, the question was just a formality.

"I'm telling myself it wasn't their blood. Ask me again when they've run the sample and I have to let go of my denial," he told the interior roof of my car. It wasn't an outright declaration of emotional turmoil, but it was honest. "What's the weirdest thing you've ever seen doing your job?"

"Don't know about the weirdest, but someone tried to dress like me and commit crimes in my image. She was too short and too not purple-eyed. When I was in the Army, though, I was asked to clear a hangar for the Air Force that had been over-run by geese. They launched a full-scale assault on the grounded aircraft with a level of training and precision even the Air Force didn't have. I think they were marched off to their death at a French restaurant." I tried to get him to talk about something else. "What's the weirdest building you ever designed?"

"Out in Idaho, they wanted me to build a Paul Bunyan and Babe the Ox rental house, with the legs being the stairs, and the residential pods were in the testicle region of both. Like clear spheres where the balls would be." He was still looking at the roof. "The drawing he gave me looked like a hamster ball stuffed in a lumberjack's pants."

"Did you build it?" I asked, and he let out a laugh.

"No. No one would allow that monstrosity in their city limits. I think he got it built near Portland." He smiled and rolled his head in my direction. "Any chance you want to go get breakfast? Or coffee? I get the impression you like coffee."

"Breakfast date?" he clarified, when I didn't immediately answer.

"Are you... asking me out?" I asked, head dropping to my shoulder. Winnie angled hers as well, neither of us certain what happens in this situation.

"Yeah... it's been a weird morning, but I get the feeling none of this is getting normal any time soon. So... might as well keep living." He offered me a warm smile that made my lady parts hum. "I feel like we might have fun spending time together and you'll have better stories than this Heather chick I dated who just wanted to talk about her nails and watch people eat food on the internet while shouting into her speaker phone."

"Shouting at who?"

"Nobody knows, but we can make up stories together. What do you say?"

I gulped at the immediate heat wave that rushed through me.

"There's breakfast at my apartment... kind of..." I looked at Winnie, who wiggled her black brow ridge in a direct challenge to my claim. "OK, there's coffee and sometimes bacon... and frozen toaster waffles. But I consider that..."

My words were interrupted by the press of his lips against mine. Just a brush, but I was effectively silenced.

Silenced and slightly offended.

"An actual date means we dine in public," he whispered, kissing me again. "Also, your brother said not to let you in my pants unless I wanted to never see you again. So, what do you say?"

"I say Seth needs to shut the heck up. Nothing that's happened in the hours since we've met has been good. Why would you want to—"

Two loud raps against the glass of my window jerked my attention away, killing the moment with the face of Daniel Kirby, Larry's older, hotter, vastly stupider brother. His cheek was nearly pressed against the window as he glared in at me.

"What?" I shouted.

He waved me out of the car just as Levi's phone rang. Much as talking to Daniel was on par with a pap smear, offering Levi privacy was the decent thing to do. Opening the car door, I climbed out to give him space to take a call.

"Who the hell do you think you are?" I snapped, pushing him backward and out of my air space. He stumbled slightly on his bare feet but got right back in the fight.

"Don't yell at me. Who the hell is that?"

"My brother's co-worker. What do you want?" I crossed my arms and leaned against my Jeep. Eyeing him up and down, I tried to make him uncomfortable, but he responded with more arrogant condescension. Daniel had been the hottest guy in high school, the "it" boy. He skated through on sports team competence, charm, and sexy hair. His wife had been his catty girlfriend, and while he had strayed more than once, she still married him.

Now they had enough kids to staff a baseball team and served as one of the Village of Sweet Pea's two deputies… or officers… but was still trying to skate by on amazing hair, sexy lashes, and stories of his glory days on the sportball field. Unlike his brother, the years had made Daniel soft, the once boyish face lined with crow's feet and smile lines, more pronounced in his sun-damaged skin than they'd been even a few months ago.

"Why are you kissing another man in front of my house? Are you trying to kill Larry?"

"This is your house?" I asked, taken aback at the level of cleanliness and quiet. I'd always imagined Daniel's house as having plastic slides and rusted bikes on an overgrown front lawn filled with garden snakes and cherry bombs. "I always pictured you living out near the chicken farms where no one can hear the screams of your criminal children slowly murdering each other while you smothered your wife with your ugly face."

"Stop dodging the subject. Why are you out here with some guy, not returning my brother's calls, and... just..." he gestured up and down and around. I felt like a kindergarten teacher standing near a kid who just discovered his emotions.

"Someone's having big feelings," I patronized him, and I saw a flash of violence in his eyes before it faded into a bone-weary look of exhaustion. "Look, Daniel, Larry and I aren't going to work out. He has hang-ups and baggage from your family that will always be a problem for us. It's time for both of us to let it go. His inability to accept my decision is another obvious example of why he is not mature or respectful enough for me to be with. A man who really cared about me would take the words coming out of my mouth as the truth and back the hell off. The more he pushes, the less likely I am to speak to him as a human, much less a friend."

"But he loves you," Daniel pouted, and I wondered if he knew what that word meant or if he'd just heard it on Sesame Street this morning and thought he'd give it a whirl.

"I'm sure we'll figure out how to be friends again some-day," I gave Daniel a reassuring shoulder pat. It was the third time I'd touched someone to offer comfort today, a new personal best, but I should probably wash my hands. Swiping them up and down my pant leg, I glanced around his neighborhood and noticed the same phenomenon I'd seen near my own apartment.

"Do you know who all these cars belong to?" I asked, tagging at least two sports cars worth more than my parent's house. A few Teslas were situated at the corner, but there were no power sources. This town didn't have electrical vehicle chargers, public or for profit, so either they were visiting people in the area, or they died and were abandoned out in the sticks.

Daniel followed my line of sight and scratched his belly.

"No... maybe they belong to that development a few streets over? I don't know what they're building, but I've seen work trucks." His brow furrowed deep into the sun-worn skin of his face as he gazed off toward a flattened piece of land just beyond the widespread rural homes.

"Have you seen any of the vehicle owners? How long have those Teslas been there?" I tried to narrow his scope and call on his skills as an investigator.

"No idea... maybe a couple days?"

Apparently, he didn't *have* any skills as an investigator.

A tragedy since he made up one third of our police force and his powers of observation had been reliable once.

"Your cousin is dating Mrs. Margot's niece, right?"

"Yeah..." he answered absently. "Living with her, too. A hacker and a computer programmer. It's like a match made in cyber security hell."

"Coding? Not construction?" I studied his face.

"Yeah. Dude has no upper body strength."

"Right... I'll talk to you later, then," I pushed off my Jeep, adding another item to my list of things about this case Mrs. Margot had lied about.

Climbing back in the Jeep, I heard Levi bid goodbye to the caller on the other end. Daniel continued standing there in basketball shorts and faded white T-shirt, naked feet on the sidewalk. He kept studying the cars on the street, pulling out his phone and either taking down their info or looking at porn while he had a moment alone.

Neither would be out of character.

Only one would I ask for follow-up on.

"So... the good news is that the blood type isn't a match to either Ferrah or Leonard," Levi stated, startling me from my Daniel observations. I processed his words while studying his face.

"That's great news... why don't you look happy?"

"Because it matches a dead guy in the morgue with a knife wound. They have him as a John Doe, and they're hoping I can ID him." His forehead was in his hands, temples scrunching under his fingers aggressively massaging. Dropping one hand, he rested it on my thigh and my heartbeat kicked up a notch.

Is it hot in here?

Am I dying?

"They're asking me to come look at the dead guy. Any chance you want to go back to Dayton?"

My phone chirped a reminder alarm, and I checked it.

"I'm sorry, I can't," I showed him the alert. "I need to get ready for work. But if you can send me a picture and get any details about how and where he was found, I'll see if there's any connection."

"You're a PI, right? Isn't this... already work? Or are you talking about that farm thing you mentioned?"

I let out a deranged laugh. "No, this is a town sponsored hobby that is trying to steal my sanity. I actually work at a dairy farm... technician-ing animals."

Nodding, he didn't ask any follow-up questions, so I figured he knew what an animal technician was or, more likely, he'd decided I was nuts and wanted to get away from me. Dropping the car into drive, I navigated us back to my building, Levi's hand staying on my inner thigh to my delight... and detriment. At least three trash cans were almost decimated while I tried to think of something not asinine to say. The Jeep slid in behind his car and I gave him a weak smile.

"You have reached your destination," I mimicked GPS.

Yup, still asinine.

He nodded and leaned across the car, giving me another kiss.

"I'll see you later, then?"

"Sure," I chirped, voice too high. Winnie let out a whimper, and I cleared my throat, hoping to get my voice down to a normal pitch. "Let me know about the dead guy. I'm curious whose

131

blood I spent the morning making period and oral sex jokes about."

Head shaking, Levi got out and moved toward his car while I scanned the street for witnesses to my awkward lack of flirting skills. It wasn't technically legal to park at my curb for more than loading and unloading, so witnesses would be bad on a number of levels.

Instead of people, all I saw were coffee mugs.

Six new ones, sitting outside my office door.

Chapter Eleven:
Unlucky Idol

There are a lot of proverbs about fortune. You have "fortune favors the bold", "fortune favors the prepared mind" and "fortune smiles upon the brave", all of which demand you stand out, stand up, and prepare for everything and then you'll get lucky.

Or dead.

I wasn't timid, and I was always prepared with snacks and coffee, but I never had an ounce of luck.

Arriving at the dairy, Joseph was front and center at the barn door, holding some manner of something orange and sparkly. When I first started here, Winnie was put to work herding and failed miserably. Then she went to work as security compliance for poorly behaved animals, who she led to freedom in an infamous uprising that terrified a horse.

It was then that Joseph, the dairy's manager and owner, propositioned her to sit in front of the dairy in a ridiculous outfit and take pictures with children. I'd told him it was the dumbest idea he ever had, and he insisted I was crazy. The former military working dog now had an impressive wardrobe, her own gourmet snacks as payment, and a cult following in the Elementary School crowd who thankfully didn't have the internet.

She'd also led more than one child uprising against Joseph, but the Winnie Photo Spot persisted.

As did the stains on his shirt from the permanent markers that had attacked him.

"I need you to be up front with Winnie today," he announced without preamble, and I shook my head. "It's not a request, but an order."

"Not a chance in hell, Joseph. You couldn't make me Fiona and you won't make me whatever the hell that is." I walked past him into the barn. It was an open building with only side walls, shelter provided on two sides for the open-air arena and animal stalls lining both long walls. Primarily, the barn was used for births, medical treatment, and staff breaks, none of which required the majority of it to be shielded from public view.

Once inside the barn, I became visible from the customer parking lot... as did Winnie. She followed me, preening for the adoring fans waiting at the entrance of the ice cream parlor who'd tittered in delight at her arrival.

"Cynthia-"

"No. You're the one who enjoys playing dress up with my dog. I've told you before…"

My protests died on my lips at the sight of Larry treating a pair of goats with at least two more stalls emitting noises of distress. At the sight of me, his face flamed red, and a sharp scowl carved into the space between his eyebrows.

"Get her out of here or find a different vet, Joseph." Spit flew out of his mouth with the words, and I stumbled backward as if he slapped me. "I'm not working near her. Not after she made out with some strange dude in front of my brother's house!"

"Why the hell do you-"

"You have ten seconds, Joseph," Larry snapped.

"I'm handling it. Cynthia-" Joseph shoved the costumes into my hand and pointed toward the parlor. Annoyed and lacking the motivation to fight, I stomped toward a small breakroom to change, passing dozens of farm hands who wouldn't meet my eyes. It hurt to know I'd caused Larry pain, however much his own actions had caused this mess. But it hurt even more to know that, at the end of the day, the people I worked with would turn their backs on me over the unreliable word of a man scorned.

Which is how I came to be wearing a glitter leaf tree costume beside pumpkin Winnie, yelling at children's parents and "ruining the experience".

I'd been bold.

I'd been brave.

But fortune was nowhere to be found.

"No! Those are the rules! You will not give her dairy products, or you will be blacklisted. There is a sign, and I know Joseph isn't letting this slide because I haven't castrated him yet. Put it in the designated location or leave. I don't care what choice you make."

"Trees can't talk!" A blonde boy shouted at me from kneecap height. It would be so easy to crush him with my size 13 feet, but I hadn't brought a spare pair of shoes.

Also, murder is wrong or whatever.

"And children who can't follow directions don't get to take a picture with my dog. Stay," I growled at Winnie. She had been belly crawling along her hay bale toward another child, trying to lure her away with the promise of forbidden treats. "You, get in line and wait your turn. There are hand wipes at the front if you're still sticky when you make it through."

"You can't speak to children like that!" a woman piped up. She looked like she walked right out of an animated sitcom where she screamed *won't somebody please think of the children!*

"Lady, somebody has to. None of these kids has ever heard the word *no* and I think I know who isn't saying it. If you want people to stop being hedonistic abominations, stop worrying about rainbow people and abortions and start looking at the nightmare that is the entitled white lady!"

"How dare you mention the *gays!*" She hissed the last word, grabbing hold of the only child in line better behaved than Winnie. He had a perfect side part, a button-down shirt tucked into his shorts and an honest to goodness bow tie.

The young man gave the filthy children in line a wayward glance and mouthed *thank you* before walking back to the car.

"Get in a line!" I ordered the kids and at least half of them complied while their spandex clad nannies and mommies tried to get a selfie with their ice cream and a cow in the background. "A line that's straight is a line that's great!"

"You're mean!" The little boy screamed while the little girl holding out a peanut butter ice cream covered hand burst into tears. Behind her, a rail thin woman sipping a slime green beverage with a pinched face glanced up from her phone.

"Make it stop screaming. Just... give it what it wants!"

"No!" I snapped, getting between the woman, the screaming child, the little boy who started the chant *mean lady, mean lady, hit her with the green* and Winnie.

"Enough! All of you! Place," I hollered, snapping my fingers and pointing. Winnie appeared, sitting beside me, ears up and giving me the look of confident obedience. A look I had earned saving her again and again, offering love, gratitude and snacks. "This is a military working dog. She is trained in physical defense and explosives detection. If you want to take a ridiculous picture with her, you will listen to me. If you don't..."

Winnie lifted her upper lip and flashed a set of incisors.

Everyone shut up and got in line, the photographer showing a lot of eye whites as I nodded that she could allow the next group to approach. From down by the barn, I caught the flash of a white lab coat as Larry went back inside.

"Smile for the camera, Cyn!" the photographer cooed, and I showed her my teeth.

She didn't ask again.

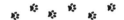

Winnie's photo spot was the most organized operation I'd ever conducted. Word travels fast, and children knew better than to let their parents misbehave if they wanted their picture... and a custom Winnie trading sticker I had never seen before. What normally took five hours to go through was accomplished in two, children and ice cream processed neatly and without incident.

I'd spotted Larry spying on me three more times, and as far as I could tell, he was still working in the barn. He'd made it clear I wasn't welcome in his company, and I'd had a long day of human interaction that ensured the feeling was mutual. Whether he'd known Joseph would send me up here with Winnie or had simply hoped to witness my suffering, the plan had backfired.

No matter what he hit me with, I could hit back harder.

Revenge might be "best served cold", but the melted ice cream coating parts of me only fueled my fiery rage and sense of vengeance.

Sitting back on the hay bale beside Winnie, I closed my eyes for a moment and pondered whether or not to just leave. Bills be damned.

"Did ya mean what ya said about that dog sniffin' explosives?" A man asked, walking up beside us. I opened my eyes and let my head roll toward his footsteps. He was wearing black ripstop cargo pants, a black t-shirt, and boots, none of which were filled out with anything remotely passable as a muscle.

My eyes had remained trained on the parking lot all day, suspicious of any car that exceeded the average annual income of the town, but every one of them had spewed a child-toting adult with a pinched face and athleisure clothing. The man in front of me had been lurking at the edge of the parking lot since the photo spot opened and I'd kept my eyes on his hands the whole time.

They'd spent what might be an inappropriate amount of time picking his nose, but otherwise had done nothing lascivious. I didn't think he was dangerous, and on closer inspection, he didn't have the look of a predator. Sandy blonde hair tucked behind his ears, a balding patch at his crown, the man could pass for grown up Opie Taylor. I estimated him as thirty, a basement dweller, who probably googled "what commandos wear" and then bought it off Amazon.

Poser, my nostrils flared above my pursed lips, and he froze, taking a small step back.

"Not meanin' to disturb, I just... need some help."

"With what?" I asked, turning back to the jovial ice cream employees who were counting their tips by the register. They'd told me the Winnie photo spot was usually still hopping long after the shop was closed, but we'd avoided all time-wasting incidents, and no one had seemed intent on dawdling.

Probably my winning personality, I thought with a menacing glare toward a teenager on a date.

He moved off the porch and away from me while Winnie let out a soft whimper of protest. I glanced beside me to see her shifting uncomfortably. I nodded off the side of the porch and she took off to the small patch of grass to relieve herself.

"With what?" I repeated, staring down at the small man who looked like a kid playing soldier. Even seated, I felt like I was towering over him.

"With..." He folded the ball cap in his hand while I worked my jaw. Sweat dripped along his temple, pooling under his arms, at the line of his belt and the underside of his soft pecs.

Under boob sweat, not just a problem for women... it would have been more gratifying if the skin there folded over, and he was in danger of getting a rash.

As it was, he was probably just going to get one less day of wear out of the garment.

"With a... what I mean is..."

He swallowed hard as Winnie trotted back, sitting beside me and demanding affection. I obliged, losing some of the tension in my shoulders and jaw in her soft fur. Back when I'd been exiled to Florida, my shirts could stand up on their own at the end of the day, and also doubled as a biome for growing bacteria.

"Do you have a name?" I asked, and he nodded, taking a cautious pair of steps toward me. "You want to start by telling me what it is, or should we play twenty questions?"

"Brad," he gave a hopeful smile that added ten years to the original age estimate I'd given him. The tan lines and worn leather look were more pronounced up close, and I retracted my accusation of basement dweller. He was mid-forties maybe, yellowed teeth so he smoked, and the red watery eyes of a drinker. In another decade, the red patches on his nose will get more pronounced and bulbous, assuming he didn't die of skin cancer due to sunscreen aversions. "Brad Bosley."

"Brad... do you need help with an explosive?" I asked, still rubbing one of Winnie's ears.

"Yeah. I kind of..." his voice dropped to a stage whisper. "I lost a bomb."

Chapter Twelve: Unprepared Prepper

B rad didn't have a car.

He'd bummed a ride out to the dairy from a tourist bus of seniors on their way from the bar to BINGO at the church. They were gambling in the Lord's house and he was now sitting in my passenger seat, giving directions. Mr. Bosley smelled like the love child of nail polish remover and paint thinner, making me wonder if he drank his vices or just wore them. There were only two turns you could take from the dairy, and he chose the one that went away from my house... and my coffee maker.

Of all the travesties sitting in the car with this man had wrought upon me, dealing with him sans coffee was the worst.

At least you're still getting paid...

With the photo spot closed, Joseph had nothing else for me to do that wouldn't put me in Larry's warpath. Despite his stalker tendencies throughout the day, an activity that once again proved he wasn't listening to me, his anger raged on. Thanks to his behavior, I was enraged *and* covered in ice cream.

His family was the reason we weren't together. Mine was no picnic, but they didn't interfere with my choices. He couldn't pick his family, but he also couldn't change them anymore than I could change mine. But I could choose not to add their crazy into my life, and his persistence grated.

Speaking of crazy things that get on my nerves... The man in my passenger seat was still talking.

"It's out past the old Huffleweiss homestead. Sure, you remember that place?" I shook my head, a muscle in my eye twitching while I rolled down the windows. "Yea, mighta been before you were back from the war."

He said *The War* like it was a coveted and treasured life experience. The man wasn't so old he couldn't have gone himself, but I got the impression even crazy Uncle Sam knew better than to give this man a weapon.

And yet... he still had a bomb...

"Few years ago, maybe five, the government took them all out for cottoning onto their plan to harvest the organs of the aliens at Area 51 and implant them into new mothers while they were laid up at the hospital. His wife got implanted with a biting vagina.

Nearly bit off his penis, but he managed to get it under control by feeding it sausages and ice. Anyway, one day, we head over with some pig's blood and it's like they got beamed up in the middle of watching their TV. Next day, seems like their house was torn down and then condos popped up. Turn right up ahead."

There was no second person in his story to account for the "we" in his pig's blood story. It also failed to explain why pregnant women needed alien parts and biting vaginas. Though if his friend was anything like him, I'd want vagina teeth to chomp off anything of theirs that came into my orbit.

Also, I was pretty sure my vagina had never been hungry before, so what the hell was the point of the sausage and ice?

My brain abandoned his running commentary, his vague instructions guiding us onto a rutted dirt road. It was decently well traveled, but we were heading deeper into the cornfields. If there was a bomb out here, I was moderately comforted by the knowledge that if it exploded, the blast would probably only kill him and scare the crap out of some crows. Winnie was in the back seat, eyes on alert as we drove into the setting sun.

Can dogs smell crazy? Would it smell like peanuts?

"That's when I got the van and purchased my parcel in an umbrella deal," he said, pointing out the window toward a tricked-out RV with bug lights, antennae and what could have been a distillery or a meth lab coming out of the bumper. "Can't drive her no more. Gave up my license when I gave up paying taxes and answering to the man. But I still hear things, skim Wi-Fi with the antenna to get the news on the dark web. I heard they were poking around out here, and I needed to prepare."

"Why do you think you lost a bomb?" I asked, stopping at a chain between two aluminum poles. To the left of the pole was an enormous expanse of nothing, and the same was true to the right. Beyond the chain, aside from the bugout van, was nothing but holes. Unlike the ones in *Holes*, these were not 3 feet by 3 feet and dug with a yardstick. Each one was a different depth and shape, a series of shovels scattered in between with every shape between round, flat and pointed. Most were oxidized beyond what any sane person would call rust; the wooden handles splintered and broken while the metal ones looked like they might turn to red dust if you touched them.

"I, uh, was getting worried about the chatter last night and started drinking, doing a deep dive into this supposed development planned for my land, but I knew it was the government. They know that I know about the aliens and they wanted my land... but I blacked out. I woke up this morning and there were..." he gestured out at the yard. "Holes. Well, more holes than the ones I had there before. Holes and there was some C4 I'd had that wasn't where I left it... Are you familiar with C4?"

I gave him a long slow blink, wondering if I myself had blacked out and woken up in the Twilight Zone.

His hands rubbed up and down on the cargos, a streak of moisture left behind in the dust coating on his pants. The fabric was not designed to absorb, but the dirt took care of the minimal wetness by making a muddy smear. Despite his nervous chatter, Mr. Bosley the Prepper didn't seem nearly concerned enough for a man who had supposedly rigged his own "yard" to explode.

I let my forehead drop to my steering wheel, sucking in air and fighting the urge to scream.

"Did you look in the holes?" I asked when I thought I could speak without committing murder. They say looks can kill, and I was fairly certain the things I wanted to say would at the very least maim him.

"Of course I looked in the holes... well, some of them. But I got a little worried that maybe the explosives might be between the holes. So, I hopped on one foot between and in the holes to..."

"Why on one foot?" I interrupted, because my sense of self-preservation did not extend to my sanity. If curiosity could kill humans as well as cats, I would be too long dead to be having this conversation.

Missed opportunities...

"In case it was pressure activated. I wouldn't weigh enough to set it off," he answered, tapping his temple in a way that suggested he was a genius. A genius would know that you weigh the same on one foot or two, and I was once again confused as to how these people knew where to find me.

Gotta check my underwear for tracking devices.

"So... you... drunkenly surrounded your house with landmines and then decided to... hop away?"

"Well..."

"Stay here," I ordered, getting out of the Jeep and opening Winnie's door. Clipping on her leash, I lead her out of the car and pointed at the metal poles, asking her to check them.

She gave both a cursory sniff and sneezed dust out of her nose.

We walked around it, Winnie scenting the ground on a very short leash. Stopping at the first hole, I let her sniff, and she moved on, tracking as far left as the holes in the soft sand that seemed to serve as the invisible property line he'd half-ass fenced off.

When we reached the beginning of a cornstalk wall, I exchanged a look with the shepherd mix. She lead me three feet inward and we started the process again to the right. Passing the aluminum poles, I peered into the Jeep to see Brad working the lid off a plastic water bottle he either had in his pockets or had found in my car. If it was from my car, it was probably sink water and might have Winnie splash back.

If it had been in his pocket, I hoped it was hot and tasted funny.

Continuing along the grid, we were two more rows in when Winnie started whimpering. Glancing at her, I measured my steps slower. Her nose paused longer at each micro step until she sat.

Winnie had stopped between two holes beside a flat edged square shovel. Her paw was angled inward toward the trailer, her nose facing slightly to the left. At her feet, the two holes were shallow and narrow, like something a gardener would dig to install sprinklers. Gently moving Winnie back into the previously searched area, I lowered myself down onto my belly to look into the opening at an angle.

Sitting under the small land bridge was a grey square the size of a brownie bite, with what looked like a pop socket sitting on top. The scissored design and metal framework were a little sturdier than the standard telescoping circle, but I was fairly confident it was a pressure activated device designed to take out someone who collapsed the land bridge and triggered the charge. Though the C4 wasn't deep enough to hold a pin, I wasn't sure it was safe to assume the thing wouldn't work.

Leaning in farther, I was able to see a sizeable gap between the top of the spring mechanism and the land bridge. Sliding my hand in, I eased it out with downward movement until it was resting in the bottom of one hole with nothing above it.

I flopped onto my back and let out the breath I'd strangled in my lungs while I tried not to kill us all.

"I need a new life," I said to Winnie, who came to lick my face before scenting the air and sitting down again. "Come on..."

Before I could get up, I heard the car door slam shut and the thunder of boots charging across the weather-beaten earth. Bolting up, I shouted, "Wait! There's..."

He sunk through another land bridge and I heard the *beep, beep* of an activated charge a few feet away from me.

"There's another device," I sighed, staring at the colorless skin of his face. "Don't move, or I will leave you. Understand?"

The would-be bomber nodded. I stood, looking at the trigger of the recovered device. Pulling the mechanism out, I separated the ignition from the explosive part and placed them into separate pockets. Hands on my hips, I scanned the ground, the trailer and the man who'd put them all here.

"How many bombs do you remember making?" I demanded. "Because it was clearly more than one."

"I don't know... I was drunk," he stammered, and I scrubbed my hands over my face, careful not to move any closer to the unsecured area. "I'd tried drunken recall, but all I did was maybe plant more bombs."

"Great. When were you last drunk?" I asked, spying something near the trailer that might work. Carefully taking Winnie's lead, I looked her in the eyes. "Find me a path and you'll get five pup cups on the way home."

Her tail wagged, and I held onto the lead, letting her move me toward the trailer. The direct path between the trailer and the gate seemed to be mostly clear, which explained how he'd survived leaving his house today. It was more worn than the neighboring stretches of desert, and I suspected the compaction would have made it harder for him to dig, saving his life and keeping his path clear.

Until he tried to do the right thing and get the bombs dug up... there was probably a lesson there. One I shouldn't impart onto Sylvia if I didn't want to do this again in my brother's backyard.

"I can't go meet the Lord with a lie on my lips. I'm drunk now," he sobbed, and I rolled my eyes at the sky, staying in Winnie's paw path. He believes in aliens, government conspiracies AND God. His obsession with people watching and judging him was a little voyeuristic, and I made a mental note to check if he'd put up curtains on the bug out van. "What are you doing?"

We were at the trailer, and I had the oversized tire in my grip. Studying its width against the breadth of my footprints, I was pretty sure it would fit, but I couldn't risk it. If I blew up in a fiery inferno because of a dumbass, Winnie was going to live on to pee on his grave.

"Go back to the car, girl," I told her, placing a kiss on her nose. "Go back to the car and cross your paws this works. If I die, you will go pee on his grave every day forever."

Her whimpered response was defiant.

"Uh uh, we can't both go. You must carry on and tell my story. Maybe make me sound cooler, yeah?"

She flattened her ears and let out another whimper.

"Go, now," I ordered, and she started slinking back toward the car while I carefully rolled the tire to Brad the Alcoholic.

"What are you doing?" he repeated.

"Have you seen Indiana Jones?" I was watching the path I'd left, as well as studying the holes for the telltale potential of land bridges. Sweat was dripping down my face despite the cooling sunset and I was chewing a hole in my lip, trying to keep the heavy tire on track to save the town's least useful human being.

I was pretty sure only the local bartender would miss him.

"Which one?"

"The first one. He was trying to get the idol out of a temple and replaced it with the bag of sand and then got chased by an enormous rock?" The tire got off course and I stopped to breathe deeply and correct the trajectory.

I need to stop skipping arm day... and all the other fitness days.

"I think so," he said. I was a little over a foot away. There wasn't a lot of room to swipe and drop which really only left running him over. Rolling the tire onto his foot, I smirked, watching him wince.

"Hold this here," I told him, moving back into the safe zone and trying to take cover without looking like a coward. "OK, take your foot out without removing the tire."

"But..."

"Do it!" I shouted and with a deep breath of his own, he pushed down on the tire and pulled out his foot. My hands clamped over my ears; eyes squeezed shut just in case as I sniffed for the acrid stench of gunpowder.

Nothing.

Peeling my eyes open, I saw Brad standing there with a stream of urine running down his leg.

"Now what?" He panted, and I shook my head.

"Now you walk to the other side of that pole and wait for the cops. This place needs to be swept and deactivated. You only have one tire and..."

A breeze came by and the tire wavered.

"Move," I demanded.

"But-"

"Move!" I turned and ran toward my car, climbing in and backing away while Brad struggled to walk around the pole and Winnie leaned into me. Leaving him behind was cruel, but my priority was Winnie and this man... well, he'd done this to himself.

"Look, it's fine!" He shouted at me, taking a step back toward the trailer.

Another breeze, and the tire fell over, releasing the trigger in a magnificent explosion that showered him in rocks and dirt.

Chapter Thirteen:
No Good Deed

T he problem with needing law enforcement in a town so
small that it was considered a village was that there was no
one competent to call. Our police department was composed of
two officers, a chief, and a pair of volunteer seniors who liked to
write parking tickets.

Like, actually write them.

On carbon copy triplicate.

In a major city, you had decent odds that a response team of
competent bomb techs and officers who knew how to set up a
perimeter would show up and keep the problem from getting
worse. I'd seen it before. A group of men and women who wisely used a robot to test surfaces and brought out bomb boxes
for collection and disposal while the untrained staff kept the

public back. Then the highly trained professionals with a list of certifications and practice runs who knew about bombs would methodically and efficiently clear the area while offering Winnie a high-five for her part in keeping me alive.

Instead, we had Barney Fife and Daniel Kirby.

I suspect Barney's mother knew what she was doing when she named him. Though he was physically the opposite of the Don Knotts character, in so many ways he was just as cocky and ridiculous. The officer was built like a linebacker and behaved like one who'd taken too many brain jostling hits. Now he couldn't distinguish between antifreeze and vodka, so I assumed he drank both. Barney's thinning hair was buzz cut to show off the large round ears sticking out the side of his head and the vacant expression on his un-lined face.

Hard to get wrinkles when there wasn't anyone home upstairs to move your face.

Which I suspected was how Daniel tricked him into being the one to find the remaining landmines.

"Didja check over there?" he asked, pointing a PVC pipe toward the trailer. "Or there?"

A freaking PVC pipe.

He and Daniel had gathered their collective brain cells and decided that pounding the ground with a PVC pipe was the way to go about finding landmines. Not asking the specialized canine and handler team trained for the job. Not asking for help from the County or Dayton PD. Not even taking a remote-controlled toy car weighed down with bricks and driving it over the landmine areas, possibly blowing the car to smithereens, and then starting again with a new car.

Nope, a ten-foot plastic pipe and an idiot to hold it were all they needed.

And by the end of the day, they'd need a new idiot when this one was just chunks of tissue clinging to the side of a jailed prepper who couldn't actually prep properly.

Even Winnie petulantly refused to leave her pup cups to show them how it's done, too insulted at not being the first and obvious choice.

Daniel was detaining the unprepared prepper, but he hadn't officially arrested him. Despite Brad's claims that he could do whatever he wanted on his land, it was not a sovereign nation under his leadership. The laws about owning and detonating explosives still applied to him, no matter how legally he claims to have obtained the components. Since the entire village only had 2 officers, however, his detainment was in the back of Daniel's car with the windows cracked. Carla had been meeting with local police leadership and when she'd tried to slip out, had been volun-told to bring them along.

It was unclear how they managed it. They had no power over her in theory.

Which meant a ten-minute drive was now a thirty-minute motorcade with potty stops.

I was ready to walk away and leave them to either clear or be taken out by this nightmare, but I was ordered by Carla to stay here and keep their dumb asses alive. Since I'd wisely already driven away to get iced coffee and the promised Winnie pup cups, it wasn't the worst use of the farm's money, but I was off in twenty minutes and the adrenaline dump was fading into exhaustion faster than Barney's sweat-soaked undershirt.

When I'd sent her a video of what they were doing, Daniel's phone rang, and he'd been getting yelled at for the past several minutes.

"I already showed you where I checked, Barney. And marked the boundary with the spray paint I recovered from the trunk of your car that you 'don't know how it got there', even though it definitely matches the paint on your ex-wife's car. If you can't figure out how to read sand paint markings, you shouldn't be standing amid an acre of potential bombs!"

"How else we gonna find them?" He shouted back while Daniel gestured him back toward the police truck with a crooked finger. Barney started stomping across the field, dragging the pipe behind him like a petulant child told to put on their coat. With every stomp, I tensed for an explosion. Every time he didn't blow off a leg, I both thanked and cursed the universe for not mutilating him because, on the one hand, that level of stupidity deserved to lose a leg.

On the other, I hated seeing bloodied dismembered limbs.

"If they're underground, they're already safe to detonate," he whined.

Winnie and I exchanged a look.

Maybe I could stomach the sight of *one* more dismembered limb.

"Come on! I own this land, I can do what I want on it!" Brad began shouting from the back seat of the cruiser parked beside my Jeep. Glancing around, it seemed like dumb and dumber were taking a break from being... well, dumb, so I decided to see if I could get crazy to say something intelligent. "Is this what you fought for? So they can just tell me what to do on my own property? The founding fathers would be ashamed of this blatant disregard for private citizens. Taxation without representation."

"You don't pay taxes. You said so earlier," I countered, and he blustered back at me.

"It's a figure of speech!"

Sand fell out of his hair and stuck to his moist lips.

"No, it's not. Not paying taxes is a felony, so I'd recommend not making that statement to anyone else. I'm also not much of a fighter," I shrugged, looking out at the farms from where I leaned against the cruiser beside his partially open window. There wasn't much out this way, but there was still a sense of activity that belied the stillness of the air.

"But you served in The War!"

He was back to glorifying The War, again.

I exhaled my urge to smack him.

It was as though people believed I'd joined the Army to do anything more than get a free dog, see the world and get out of a boring life in the farmlands of Ohio. It was one of the biggest misconceptions about people who joined the military. Some were gung-ho, life's calling, but most of us... we just didn't have other options. I didn't have a calling, purpose, or direction. I'd majored in Animal Science because I thought I could do an equivalent of Noah's Arc and rescue all the dogs from the asshole humans who didn't deserve them... and also make genetically superior super critters who could rightfully get vengeance on those people. When that fell through, I enlisted to avoid moving back in with my parents and working at the dairy.

Both of which I ended up doing anyway, so all I really got out of this was Winnie.

Best decision ever.

"Tell me about the Huffleweiss house. You said they one day up and left. Did you go inside the house?" I asked him, deciding not to share my own personal revelation.

He wouldn't get it if I tried.

"After they left? Nah. I was worried about the fallout. I walked past with an EMF detector, and it was cackling like an AM radio. Probably spectral traces and nuclear waste... heard the people who moved in were getting sick. Like living on an Indian burial ground..."

"Do you know the address to where it was?" I was going to ask who bought it, but I was worried he'd give me a rambling story about Walt's frozen corpse coming to him in a dream.

"It was out on route 68 or... maybe 72. 234? It's definitely still in Green County," his slurring was getting steadily... slurrier and I glanced back at the officers who were still standing there, staring at holes.

"Do you have booze back there?"

"Yeah. Need a nip?" He tried to pass me his flask through the steel grate of his window.

"No, I'm good. Thanks." Pushing off the cruiser, I made my way over to Beavis and Butthead take 2. I'm not sure why I cared whether Brad got to keep drinking, but I was not in favor of him getting what he wanted most while I couldn't do the one thing I wanted.

Go home and take a shower.

"So, did you leave him with the flask, or did whoever put him in the car forget to do a pat down?"

"Wha-" Barney started, looking over their prisoner.

The man saluted him with the metal flask.

"You checked him for contraband, right, Barn?" Daniel asked, but his sudden imitation of a fish was confirmation he had not even considered the man who booby-trapped his own home might need to be frisked. "Damn it. Go frisk him! Before Carla gets here and chews our assess out."

Barney bustled over, awkwardly sputtering as he tried to get the man out of the car.

"Let me guess, you wanted to get rid of him to ask me a question?" Daniel smirked, glancing over the mirrored lenses of his aviator shades. Though he was getting soft, the Village of Sweet Pea police uniform he wore was tailored to show off his assets, including the almost too-short shorts he wore in the summer.

The man was basically an extra on *Reno 911!* just waiting for a call back.

"Are you going to shout at me for telling Larry about your stunt? Because..."

"This isn't about Larry. Did you check on the owners of the cars in your neighborhood?"

"Yeah... they don't belong to anyone," he brushed down the front of his shirt. "None of them had plates and when I took pics of a few VINs, they all came back as having no registered owner.

I think it might be overflow from a dealer lot, but we can't figure out which one."

"Huh" I filed that away for later. I wasn't aware of a dealership in the area that could accommodate electric car sales, but it didn't mean there wasn't one. "Brad was going on about some place called the Huffleweiss place. You heard of it?" I asked, not letting on that my curiosity was based on a very real blood stain in a very similar "suddenly missing" situation.

"Yeah... well, kind of. A decade ago, a developer wanted to buy up all the farms out here and build tract housing." Daniel's demeanor changed from smug assurance to storyteller. Though the man was a massive thorn in my side, he'd never left Sweet Pea, which guaranteed he had access to all the old gossip. "He thought all the people out here were dumb hicks and tried to low ball them on the offers. Dude didn't seem to understand that if they sold him their land, they were selling him their livelihoods. He made a huge, whiny scene at town hall, but this out here isn't Sweet Pea. It's not quite anything besides County, and the county meeting is closer to Fairborn, but the video made the rounds."

"He? Who's he?" I asked, annoyed again that people wouldn't tell me a name I could Google.

"The developer," he answered with an eye roll.

"No, what's his name? Did you see him? Can you send me a video?"

"Yeah, a couple times... His name started with a J or maybe a G? It was a while ago and he never made it very far. Eventually he lost steam, but there was a yellow and white colonial style about 10 miles that way that got torn down. It's been under construction a long ass time..."

"This yahoo said people were getting sick. Did it ever get finished?"

Daniel scratched the back of his neck, flexing his biceps for a reason that would probably make me want to barf.

"I don't think so, but I can't be sure. You'd know better than I would since you've actually been there."

"What? I haven't been on a construction site... I don't think. Have I?" I asked Winnie, and she gave me a few eyebrow wiggles that said *I've been everywhere, man*. Which was not inaccurate, but certainly not completely true.

We'd never been to Alaska.

"Yeah, you have. When all those people Stella called drama kids were running around town, and Penny Plootz teamed up with the old Sweet Pea principal, Cummins? Larry said some guy brought you out to look at toilets and water or something..." He pulled a water bottle out of the cruiser behind him and took a drink. Barney had gotten the door unlocked, his keys still hanging in the lock where I imagined him forgetting them until panic showed up at leaving time. Mr. Bosley refused to give over the flask, but Barney wasn't giving up. Instead, the deputy officer was pulling on the drunk trying to get him out of the car, while the seat belt kept pulling him back in. All the while, the burier of bombs kept his mouth suctioned closed around the opening of his flask. Every tug to and fro, he suckled harder until Barney admitted defeat and let go. Both men fell over, Barney landing flat in the dirt and Brad falling over, upside down, on the plastic seats. We heard the flask hit the floorboards right before the prisoner heaved out everything in his stomach somewhere in the back of the cruiser.

"Son of biscuit," Daniel whined. "I don't want to clean that."

"Sucks to be you," I tossed back offhandedly. My mind was already elsewhere. Pulling up memories of the time Sweet Pea lost power and clowns ransomed me.

Honest to goodness, circus clowns.

The development in question had been somewhere between Yellow Springs and Dayton, about ten minutes from my office at night when no one could see how fast I was driving. It had been months since I'd driven out that way. It was a bit off the beaten path, less than this field of mines, but still out there. I'd just assumed the thing had been built in the time since I'd last seen it. I never once considered that a crappy contractor who hired unlicensed plumbers would have gotten on the project from a shady developer trying to drown out the thing indefinitely.

"Any idea who the developer was?" I asked him again. "Besides the J or G? Maybe a business name?"

We were watching a fleet of police vehicles pull up the drive and line up neatly behind my Jeep. All of them took a minute to collect... whatever police leaders need to have on a crime-ish scene. Exiting their cruisers, they pulled ball caps onto shiny heads to stand with their hands on hips, facing the property before us.

Guess I don't get to leave... a thought that was confirmed when the occupant exiting the vehicle behind mine was Carla. We shared a look during which I tried to tell her *Look, I kept them alive* while hers suggested that an officer on the ground and the rank smell of vomit were good indicators I could have tried harder.

"Cyn," she greeted me, waving me over with a crooked finger the same way Daniel had to Barney. I crossed my arms tightly against my chest and leaned against Daniel's car, digging in my heels. "Now, Cyn."

I drank my coffee and glowered.

"Please?" she asked with an eye roll, and I shuffled over. A bunch more men climbed out of their vehicles in shirtsleeves and trousers, almost all of them taller than Carla but much shorter than me. Their fitness levels varied from marathoner to couch potato, but they all wore the same world-weary expression above a glad-handing smile.

Politicians, ick.

Each man had an assistant in blue or brown, directed to the trunk of their respective cars to pull out equipment. These individuals moved efficiently, both with and separate from the others. A semi-circle was erected around the property inside my painted box of safety, though it was getting harder to see.

The sun was sinking below the horizon, and I wondered how they planned to defuse the bombs without any light. In a blink, the hum of a generator filled the night and a half-dozen flood lights lit up the scene.

It looked worse in the artificial light than it had in the sun. Shadows cast long and menacing from hole to hole, and the trailer had taken on a sinister glint in the slanted highlighting of indirect light. None of this was my idea of a good night activity, and my phone buzzed in my pocket.

Opening the message, I saw a corpse on a metal table. The man was in his late forties, hair thinning on his head and extra thick on the chest. The sheet stopped just above his nipples, but the Y incision was visible and stitched closed. My brain's first thought was *all his organs were just dumped back in there like a poorly packed suitcase*. My second was that I might have seen his face before, but I couldn't place it.

"Is that a dead guy?" Carla asked from beside my elbow, and I lurched away.

"Geez! I forgot you were there."

"Is that a dead guy?" she asked again, taking my phone and staring at the open image.

"Yeah. We entered Leonard and Ferrah's house, and the kitchen had a giant pool of blood. The forensic people took a sample, and it matched this dead guy. It's not Leonard, which is good, but... he looks familiar."

I turned my head left and right while the miniature strike team of police leadership assistants returned to their commanders for additional orders. It would have been cool if they didn't look like robots obeying their mechanical overlords.

I should really go home and sleep...

"Any chance you'll move your car and let me leave?"

Carla chewed on her lip before slowly shaking her head *no*.

"You are being hired, temporarily... to find the rest of the bombs."

Chapter Fourteen: Regional Planning

I t was too early to be awake.

Carla had Winnie searching for bombs until nearly midnight. We found three more, bringing Brad into league with domestic terrorists and burned spies trying to save Floridians.

In the kitchen, my burbling coffee maker gave me hope for humanity. I'd been seconds from collapse last night, but I'd still remembered to program the coffee maker. Few things in life were as important as remembering to set up my coffee maker and feeding Winnie.

If I forgot either, people could die.

Beside me, Winnie was still out.

She had been methodical, sniffing every last inch in twenty-minute blocks before she rested and played. Then we refocused and carried on until the whole of a two-acre lot was searched. Winnie hadn't had that much focused work in almost two years, Florida being a punishment and not a job where she could use her skills.

It took us a minute to get back into our routine, but finding bombs was a game to her and I needed to make it fun.

It's hard to make possibly blowing yourself up fun, but we managed.

Once we'd swept the grounds, a tow truck arrived, and all of the vehicles and lights moved so it could hitch to the bug out vehicle. When I'd suggested we clear it of bomb supplies first, I was told we could not enter the man's residence. The trailer wasn't searchable without a warrant, but they could tow it for being "on a crime scene".

Sounded made up to me, but it was hard to argue with that many police chiefs. My only option was to send a silent prayer to the universe that should it blow up on a road and decimate the pavement, it was not the road I'd need to travel to get home.

"Winnie?" I said, rubbing her shoulder. The canine twitched but slept on, not caring that I got up or that I had gone into the kitchen.

Nothing wears a working dog out more than having an actual job.

I'd wanted to stop at the construction site, but there wasn't time, light, or energy by the time we were done. I'd googled the property during one of Winnie's mandatory re-focusing breaks and got a few hits on a planning department website about applications associated with the address. There were weird alpha-numeric designators that expanded into a permit for something or other, but I couldn't figure out what I was reading. I was fairly certain the documents were written in English, but my definition of setbacks had to do with falling behind... somehow this group used it to measure a distance. Nothing showed who owned the property or who had gotten the permits to develop it... at least, not in a way I understood.

"Alexa," I addressed the robot and waited for the little lights. "What day is it?"

Pouring coffee into a mug, I waited for the machine to think while I perused my coffee flavoring options.

"It is Thursday, September 10th. It is currently 52 degrees, with a high of 72. Would you like me to provide you with breaking news updates?"

"Not at all, thanks Robo-lady."

"I'm sorry, I don't know that. Would you like breaking news update-"

"No thank you," I spoke clearly, and she powered down. "Thursday... Thursday..."

I pulled out my phone, looking again at the day of the week while I drank coffee. There were a few text messages that had come in... at some point. The first was from Carla with a stern reminder that I was expected to be at lunch with the two Mrs. Margots.

I responded I would rather eat my own arm, but I'd be there.

Another was from Stella, my autistic former intern who'd taken it upon herself to find me a replacement.

Whom Winnie took it upon herself to refuse.

Stella: *Hi Cyn, this is Stella.*

Stella: *Would you be able to meet with me sometime today? I would like to talk to you about something weird.*

Stella: *It is not the type of weird we talk about at your parents' house.*

Stella: *I also have more resumes as I received word from all candidates you did not contact them.*

Stella: *Please confirm our meeting.*

Me: *Hello, Stella, this is Cyn.*

Me: *I'm having lunch with Carla, Mrs. Margot and her sister. Would you like to join us?*

Me: *We will probably be talking about a dead guy.*

Me: *If you agree with these terms, our meeting is confirmed, and I will tell you the time and location when someone tells me.*

The next one was from Levi.

Levi: *I had a dream about you. Hope to make it come true soon.*

Me: *If it involved coffee or dogs, I'm already living it.*

I snapped a picture of my coffee mug with Winnie in the background and sent it along. It wasn't sexy or flirty, but I was tired, and sometimes sending a random picture saved me from using more words.

It also helped weed out people who'd accidentally mistaken me for normal. So, two tennis balls, one dog... or whatever the saying was.

Last night was the first time I'd gotten non-substance assisted sleep this week, and I honestly felt worse than I had with no sleep... though walking a grid pattern for 5 hours probably had more to do with it than the actual sleep part.

My last message was from Joseph, informing me that he was implementing an employee fraternization policy that I was expected to sign, and that Larry would be at the dairy in the morning and could I please start work later to accommodate the man. There was also an accidental voice memo where he was shouting at what might have been sunflowers, but we also had a cow named Sunflower, so no real conclusions could be drawn.

"I should just quit," I sighed, sending Joseph a middle finger emoji. Then, since he was unstable, an *thumbs up emoji, pretending the first one was a typo. "That man is exhausting, and I don't really need much money..."

Abandoning the phone, I pulled Winnie's dish down and started preparing her breakfast. She lifted a single sleepy eyelid, but didn't seem inclined to dance under my feet in the kitchen. It was the first time I was able to accomplish the task without a pain-filled howl when I stepped on her or a string of swears when I slipped in her drool and fell down.

It was weird, and I didn't like it.

"Winnie?" I called out to her, and she slowly rose, doing a big stretch first forward and then backward. Shaking out her fur, she gracelessly leapt to the floor with a *thump* and walked over on clicking claws. I set the dish down and she became slightly more alive, eating with intent and significantly less gusto than normal.

"You up for a day of government buildings?" I asked her, grabbing more coffee. My phone chimed with a message from Stella stating that she would join us. I let Carla know, and she advised it would be at Gertie's little backyard house at noon. My shift at the dairy started at 1300, so I asked her if we could make it earlier. I was then informed we would meet at 11 and I gave all the info to Stella.

"This is a lot of texting for the morning," I grumbled, getting coffee number three prepped and ready to drink. Winnie finished her breakfast and let out a wide yawn that showed all of her teeth.

"Yup. But we can't go back to sleep," I warned her, heading into the bathroom before I let her outside. "We need to go talk to the government. Won't that be fun?"

Winnie sneezed at me and laid down, anyway.

Yup... fun.

The planning office was on the main level of a short brick building near Fairborn. Winnie and I arrived at ten past eight and there were already four people standing in the lobby beside a reception desk. Three of them were holding rolled up papers with a slight sheen, held into their tight rolls by a single rubber band. There appeared to be a mandatory uniform of work boots, jeans and some manner of construction debris to be in this line and I met none of those requirements, but stayed in line anyway.

In front of us was a small woman with black hair, an athletic build, and a powerful aura of *mess with me and find out*. Which was to her credit, since at least two of the people in front of me were wearing *I'm king of the world and all will do my bidding* face. It would make my morning to see her in action.

Apparently, this wasn't their first trip to her counter because when she told them to sit and wait, they did.

"Can I help you?" she asked with a smile that could go either way on the customer satisfaction survey.

"I..." I looked down at Winnie and then back up at the woman. Her name plate said Sharon, and she looked at Winnie but didn't comment for or against her presence in the building. Usually, government buildings had signs with a list of prohibited items like guns, drugs, nipple piercings, and dogs, but this one was lacking. "I wanted information about the owner or developer of a project under construction? I searched the website and found some... things, but I couldn't read them and I didn't really know what I was looking at. Kinda hoping someone smarter than me could tell me how to read the things?"

Sharon let out a little laugh, and my shoulders loosened slightly.

"Yeah, I think there's a planner I could set you up with. Take a seat at one of the desks behind me," she gestured to her right, and I leaned to the side. There were four little cubbies with workstations facing three quad sets of chairs in the center of the room. On the opposite side was another set of workstations. The four people before me were sitting in the waiting area, and I lowered my voice.

"Will they be mad if I go first? I'm not in a hurry."

She let out another laugh, this one accompanied by a bright smile.

"They need other people. But honestly, even if they also needed a planner, it's their turn when I say it is." She stared down an almost seven-foot man whose knees were nearly at his ears in the average sized chairs. He was easily three hundred pounds, but he shrank under the gaze of the under-five-foot woman who might have weighed less than Winnie. "Grab a seat."

Not wanting to get on her bad list, I sat down at the second station and waited quietly for my planner. There were two chairs facing a solo chair with two screens, one facing the employee side and the other facing the customer. Only the employee side had a mouse and a keyboard. Winnie hopped up on the chair next to me and I stroked her fur.

"Hi, I'm Crystalline Rainier. I heard you need a planner?" A woman had floated over soundlessly in a tiered bohemian skirt and rainbow sleeveless shirt. Her dark curly hair draped around her shoulders, showcasing tarot card tattoos and images of forestation over time. Her short, choppy bangs ended an inch before her eyebrows, drawing attention to pale green eyes that were intelligent and kind.

"Um... yes. Are you... a planner?" I asked, thinking the woman belonged somewhere else. With such a kickass name, I wanted her to be a woodland woman leading jerks to their death.

"Yes. You look confused."

"Your name and look... don't really scream 'government employee'. I feel like you could be... a cult leader or like... an artist who uses an arc welder and makes sculptures that are basically giant vaginas but claims to be something else. Then make rich white dudes pay you to put them in conservative buildings and mess with the people."

"Well, that's oddly specific and now I kind of wish art was one of my skills. As far as this goes, everyone needs a day job. I find my purpose outside of work," she floated into the chair in front of me, every bit the mythical creature in a bland beige office space.

"What do you do outside of work?" I asked, petting Winnie. The woman shrugged.

"Ritual human sacrifice."

I nodded.

"If you ever need more... sacrifices, I know some people who could stand to bleed out."

"Exes? I get a lot of offers for exes."

"I'm more into petty vengeance for people who've wronged me personally. Why let them die quickly when you can subject them to a lifetime of minor inconveniences?"

"Why indeed? I personally choose to only sacrifice plants, but they often kill themselves, so why not eat them? And you are?"

Her gaze fluttered between us and I wished I owned something besides T-shirts and cargo pants. I'd owned a dress once, but it was involved in a hand amputation incident that left it stained beyond cleaning.

"I'm Cyn Sharp, this is Winnie. We used to be government employees, but we were terrible at it. I almost blew up Florida... Or she did? So, now we work at a dairy... well, I do. She's a social media influencer in the K through 6 demographics."

Crystalline accepted my hand, and then Winnie's paw, before settling her steepled fingers on the desktop. Patient eyes beneath large circular glasses encouraged me to continue without the pressure of words.

"We live out in Sweet Pea. Earlier this year, we were at a construction site and this guy bought cheap plumbing fixtures, but I heard a story about someone sort of bullying the old owners into selling and trying to buy up the area, but the guy I was talking to said they sort of disappeared. My source is... spotty with reality, but it's a little too similar to an incident I'm looking into, which is the second address that has an accessory deal-occupant's words. I was wondering if I can find out who owns the building at this address, who's developing it and... I don't really know how buildings work, but... anything that might explain a link between real estate and missing people? Also, if you could show me how to use the website, that would be great. What's a setback when not referencing a shortcoming of some sort? Or mylars? And easement vacations?"

My lungs begged for air as I pulled some in.

Note to self: it's OK to breathe while talking.

I passed her the post-it with the address to the apartment complex and Ferrah and Leonard's house on it. Winnie and I had driven past the construction site. Cones and chain link kept us from getting very close, but it was still partially crumbled. There was a work crew on site, and several pickups that looked like they were personal vehicles owned by the loitering workers wearing hard hats and safety vests. There was still half-melted drywall, but the broken plumbing fixtures had been removed. When I paused too long at the fence, all the men took notice and at least two pulled out cell phones, calling while staring menacingly.

"Sure. First, a setback is the minimum buffer distance between the property line and the structure, and I think an 'accessory deal' means an accessory dwelling unit or ADU. Mylars are paper copies of plans filed, and an easement is an agreement that someone has permission to access private property."

Her long fingers danced across the keyboard, entering the address I'd given her. Accessory dwelling unit didn't sound any more informative than "accessory deal", but I felt justified assuming she didn't know what SNAFU meant, so it was fine that I didn't know what an ADU was.

All of her other explanations sounded like government doublespeak, so I just nodded and pretended it all made perfect sense.

"Second, most government agencies have GIS for location info for the public and a public portal for viewing apps." She pulled up the screen for searching and I nodded. "You'll want to adjust your dates and put the address in."

The date range was 10 years, and she entered the address of Ferrah and Leonard's house. Then opened a new window and did the same thing to see the location of "the old Huffleweiss place".

"Hopefully it's not older than ten years because those aren't digital... or located here. Major subdivision, replat," she clicked on an application and blinked twice at the words.

"Any chance replat is short for platypus and is a design term to make buildings look like a platypus or a collection of platypae?"

I asked, hoping to sound smart. This woman was insanely cool, and I wanted her to be my friend. Maybe teach me about planning and how not to be awkward.

"I think the plural of platypus is platypuses... Also sounds wrong but in a different, convo with HR kind of way. A plat is a picture of how you plan to divide a parcel. It's like the picture on the front of a puzzle box that explains what the puzzle will look like when all the pieces are put together. You have to split a property to put multiple buildings on it so each gets its own address..." she paused in her talking while opening another screen and entering the second address. On a third tab, she pulled up an internal system window, her mouth opening and closing while silently reading the words on the screen.

"Son of witch's tit," she exclaimed, leaning back in her chair. "That asshole."

"Who?" I looked between Winnie, the screen and Crystalline. "What's happening?"

"The developer who submitted the application for that subdivision, the accessory dwelling unit on that house, and two more subdivisions I got calls about today where there was unpermitted work, are all owned by the same person."

"He owns the falling down complex and Leonard and Ferrah's house?" I asked, looking at the name listed as applicant: Jayam, LLC. It was a dumb name, but not really sinister in any way.

"It doesn't look like he's listed as the owner, just the appli cant... Owner is..."

She clicked around but only made a face.

"Owner isn't listed. I'll have to check another database. The sub out in Sweet Pea, what did you say the names were of the people who owned the property before?" She opened a fourth browser window.

"Huffleweiss," I said, and she stared at me, fingers poised over the keys.

"How do you spell that?"

"No idea..." I answered her arched eyebrow. "I've just sort of been picturing it like Hufflepuff without the puff and Weissman without the man... "

Shrugging, she tried my way and a single result popped up with a link to another county website.

"Where does that go?" I asked, though she had already clicked on it to find out. It took a moment to load, but we were in the county branch of the Bureau of Vital Records, looking at two death certificates. A Mr. James Huffleweiss and a Mrs. Lilly Porter-Huffleweiss, deceased... I looked back to the screen beside it, displaying the subdivision application information.

"They died the day before this application was submitted?" I looked between Crystalline and the screen.

"It gets better. Check the name."

The name below Jayam, LLC, was a Jay Gitt. The person listed on the death certificate as discoverer of remains was... "Jay Gitt?"

I googled it on my phone and found a picture of Jay Gitt.

"He looks like someone I would punch in the face," I mentioned, clicking through the databases and seeing shot after shot of a weak-chinned man with a poorly executed goatee and sideburns. His hair was thinning, worn swept back to give the illusion of volume. There were only professional glamour shots, stopping at mid chest, but his shoulders looked narrow and slim, hinting at a smaller build. "Do you know much about him?"

"Some things... mostly just hear some stuff. He's a complete tool bag, constantly in here with crap apps for crap projects, but look what he named the subdivision." She double clicked to highlight the crucial piece.

Termination Point.

"Which means..."

We shared a look, not daring to look at the remaining address on the post it in front of her.

"Which means... he might have a habit of killing people... or arranging their deaths."

Chapter Fifteen: Lively Ladies Lunching

"**Y**ou got what you deserved, you old bat!"

I ducked just in time to avoid a glob of egg salad to the face. It splattered on the doorframe, retaining its spherical structure and sliding downward like a slug. The sulfuric stench polluted the air, and I fought the urge to gag while I took in the carnage. In front of me, Gertie was squared off against Mrs. Margot on the other side of the dining room table. Stella sat immobile on one of the cream couches and Carla was in the kitchen trying to remove the cork from a bottle of wine.

"Gheblout," I told Winnie, and she let out a super bark that rattled the windows of the accessory unit. Carla and Stella snapped to attention while both Margots fisted their hips and spoke at the same time.

"What was that?"

"Honestly, Cynthia!"

Side by side, I finally saw the family resemblance. While Mrs. Margot's severe grey bun stood in sharp contrast to Gertie's silver ringlets, they shared a firm set to the mouth from years of suffering fools. Though she used a walker, Mrs. Margot didn't have any more wrinkles than Gertie did, a fact I attributed to their vampirism.

"I need to carry garlic," I muttered, swiping my finger under the egg salad glob and carrying it to the table. Flicking it onto a napkin, I looked between the two older women and then joined Carla in the kitchen. "Why are you trying to open a wine bottle with your keys?"

Carla looked down and then back at me.

"I thought it was a corkscrew," she answered, chin tucked. I noticed the exhaustion coloring her sheepish expression, and I took over the wine project while she sat next to Stella.

"Alright, aside from your signature sulfur salad, what the hell is going on here?" I asked, delighted when Stella piped up with her own signature brand of observational verbal vomit.

"Gertie and Mrs. Margot were married to male twins before the Margots. Though there is only a three percent chance of any pregnancy resulting in twins, I know that Gertie and Glen's mother was over forty at their conception, so it was more likely even before taking genetic factors into consideration. I don't know anything about the first set of brothers they married. It appears that they were each interested in the man who was dating the other sister and the night before the wedding, each couple switched. Only the grass was not as greener as they thought, and they've been fighting about minor things for years to avoid dealing with the reality that they spent years of their life with the wrong man because they were both too proud to admit they were wrong. Then the men requested divorces, which was apparently a blow to the pride of both. Gertie especially because though she is bisexual, she's never taken rejection from men as well as she has from women. Though they've remarried and made it to the 'til death' part, there is still a lot of bitterness over that first marriage. This particular bout of deflection was about..." She looked slightly to the ceiling, reading notes in the book of her mind. "Whether or not any of us actually like the other one or are only tolerating them out of social courtesy."

"Well, I can answer that one. You're both a major pain in my ass, but without you I would have more free time to ponder all the ways I've disappointed myself, my family, Larry, Ian, Winnie... Everyone. So, thank you for saving me from that depressive existential spiral. Will someone please put a lid on that egg salad before I toss my cookies?"

"It smells fine!" Mrs. Margot snapped, and I shook my head.

"You have the walking farts and are too deaf to hear them. If you can't smell them either, I'm not accepting your opinion on any olfactory associated assessments. Show of hands: who would rather have a fistfight with The Hulk than smell that?" I raised my hand, as did Carla and Stella.

"You are in quite the mood," Gertie grumbled, pushing the lid onto the egg salad. "There's nothing wrong with Glen's egg salad. Except that she made it."

The sisters made a weird telepathic face apology, and the room seemed to settle. I opened the Chardonnay using an actual corkscrew and poured some into the four waiting stemless wine glasses. Carla collected hers and I took one to each of the sisters Margot, where they were seated at the table. Aside from the now quarantined egg salad, there was a spread of cheese, meat, bread, nuts, olives, and Jell-O.

I put a little of everything on two plates and took the second to Stella on the couch with her glass of wine. She accepted both the plate and the glass while I stood awkwardly.

"Before we get started with... anything. Does your niece's Canadian actually know Leonard, or was that a ruse to avoid telling me Gertie is still alive?"

"They're... acquainted." She hedged, and I rolled my eyes. "They both work construction."

"No, they don't! Daniel says his cousin is doing coding!"

"I don't listen to *everything* my niece says. It seemed like something a Canadian would do," she sniffed. "Like I said, I hedged."

"You mean you lied?" I crossed my arms and glared down at her.

"You pretended my daughter was the one who knew Leonard?" Gertie snapped. Before I could process that Mrs.

Margot's niece would have a parent related to her, Stella pivoted the conversation away from touchy subjects.

"What language did you use to make Winnie bark?" Stella asked. Looking down at the dog, she preened at the mention of her superior barking skills. I made a mental note to revisit the whole "niece" thing, just in case the sisters had another, more stable sibling.

"German... I think. Though Google says speak and bark are completely different words, neither of which looks anything like gheblout."

"Keyb-L-OW?" Stella tried, putting extra emphasis on the OW. Winnie sneezed at her and I shrugged.

"You were close enough, but she only listens sometimes. Which reminds me... she ate the resumes you sent over, so I don't think I'll be taking on another intern while you volunteer at the school."

"I could send the applications again. When they all informed me you hadn't contacted them, I assumed you had found them unsatisfactory, and I was working on acquiring you a new crop of humans to consider. Similarly, I also learned from our therapist that you've been ghosting her calls and, considering what new atrocities you have seen, I really think you would benefit from resuming the conversation."

"No, I think we'll keep the team at two and my emotions shoved down until they erupt unexpectedly in the cheese aisle at the grocery store. Still seeing the pizza man?"

"James? Yes, though I will allow the topic to change this time, you are not off the hook regarding therapy. James and I have engaged in intercourse and, after the initial gross factor of sweat, it was rather enjoyable. I find I need to know more about what I am to understand is referred to as oral..."

I slapped my hands over my ears and hummed.

"I told you to ask my mom about sex. Do not ask me, I cannot. I am a repressed millennial who was taught to be curious about sex but never, ever, talk about it." I followed my declaration with some humming that ended when Winnie shoved her head against my knees, and I discovered I'd closed my eyes.

"Is it over?" She nodded, and I dropped my hands. "How's it going at the school, by the way? Have you taught those kids how awesome it is to be different? Are you excited about your last year of college?"

Stella's fingers tapped on her thigh. Index, middle, ring. Index twice, middle twice, ring twice... With her other hand, she grabbed her ponytail, the black hair smooth and glossy beside her brown skin and almond eyes.

"Stella?" I asked, but her tapping increased in speed.

"It's not going well," she admitted. Winnie went to her side, letting Stella self-soothe by stroking her fur. "My work at the school, college is fine aside from a very creepy police officer who keeps trying to see the female students nude in compromising positions. As you know, I was very interested in special education and assisting children similar to me. My personal experience was less than desirable, especially when autism was treated as a disease associated with vaccines and leveraged as a source of shame. That sentiment continues, which is awful on its own. However, there seems to be an increase in the number of children in the special education program. An average of fifteen percent of students in the public school system are in programs funded by Individuals with Disabilities Education Act. Ohio is slightly higher at sixteen percent, but that would equate to about 80 students in the 3136 schools over all grade levels. In my school, there are 35 kids in the fourth-grade class alone with developmental challenges limiting brain and bodily functions."

"Bodily functions?" I asked, not catching on as quickly as I should.

"Uncontrolled urination and muscle movements in addition to irregular growth."

"You think somehow they are being harmed?" I asked, sitting beside her on the couch with a sufficient buffer for her aversion to touch. Stella picked at her plate of nibbles, alternating small bites with sips of her white wine.

"I do not think they are being harmed intentionally, but..." She took a long pause, considering. "If I confess to a crime, are you required to arrest me?"

Stella directed her question to Carla, who startled, droopy eyes indicating she'd been slightly asleep.

"Huh?"

"If I confess to a crime, are you duty bound to incarcerate me?"

"Did you do it in Sweet Pea?" she queried with a yawn.

"No. It was here in Fairborn."

"Then it's out of my jurisdiction. Carry on, confession queen," she waved, and Mrs. Margot tutted at her. "Shut it. I care about Stella, but after Cyn and Winnie found four bombs last night, I had to book the three that didn't go boom and write a report. I've had 3 hours of sleep. I can promise no one will harm Stella, but I cannot promise to know what she's talking about tomorrow."

"I accept your terms." Stella stroked Winnie faster, and we all had to wait for her to find words in her own time. "During a trip to the administrative office, I found the student files... lying around. I collected a few for some of my students and scanned their information. Then I intentionally pulled a few more until I had the addresses of all 35 students in my class."

Stella gave a far-off look, pausing to choose her words rather than for dramatic effect.

"Many of the students had only moved here in the past two or three years. Before that, their records show normal development and mental acuity. Then... they regressed after six months in the area. None of the parents indicated upon registration that they had any such history with abnormal development, so I looked closer."

Her fingers resumed their stim on her thigh while the other hand continued to stroke Winnie's fur.

"They all live in the same apartment complex. I went out there yesterday, and there's a smell... like metallic but sweet... I can't explain it. When I saw some of my students, they said they couldn't smell anything. Perhaps they have gotten used to it, which is far more alarming."

"Did you ask the manager of the complex? Or get information from the owner?" My scalp was itching, and my skin felt crawly.

"No. I wasn't sure where to go with my concerns. I had planned to look into it more this weekend and was going to ask you for help." She gave me wide doe eyes and I melted.

"Yeah, I can help. What's the address or name of the apartment complex?"

"What about Ferrah and Leonard?" Gertie asked, horrified that I might not locate her landlord.

"I'm still looking into that, too." I scrubbed my hands over my face and pulled out my phone. My text thread from Levi was up. He'd sent me a GIF about a woman hoarding dogs, and I scrolled back to the autopsy photo.

I've seen him...

"Is that man dead?" Stella interrupted, and I glanced back at her.

"Yeah. Sorry. This is the guy whose blood is in Leonard and Ferrah's kitchen."

The rest of the women came over and took turns checking out the image, discussing amongst themselves while I tried to put the man into context, but all I could think about was children wetting themselves near shattered toilets.

Toilets... broken toilets.

"That's who he is!" I gasped, trying not to happy dance that I remembered who the dead guy was. "He's the man who got swindled on the plumbing fixtures. Back when the roadside carnival was in town," I jiggled excitedly until I remembered he was dead. "So... why was a construction foreman stabbed in Leonard's kitchen?"

Hearing silence, I entered Stella's address into the permit query form, looking for a subdivision application. Sending the photo to Crystalline with a quick 'look familiar... but not dead?', I was well aware of the ticking clock until I was needed at the farm.

"Any leads on where Mr. Bosley got the explosives?" Carla blinked at me like a newborn unfamiliar with speech. Running over the words in my head, I couldn't come up with another way to phrase the question. I made a mental note to ask her later.

"Never mind, I need to head back to the dairy for work. We good?" I made eye contact with each one in turn, ending with a sleepy Carla. Sleepy because Winnie found four bombs, and she had to book the components of three....

"Winnie found five bombs," I told her, and she jerked upright.

"What?"

"Winnie found five bombs... You said you booked three and then one went boom. She found five... so there's another non-exploded one... somewhere. Might be in the pocket of the pants I was wearing yesterday. Well, pockets. I separated the trigger from the C4. Remind me to get it to you?"

I said the last part from the safety of the front porch with the door only slightly ajar.

"Cyn!" Carla shouted, and I made a dash for the Jeep with Winnie on my heels. We jumped in and I started the engine, reading the text back from Crystalline.

CR: *Yup, that's Ely Mollusk. He's not a general contractor though... I think he's an assistant. I called up the morgue and sent* *them down the right path to an ID. Which reminds me, the house is owned by a shell company. Sheriff's are helping with the layers.*

Me: *You knew the blood donor?*

CR: *Yeah, sorry. Ely was the right-hand man to Jay Gitt... who also owns the subdivision you sent me the address for.*

CR: *He was on my human sacrifice list... I'm a little disappointed.*

Damn it.

I scrunched up my face, trying to find my next move

Me: *Me too... Do you know where Jay Gitt lives?*

CR: *No... Just his work address?*

Me: *Hate giving up the home field advantage. Any chance you can trick Jay into your office tomorrow? And send me the addresses of all his current projects.*

CR: *Yup. Send me your email. It's too much to text.*

CR: *He'll be in tomorrow at 11.*

CR: *Don't punch him in the face. It's a government building, and he's a little bitch.*

Chapter Sixteen: Nothing but Nuggets

J oseph texted I couldn't quite come in yet, but I was "on the clock". Instead of cursing him and Larry, I took a detour to some of the construction sites Crystalline had given me the addresses of. Starting with the two she reported receiving complaints on, I plugged them into GPS and followed the robot lady to my first destination.

In about 5 minutes, I was looking at a fenced off rectangle of dirt between a grocery store and a highway entrance with the highway itself running behind.

There were no workers on site, but tire tracks criss crossed back and forth across a dirt driveway that separated two parts of a sidewalk. A storage container sat on the far edge, most of the tire tracks going that direction. Six greenish tarps billowed from the fence behind it, weather worn and fraying at the edges... but only on two sides of the fence, the one butting up against the grocery store parking lot and part of the space visible from the highway.

The front had a sign that said there was a public hearing on the parcel next week. Construction had already started with excavating the land to pour foundation, but the hole was as deep as a home pool, about ten feet. When I'd researched foundations, it only required 12 inches below the top layer and/or frost point. Unless they were digging underground parking, and then it was about twenty feet too shallow. Searching for the address like Crystalline taught me, I located the submitted site plan. It was a rough group of rectangles on a stained napkin with numbers I assumed were the intended final dimensions.

"No basement in the plan," I said, looking at Winnie in the back seat. Her eyes were closed, and her interest was waning. I drove to the next site, and aside from being between a strip mall with four out of six storefronts empty, it was the same.

Same deep hole in hole in the ground, same storage container, same submitted site plan when I entered the address into the plan review system.

Based on the stain, it may have even been the same napkin.

"This is weird..." I said into my rearview at Winnie. The tarps on this property covered the fence to the rear and beside the strip mall. This storage container was again at the intersection of those two tarped sections. Behind the property, a sea of grey roof tiles and the occasional chimney poked up from a housing tract with brick walls to the rear.

While I stared, something moved.

Cutting the engine, I listened for something besides the slapping of tarps against chain link.

Dirt crunched, and the metal door to the storage shed creaked open. Climbing out, I leashed Winnie, and we tried to look natural as I crossed the street and entered the pathway beside the railroad tracks.

Just a woman walking her dog...

We creeped along the outer edge of the fence, minding the railroad tracks to see behind the storage unit before we could disturb whoever might be over there. A loud thump came from inside the container, and I hurried toward the entrance as quietly as possible. Once in line with it, I focused on breathing quietly while Winnie panted beside me.

"Shh" I whispered. Her eyebrows wiggled in annoyance, and she panted harder while sweat pooled in my armpits.

The door of the container stood open, blocking the side view of the entrance. When no other sounds came out of the container, Winnie and I hustled forward toward the rear wall of the housing tract. I couldn't get a good angle without climbing onto the wall. Crouching low, I watched the door and waited for whoever was inside to emerge.

"Hey!" someone shouted from somewhere to the right. I popped up and looked around, catching sight of a man running over from a matte black truck with an extra-long antenna protruding from the cab roof.

It was also now blocking my exit beside the railroad track.

The stranger had blonde hair and blue eyes, wearing denim pants and a T-shirt that bulged awkwardly at his right hip. Nothing about him looked like official security or law enforcement, but that didn't mean he wasn't carrying.

Ohio state law lets almost anyone conceal carry.

"Hey?" I said, looking around me. His hand was twitching near his hip, more confirmation that what he kept there wasn't just a flashlight... or his penis.

"You're trespassing!" he snapped, looking like a 90s teen heartthrob with an attitude problem. His blonde hair flopped over one eye, reminding me of Levi. Their builds were similar, but this man clearly spent more time on arm day than intellectual pursuits, skipping leg day altogether, and had a fondness for beer that was visible above his beltline.

Mine was made of cheese, so I got it but I doubted we'd bond over vices.

"We were... on a walk." I held up Winnie's leash. "Who owns the land beside the tracks? I thought this was a public pathway."

"Why were you spying?" He ignored my question and the metal container slammed closed. I chanced a look in that direction and spotted a slight man with dark salt and pepper hair in a suit, his back ramrod straight as he disappeared back toward the strip mall.

"Answer me!" He shouted, and I allowed my vision to boomerang his direction again. Shirt pulled back, I saw the black handle of a semi-auto handgun poking out of a brown leather holster, his hand resting on the butt. His fingers twitched, but otherwise his hand was steady.

He was hoping for someone to shoot.

"We were looking for her ball," I gestured toward the fence line. "Yesterday we were playing fetch in the backyard and the ball went over. So, I was walking by and thought I'd check to see if it was here. Spying though? Is there something secret over there?"

I did a dramatic review of the area, searching my brain for a joke to make light of his accusation. Winnie's leash stuck to the sweat on my palms, and the norepinephrine surged in my system.

My body was ready to fight or flight... but my brain was like one of those windup monkeys waiting for someone to crank the handle and bring him to life.

"You know damn well you shouldn't be poking around. Didn't I see you yesterday poking around at-"

My phone chimed in my pocket and I twitched uncomfortably toward the device, wondering if I could throw it at his head to get away if I needed to. Holding up a single finger, I interrupted his words and prayed that the interruption would dissuade him from connecting me with me being at the other subdivision.

Through the cracks in my screen, I saw a message from Joseph ordering me into work.

I replied with a thumbs up and my location tag, just in case I disappeared today.

"Whelp, that's my boss. He said to come into work and I sent him my location so... he knows how long it will take me to get in. Micromanagers, am I right?"

Slowly, I approached the man and his truck, angling closer toward the train tracks as I walked back toward the street. Truck man's hand remained near his gun, but he didn't pull it out as I walked, hands raised and pointed toward him at chest level with Winnie's leash looped over my thumb.

"If you find a ball, just... throw it back over the fence, please?" I kept walking as I spoke, coming level with him and then blowing out my breath when we made it behind the truck. Winnie kept glancing behind her at the man, but she knew better than to growl or bark. At the sidewalk, I chanced a backward look and saw him with a phone pressed against his face.

Waving, we ran to the Jeep and jumped in, gunning it out of the neighborhood.

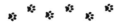

The dairy was eerily quiet when we arrived.

Out in the dirt lot, all the usual suspects had cars on site. Many of them drove older pickups and small passenger cars, all of them with peeling paint and tires held on with rust. During the snowy season, the compact cars would lessen, either due to carpooling or other alternate transportation. But it was not the snowy season, and getting out of my car and halfway to the barn without seeing a single person was creepier than my mom's nightstand.

Taking stock of each paddock, the animals were all enjoying a snack and appeared to have had their daily grooming. All the gators were parked in a neat line beside the ice cream parlor, in front of which a group of kids waited in a perfectly straight line, facing the hay bale upon which Winnie was scheduled to arrive in ten minutes. They were facing the other way, but it felt like I was being watched.

Scanning the roof of the barn and the hills that lead to the back forty, there was nothing but that sense of something darting out of the periphery. Like a fight at the OK Corral, the town was watching. I didn't see any eyeballs peeking out, no wayward meandering children getting yanked into shops... but I was walking into a fight of sorts. One where I was the bad guy they'd all been waiting for to roll into town and get shot.

If I heard a soprano recorder or saw a tumbleweed rolling past me, I was getting back in my car and driving until I reached Canada. Then changing my name to Catalina and opening a roadside stand selling poutine.

My life did not need to be scored by Ennio Morricone.

At the barn doors, I stood poised to flee in the entryway. I was scared to walk in any farther until I saw someone. I could sense movement inside, but like the paddocks, I couldn't see anyone. The main arena had dust lingering in the air, a stall door swinging slightly on its hinge, and the low hum of milking technology formed an unpleasant image of sudden disappearances. The whole situation gave me hardcore Afghanistan flashbacks... right before I accidentally blew up a marketplace.

Please don't let me blow up the dairy.

Despite my Joseph issues and the general opposition to the overly machismo farm hand behavior, I would be sad if the dairy was gone. The animals did not deserve that kind of ending. While some farms were just this side of animal cruelty, these creatures received incomparable care and no one was eating them... at least not anytime soon.

"Cynthia," Joseph called out, clearing his throat with a nervous shifting of eyes. He'd appeared out of nowhere, moving more quietly than he had in all the years I'd known him... which was all the years I'd been alive. His too-new cowboy boots had been swapped for running shoes.

Interesting....

"Joseph," I said back, crossing my arms under my chest and standing with my feet shoulder width apart. I balanced my weight on the balls of my feet, ready to run the second something looked amiss. "Where is everybody?"

I saw someone scurry out of sight in my peripherals, but when I turned, there was nothing there.

"Before I answer, I want you to know that..." he paused, shuffling his running shoes. Joseph was a short man with a large belly and work clothing that was always clean, creased and just a size too small. His balding scalp lived under a brimmed cowboy hat no ranch hand would get caught dead in. Normally, I'd be more concerned with getting hit with a button from his forest green and blue flannel shirt, but today, the bigger threat was his bulging eyeballs.

I wasn't even sure he could blink without popping one out.

"You want me to know that..." I prompted. His tongue flicked out to lick his lips, left hand scratching at his denim clad leg, a junkie trying to fight his addictive need for another hit.

"You are a valued employee of this dairy. But we are also a business. In order to stay in business, we need to keep making money. Ice cream, though enjoyed by all ages, is most often requested by children." He paused again. Pulling a paisley bandanna out of his pocket and mopping his brow, I noticed his other hand was tucked behind his back. A shadow loomed boxy and large, beside his figure on the ground.

"No," I answered, taking a step back. "No, no, no..."

"They're asking for you," he pleaded, eyes somehow wider than Jim Carey in *The Mask*. "Posts with you in it get a lot more traffic than Winnie alone, and she is pretty popular as it is."

"Joseph, I'm a college educated animal technician, trained in weapons and defense tactics. I've punched asshole men in the face on three continents. And you want me to stand beside a hay bale in a dumb, glittery outfit so you can sell ice cream?"

"Well... I uh... It's not a glittery outfit," he held out the bag. "You're going to be Winnie's secret service detail. She'll be... President of Ice Cream Land."

He slipped aviators onto her nose and hung a tie around her neck while I looked into the bag he'd brought. Inside was an all-black suit with a white undershirt and tie. It was sadly an outfit I actually owned because I did some dignitary security both in and out of the service. While Winnie looked cute, I knew that whatever size Joseph had chosen for me would not look cute. Either I'd be an over-stuffed sausage, or a skeleton draped in rags.

"If you do it, you can be off the rest of the week?"

"It's Thursday!"

Winnie sat beside me with her tail curled, looking every bit the presidential leader.

"So, we'll be off Friday and Saturday in exchange for this?" I asked, and his trembling lip told me I was mistaken. "What? The week ends Sunday."

"Technically, our work week is Saturday through Friday. So... You'd be off... tomorrow." He flinched, and I rubbed a hand over my face.

"I want a raise. Three extra dollars an hour and a stipend for Winnie."

"Deal," he answered too quickly. It wasn't enough of a pause; he'd been prepared for this.

"I hate you," I grumbled, swinging the bag harder than necessary, hoping to hit him with it.

"One more thing," he held up a hand, and I loosed a growl, daring him to say out loud the thought in his head. "You need to bring your battle dress fatigues on Saturday. The flavor is combat cocomo-it's a coconut mocha, so you'll probably like it."

And then he walked away... with no grievous bodily harm.

***

There was no time to think through what I learned today as I spent the next four hours silently glaring. It should have been an easy shift, silent glaring was basically the number one skill on my resume after blowing things up by accident, but these kids seemed to have watched a few too many English movies and treated me like the queen's guard–something to be tested.

"Uuhnnn," a kid blurbled at me with his tongue hanging out, fingers in his ear.

"No, like this!" A small girl turned her back toward me and let one rip, wiggling her backside to spread the smell.

"No way, we need to," a child raced toward me holding an ice cream. Extending my arm, I barricaded him from passing. Though he weighed next to nothing, his motivation made holding him back harder than it should have been. If Winnie wasn't too exhausted to be a pain in the butt, she'd have that ice cream and all the dribbles on the kid's shirt. His sandy brown hair and green eyes were a little too familiar, but my ID was cut off by a sound I knew far better.

"I have cheese!" Sylvia screeched, and Winnie rose. My gremlin of a niece parted the sea of children attempting to breach my stoicism. In one hand, she had a slice of American cheese in all its artificial cheesy glory. In the other she had... something small and brown.

Chicken nuggets maybe?

"No!" I ordered the same way I did with Winnie, but Sylvia was immune to attempts at obedience. She collided headfirst into my abdomen, stealing my air and my balance. We crashed to the ground, her giggling form wriggling on my chest as I tried to pin her arms in place and keep some semblance of order.

"Syl! I'm open," the sandy-haired boy called out, and she tossed him the chicken nuggets. Winnie intercepted the pass, swallowing one whole before leaving her perch to locate the rest. The whole porch was cheering and chanting.

"Sylvia! Sylvia!"

A boy shouted, "Nothing but nuggets!"

And that's when I saw it.

He was a mini-Daniel Kirby.

"You!" I snarled, standing up with my niece still locked in a vise grip. Her chaotic movements bruising various organs in my unprotected abdomen. "This is a No Kirby Kid zone. I have a sign!"

I swung Sylvia's leg and used it to point at my hand drawn sign.

"And where is Seth?" I asked my captive as Winnie re-took her place upon the hay bale, satisfied at having gotten all the scattered chicken nuggets. *At least it wasn't the cheese*, I decided, noticing Sylvia's orange-stained hand.

"Get in the van," Daniel's wife called out, her sharp manicure a threat to all who dared to disobey. "Sylvia, say goodbye to your aunt."

Her death glare was far better than mine. As were her clothes, hair and make-up, but I really only envied the death glare.

I could buy a lot of things, but there wasn't a store that sold angry eyes not meant for anthropomorphized potatoes.

"Bye Auntie Cyn! Have fun with... ew! Are you wearing a diaper under your pants? Only babies do that!" she screeched, and I looked at the little boy at the front of the line. His ears burned and the Kirby kids started laughing.

"No," I snapped at Sylvia, taking hold of her arm and dropping to meet her gaze. "No. You are not bullying other kids. There is never a reason to draw attention to someone else in a negative way. If you do not stop this behavior, you will be forced to come serve community service with me at the VA hospital. We help people, we don't tear them down. Do you understand?"

Sylvia's eyes misted, but I offered her zero reprieve. This was my responsible adult line in the sand and for the first time, she seemed to acknowledge that.

"Yes, Auntie Cyn," she sniffled and looked back at the boy in line. "I'm sorry."

I scraped the cheese off her hand and tossed it in the trash, looking at Daniel's wife, who was telling off the remaining kids. They all also apologized with a surprising amount of sincerity, and she gave me a look of begrudging respect. It was uncomfortable to see something besides disdain there and I had to look away.

"I've got it from here," she advised and swept all the kids into a minivan. I fired off a text to Seth with a warning that his kid was on my list and until she behaved like a decent human, I wasn't babysitting anymore. Also, she was going to be serving mandatory community service sometime soon.

"Hey," I said to the kid, waving him over. He was wearing a T-shirt with a velociraptor over tan shorts that appeared a little awkwardly filled out. Hesitating, the boy looked between me and his slightly distressed mother, light brown hair flopping awkwardly over one eye. "You can come over. This is Winnie."

My furry friend lifted her paw and offered it. Dino kid giggled and walked over to give her a shake.

"Have a seat," I gestured to the open spot beside President Winnifred.

"I..." He looked around, ears flaming red. "I had an accident. I might... smell."

"Don't worry about it. This dog has rolled on her back in cow poop at least twice this week. She doesn't notice or care about things like that." He met my gaze, and I gave him my most reassuring smile. "And neither do I or she'd get A LOT more baths."

Dino kid wrung his hands for another minute until Winnie leaned forward and licked half his face in one swipe. Laughing, he sat next to Winnie, hugging her while his mom snapped a couple of pictures. The photographer joined her while I did my best impersonation of Secret Service in a cheap, ill-fitting suit. My partner smothered him in love and then sat in a perfect presidential pose when the photographer held up a treat. I touched my ear and looked like a professional.

"I didn't used to need these," he whispered, though I couldn't tell if he was talking to me or Winnie. "I was good before we moved..."

His fingers convulsed in her fur, and I looked up at the woman. Her eyes were a little misty, watching his hand and the sidelong glances of the kids in line. I wasn't sure which expression was threatening to rip my heart from my chest harder, but I needed to learn more if I had any chance of making this right.

"Maybe we should have a photo break and get some ice cream," I told them, waving to the photographer, that she put up the rope and close the queue. "Where do you live?"

Chapter Seventeen: Booked on a Feeling

"We moved here after my husband left," Elise began, taking a bite of butter pecan ice cream. Her chaotic curls highlighted high cheekbones and sad eyes somewhere between brown and green. She looked like a woman who'd seen it all but still had compassion left for the world. "I was offered a job heading up the marketing campaign for a business owner in town, well, just outside. The apartments, New Classic, were the right price and convenient to a local school so we could walk to and from there together. I was allowed to work remotely which meant more time with Elvis. It was like all my dreams were finally coming true."

She pointed to Dino Kid, who was eating ice cream with one hand and furiously coloring a paper with the other. Winnie gave Elvis her full attention, eyes bouncing between his hands as she pondered which held the more interesting item she wanted to steal-ice cream or crayons.

I'd seen her eat both with equal gusto.

"Before we moved here, he was considered by doctors to be developing on the upper end of the development bell curve for children. Not in the upper quartile, just upper middle." I nodded like I knew what a bell curve represented in relation to child development. I was familiar with the concept, averages and standard deviations from that center, but children were a mystery to me. They all just looked trip hazard sized from my lofty height of six feet and mask of adulthood. "After about a month of being here, he developed tremors. Nothing too intense. I'd thought he was just nervous and shaking. Being the new kid can be hard, so I didn't draw attention to it. But then he stopped gaining weight and started having trouble remembering things. Six months after the move, I took him to the doctor, and they called child services."

A few tears streaked down her face.

"They asked him if he was being abused. Using leading questions and horrifying examples of what could be happening at our home that was built entirely of love... It was weeks before he stopped crying and could sleep in his own bed. They made him talk to a psychotherapist and go into the school counselor's office twice a week to report on what we'd done, all the while asking questions meant to accuse me of something to see if he'd agree. Then the bladder issues started, and they pulled him out of the regular classes. He was placed in a room with other students who'd been having this problem for a few years. Initially, I'd thought it was just a reaction to the trauma, you know, regressive behavior. The teacher... she treats them like infections, the consequence of amoral behavior, but I can't take him to another school." Elise's voice broke, and I passed her a napkin. "He desperately wants a pet and I'm terrified that if it gets sick too, they'll take everyone away from me. I'm just so scared all the time."

Tears streamed freely down her face and I tried to give her a little cover. Angling myself between her and Elvis, I gave her a moment of privacy to collect herself while I talked with the small human.

"What grade are you in, Elvis?" I asked, looking at the picture he was coloring. It was a page from a book based on that dog show, where all the dogs have jobs and are very competent.

Unlike mine, who was really only good when she wanted to be.

"Fourth," he answered, pressing harder with the red crayon and making a pool of wax under... a dead stick figure he'd drawn in a dress like the one Sylvia had on. It didn't look like an actual murder plot, since she wasn't impaled on anything, but the X's where the eyes should be let me know she wasn't swimming in jelly.

Yup, that niece of mine is cleaning trash on the side of the road every weekend until I die.

"Fourth? I have a friend who wants to be a teacher, and she helps out in a fourth-grade classroom. Her name is Stella," I began, but his face lit up and answered the question I hadn't asked.

"I love Miss Stella! She taught me about different dinosaur teeth and how they change based on what they eat. Did you know that the hadrosaur, this duck-billed dino, has the most teeth of any dinosaur, but the herbivores could replace their teeth and get new ones like once a month!"

Elvis had come to life and his mother smiled for the first time since I saw her. I nodded along, pretending I knew what a hadrosaur was.

"Who's your favorite dinosaur?" I asked, replacing his Sylvia murder picture with a coloring sheet for a dinosaur. It had been lying on a neighboring table and I snagged it before a new family sat down. I tucked the murder picture in my pocket. Somehow, I was using it to remind my delinquent relative her words have consequences.

"Stegosaurus! Did you know the plates are actually scales on bony core stuff? Miss Stella brought me a book all about them, but our teacher took it. She stole it back and put it in my backpack, and now I can read it before bed."

Elise looked slightly alarmed, but I felt myself smiling. Stella had been fully grown when we met, but I felt like she learned the morally grey art of sticking it to the man from me. Now I just needed to get the teacher's name and stage an intervention that looked a lot like an abduction with the possibility of murder if she didn't change her tune. I was going to have some not-so-kind words to share with her about stealing books from children.

"Mrs. Bolton took your book? Won't Miss Stella get in trouble? Maybe we should give it back so Miss Stella doesn't get fired."

"She'll be OK," I assured Elise, filing the teacher's name away for later. "Stella is volunteering there, so she can't get fired. Also... she's not really easily intimidated, insulted, or bullied. Not the least of which because the human idiom means absolutely nothing to her and shortly after we met she got abducted and almost murdered, so... mean, tyrannical people sort of lost their power with benign threats and insults."

"I told her I had ants in my pants and needed to dance," Elvis laughed, coloring the dinosaur sheet with less aggression than he had the dogs. "She panicked and told me I needed to go to the bathroom and change before they bit me."

Elise was a little more focused on the attempted murder part. "How did that happen?"

"Well..." I tried to find a way to tell this story that wouldn't be traumatic. "There was this mean, anti-special ed teacher who became a principal that was stealing stuff and she turned him in. He joined up with this psycho lady and they were trying to get revenge... It's a little hard to explain, but they're all dead now."

She did not look any less concerned.

Crap... social interaction is so *not my forte.*

An angry specter appeared at the end of our table.

"What are you doing?" Joseph glowered down at us. "Why aren't you outside?"

"Government mandated break," I volleyed back at him and slid out of the booth. "Just talk to the president if you have a problem."

I slid on my aviators and offered Elvis a fist bump. With a finger pressed to my ear and a darting look around the area, I waved my partner forward.

"Madam president, you are clear to proceed." Winnie joined me after slobbering on Elvis, and I returned her sunglasses to her nose. Looking back at the mother and son at the table, my pulse quickened. I had the shadow of an idea... but I'd need some help.

The light was on in my apartment when I got home, and a shadow moved behind the curtains. Sitting in my Jeep looking up at the window, I was torn between calling for help and going up to handle the intruder myself.

On the surface, calling for help was the smart decision. In reality, help was a pair of babbling idiots who would probably make the situation worse. They would also likely take forever to get here, make a mess, and then refuse to leave.

I wasn't fond of dying, but I was even less fond of not getting any sleep tonight.

A curtain twitched and Levi waved down at me, Stella beside him with a third person I didn't know. None of them were holding weapons or wearing ski masks, so I decided they probably wouldn't murder me the second I got upstairs.

Stella's right, I really need to go back to therapy. Not everyone wants to murder me...

Lies. Just because you're paranoid doesn't mean people aren't out to get you.

My phone chimed, interrupting my inner turmoil.

Stella: *Please come upstairs. Bea, my friend who is a chemist, has a limited amount of time. Their pronouns are they / them and while you would be forgiven any errors, I would prefer if you just got it right to begin with.*

Stella: *There is also a man who followed us in. He says he knows you and he kissed you, but I've only met Ian and Larry, so I placed a knife in my pocket in case he is a liar and I need to stab him.*

Gotta love Stella.

I sent her back a "don't stab him, I'm on my way up" message and climbed out of the car with Winnie. It wasn't a trash day, and the library wasn't expecting any deliveries, so I left my car in the alley and pulled open the heavy fire door. It was a straight shot up the staircase into my living room.

I need a door.

Since Mrs. Margot's son, the original owner and resident of this apartment, had given everyone and their mother a key, the door could have two deadbolts.

And no one would get a key.

I would finally have privacy... and security and...

Winnie bounded up the stairs, her nails scraping the floor before someone said "oof", and something crashed to the floor with a wall shaking *thump*.

"Everyone alive?" I called out, climbing the first few steps.

"Yes," Stella called, appearing in the wall opening where I wished a door existed. "Winnie has thoroughly interrogated Levi and I do not know if she's signed off on him yet, but his face and crotch region are quite damp with her slobber."

Reaching the final few stairs, I arrived at my apartment to see Winnie on Levi's chest, her nose working in Bea's general direction.

"Hello... people," I decided, not sure how to make the acquaintance of guests already inside my home when I arrive. "What's the uh... word?"

I swallowed my discomfort. It had been a long day of playing secret service to Winnie and I hadn't been able to shake the feeling of impending doom whenever I thought of Elise and Elvis. I was hoping for quiet to sort through my thoughts and maybe write out a plan. Instead, I had an audience to entertain and eyelids to keep open.

"You... look like you need a drink," Bea stated and retrieved a bottle of wine from the canvas tote by their feet. Bea had short brown hair cut tight above their ears, a button stating they/them on the lapel of their jean jacket that hung open over a Black Sabbath tee and jeans. The jacket had hand-painted scenes on the sleeves that reminded me of Anne McCafferty's *Dragon Riders of Pern* series.

Why is everyone I meet today so much cooler than me? But really, that was every day I wasn't standing next to Daniel or Joseph.

They unscrewed the top of the wine, Stella brought coffee mugs from my kitchen and Winnie made sounds of protest on top of Levi. Before attempting to distract her from maiming my... *lover? make-out buddy?* Whatever he was, I couldn't help him before coffee.

Depositing the paper filter into the plastic receptacle, I added grounds and started filling the carafe with water from the tap.

"Should we not pour you any wine?" Bea asked, and I looked at them.

"No, I can have wine." I answered while pouring the tap water into the water reservoir.

"But... you're making coffee?" Their words sounded perfectly reasonable, but the inflection suggested that maybe I had threatened to use a skull as a coffee mug.

"Yeah?"

"So... you... nevermind." Bea blinked at me and tried to shrug it off. Once the percolator was percolating, I looked down at Winnie, Levi red faced and slobbery beneath her. While he appeared to be tolerating her tongue bath, it seemed like the correct time to intervene.

"You want dinner?" I asked her, cleaning out the dog bowl. Stella had assembled the coffee mugs on my coffee table and started pouring from the open bottle while I scooped kibble into the metal dish and crumbled a treat on top. Winnie sat drooling at the edge of the room, adhering to my rules about dogs in the microscopic kitchen that she willfully ignored in my mom's house. Drool pooled from the corners of her mouth, front paws tippy tapping, a sure sign she was finished being mentally exhausted and back in full food-a-saurus mode. "Eat."

Her loud crunching followed me the three feet into my living room where I helped Levi off the floor.

"Does that mean she likes me?" he asked while Bea stared at the coffee cups Stella was pouring wine into.

"Honestly? I'm not sure. Did she pee on you?" I checked him over, letting my eyes linger inappropriately on his backside. "Nope. So maybe."

"Why are we using coffee cups for wine?" Bea finally asked, unable to keep the confusion out of their voice.

"I don't own wine glasses. Or small cups... I have coffee mugs and metal tumblers for water. There isn't really room in my apartment or life for specialty glassware." I shrugged and flopped onto the chair beside Stella. She was sharing the couch with Bea, Levi lingering in the periphery, hoping to be invited to sit somewhere. "Just sit, dude. Everything has dog hair on it, so no space is cleaner than any other."

He smiled at Winnie and settled on the ground in front of my chair, his shoulder warming my thigh while light fingers brushed my ankle. My partner trotted over, stuck her nose in his ear and then leapt soundlessly onto the couch beside Bea.

"Can you tell me about Mrs. Bolton?" I asked Stella, my mind still focused on Elvis. I took a drink from the pink coffee mug she handed me. It said Haw-Horn Heights above a group of emo unicorns with black floppy bangs and instruments with *cut my hooves and black my rainbows* surrounded by music notes underneath.

"Later, yes. She's... a work of nightmares."

I tilted my head, and she repeated the words to herself.

"I'm not sure what I meant to say, but she's definitely not someone I want to be near me or children." She bobbed her head at the declaration, and I assumed we would get back to her. Looking at Bea, I framed a new question.

"Did Stella fill you in on the school and her... inclinations?" I asked, trying not to sound like a conspiracy theorist. It couldn't just be a coincidence that Elvis got sick after moving here. While I wasn't suggesting it resulted from anything supernatural, or even intentional, there was a fine line between thinking someone was poisoned and thinking they were poisoned by a house.

That line was the difference between watching *True Crime* and *Casper*.

"Stella took me by the apartment complex where the students live, and I collected some soil samples. She's right about the smell, but I can't place it... definitely had a headache after a few moments over there. Have you been out there yet?" I shook my head and Bea continued. "It's newer construction, maybe five years old, though Stella said you knew someone down in planning who could confirm. The buildings are already showing signs of wear and when I moved the dirt in the planters, I encountered a completely different type of soil layer. I sent a picture to my friend who is studying environmental science, and he gave me guidance on how to take a core sample to get all the layers for testing."

Bea pulled out a mason jar and showed us the color gradations. We all stared at it, sipping wine and trying to pretend it was interesting. My brain screamed, *I got a jar of dirt*, but for once I kept something inappropriate as an inside thought.

"Were there any plants growing where you collected this from?" I asked, noting that there were no insects or evidence of worm activity. In my experience, planters were filled with small crawly things that wanted to make your skin prickle.

"There wasn't. Just some scrub grass and rocks. I think toward the back I saw some trees, but they didn't look too alive. Could be autumn, could be soil toxins, we'll have to wait for the test."

"How long does testing take? Do they know what to test for?" I rapidly fired questions at Bea, but they didn't seem to mind. "Can we do anything to help before that?"

"It takes a day, maybe longer. The tests for arsenic, cadmium and lead are pretty fast, but if those come back negative, he'll need to wing it. Without the results as leverage, I'm not sure we can do anything yet... It would help if we could ask around, but the complex manager we ran into started shouting at us, chasing us off when Stella started asking questions."

"What kind of questions?"

"Stella style questions. Where she lists off statements of facts and observations, then shares their relevance and watches the people get squirmy."

I looked at Stella and she chewed on her lip, nervous about sharing a speculation without proof. Stella lived in a world of facts and testable hypotheses, but sucking in a breath, she shared quickly.

"I think that apartment complex was built on top of hazardous chemical waste, and I was trying to get him to tell me what's buried there."

Chapter Eighteen: Unnecessary Ruff-ness

S tella's words echoed around my apartment after she left.

There were two possibilities that came to mind. Either the landowner had gotten a killer deal on the piece of dirt because it had previously been used to store or dispose of hazardous waste, or they were selling the space as a dump site and then developing it. Neither sounded legal, nor easy to prove.

Pulling out my ancient laptop, I went to the county's planning website and searched the address of the apartment complex Elvis lived at. There was an application to subdivide, and a planned unit development to make the apartments. The summary definition called it a multi-family residential, and I had to swipe at the boredom fueled drool seeping from the side of my mouth.

"I don't understand planning," I said to Winnie, but she was in dog-ball form, curled up around a Gingerbread tear-apart toy my mom got her for the birthdate listed on her discharge papers. "If the place was residential, probably toxic waste wasn't allowed to be dumped there."

She burrowed deeper, tucking her nose under her tail and sniffing aggressively.

"So... if it was an illegal dumpsite, we need to know if the seller, buyer or developer knew before they built and whether the groundwater has been contaminated..." Winnie switched from sniffing her own butt to stretching all the way backward, curving her spine to nudge the cargo pants I'd left on the floor. They must have been from yesterday, speckled in melted ice cream from the dairy and dust from searching Brad's land for bombs. "Who owns it?"

The entry said it was an LLC that came up with snake eyes when I googled it. If it was a legitimate business, it didn't actually do business under that name. Checking my texts from Crystalline, it matched the owner of Leonard and Ferrah's house as well.

"Is there hazardous waste under that house, too?"

Winnie went back to licking her butt. The loud slap of her tongue sent my skin crawling, and I shut down the laptop. Replacing my coffee cup with a lidded tumbler, I refilled it and pulled my keys out. My canine partner was on her feet, tail wagging above a damp bunch of fur.

"Lets go look for ourselves," I decided, and she pranced to the hook by the stairwell, taking up her leash and leading the way downstairs. My Jeep was still in the alley, and we were on the road in a matter of seconds while I tried to remember anything about earth science. Aside from the *Water Cycle Boogie*, shifting plate tectonics cause earthquakes and Pangea, nothing had really stuck.

In biology, osmosis described water moving through semi-permeable membranes from where it was more concentrated to less concentrated. If ground water worked the same, a liquid dumped in the earth, or moisture built up by trapped heat of reactions underground, would be sucked from the damp soil into the dry soil.

It could kill the plants. Could cause physiological harm to children... why not the adults? Size? Amount of time spent outside?

My car announced our arrival at our destination while my brain whirred, and I was immediately disappointed at the sight before me.

The New Classic apartment complex didn't even have the decency to look sinister or classic. Grey buildings with black accents rose out of a hillside, groupings of four or six sharing a plaza with a staircase joining to the next for three tiers of boring. Even the plazas had large planters in the center with fake plants, the plastic leaves catching the streetlights with an unnatural color that even toxic ground water couldn't replicate.

Wrought-iron gates guarded two driveways, each blocking the vehicle's entry point with a flimsy metal code box. The metal was equal parts rust and black paint, a combination that made me suspect we could probably kick it over, but there wasn't any need. Sitting beside the vehicle gate was a pedestrian entrance held open with a bungee cord and a broken bolt laying on the ground.

It probably would have been more useful *inside* the gate, but what did I know?

"Not really a security conscious bunch," I said, parking in visitor parking and shuffling out. Winnie waited at her door and when I opened it, we attached her leash before allowing her to leap out onto the smooth asphalt. Closer inspection showed that the paint was peeling on the sides of the buildings and the sidewalk was more cracks than concrete.

But the parking lot looked brand new.

Quietly, we entered the gate and took the short incline toward the leasing office, where a single patch of grass clung to life. It was a brownish green that sagged under the moonlight, and even Winnie's bladder watering didn't make a difference. I took a long inhale and immediately regretted it.

The air smelled like natural gas, open sewage, and something sickly sweet that tethered to my uvula and hung out in my throat.

Beside it, the windowed box labeled Office had a single desk lamp on. Four different desks occupied the space, one in each corner with the chairs toward the windows. The spaces were impersonal and generally clean, telling me either no one who worked here had a personal interest or none of them had worked here long enough to personalize their space.

We crept along the walkway, taking care not to fall into any of the cracks in the walkway. In the plaza between the second and third floors, the lights flickered above a bank of mailboxes. Then the rest of the lights flickered, and all the exterior lighting blanked out into an inky blackness. The quarter moon above us struggled to illuminate the small bit of space in front of my nose, forcing me to shut my eyes and listen.

Beside me, Winnie did the same, her satellite dishes facing multiple directions to get reception on the danger channel. The sound of her panting slowed while my own lungs pulsed slightly at the air reduction and then kicked into overdrive when a pebble skidded toward us and bounced off my shoes.

From my right, another pebble skittered, and I reached into my pocket, searching for my phone or a flashlight. Instead, I found my keys, a penlight dangling from the ring that had died in 2008. Unscrewing the cap in the pitch black, I shook out the two disc batteries and reversed their order in the ambient light of the moon and the streetlights below. Unfortunately, the light didn't touch the area between the buildings. A rumbling reverberation echoed in the passageway while the scrambling rocks got farther away.

"Please work, please work," I whispered, reattaching the top. The light flickered on, briefly casting a glow into the shadows while something large darted down the stairs. Winnie looked at me and we tried to determine if we were big enough not to die by curiosity.

Metal slammed against heavy plastic, the sound echoing off the buildings with a murmured shout.

Smacking the light again, it showed the passageway was still clear, and we ran down. Emerging on the far side, we arrived at the top of a staircase in full view of the road below. The staircase descended over the opening to a parking garage, the voices below getting louder but not any more clear.

Going down slowly, we paused every few steps; the voices growing more agitated the closer we got. At the bottom, I saw a small service drive that connected this side to the far one where I parked, and I filed that away while slinking beneath the staircase toward the large cutouts in the side wall.

"We can't un-bury it and line it now. The damage is done!" A slimy sounding male shout whispered. "We lined the last bunch. How the hell was I supposed to know this would happen?"

"I told you it would happen!" Another man hissed back, his voice hinting at an accent he'd either trained himself out of or barely developed. "It's fourth grade earth science."

"You're the excavation monkey. I don't pay you to think." The first man was back to sounding infinitely more punchable. Another metallic thud bounced off the concrete walls, disconnecting the words "stabbing" and "payout". "Shut up! You don't know who's listening!"

My partner and I were nearly at the vehicle opening, sitting below a cutout beside the large pillar that supported the platform above us. A few sets of shoes shuffled away, an unknown breeze rattling the metal dumpster just beyond the cut-out in the wall. It shuddered, and another clank sounded from within.

"We should close it! Get the people help," the second man was pleading. "We have the other locations. Build there and then demo this. You know it's the right thing!"

"Those are spoken for. Do you not understand how making money works?" The first snapped just as Winnie started whimpering beside me. "What's that sound?"

I covered her snoot, but her ears remained upright. Beneath my hand, she started growling, eyes on the spot beside my head. A semi-familiar titter preceded another growl, and I whipped around to find a raccoon mere inches away from my face.

The grey and black bandit stood on its rear legs, snarling and spitting. Feet joined the noise and two men emerged from the structure, fumbling with guns at their waistbands. Underground parking lights backlit the shapes, obscuring their faces. Short and skinny were the only two characteristics I could pull before being jerked back into the moment.

Winnie lunged, knocking me over onto the sharp corner of a brick. The sound of something tearing barely audible over the snarling animals and the men shouting about what to aim at first. Eyes on the raccoon, I grabbed Winnie's leash and ran toward the service road, a cool breeze caressing my exposed backside.

Chapter Nineteen: Cat-tastrophe

B *eep, boop, boop, beep da daaa...*

Music was blaring from all directions, the penetrating darkness broken by the electronic samba I'd been buried with.

Buried?

A flashing light joined the samba, strobing into my dirt fortress and pulling me from... bed.

Winnie was half sprawled on my chest, her weight a comforting pressure that accounted for the sensation of being buried alive. My phone on the nightstand was the source of the light show and serenade, neither of which I'd asked for. Slapping the wooden table, I tried to find the offending device without disturbing the furry menace.

The phone went silent.

Snuggling back down, I yawned widely and tried to return to the dream I was having about being a coffee mermaid when... *beep, boop, boop, beep da daa...* Winnie stirred on my chest, which meant she'd want to go outside soon and sleeping time was over.

Grabbing my offensive device, I glared at the caller ID.

"I'm sleeping, Mo," I said in lieu of a greeting. "I just got home and I'm sleeping."

"Cyn, they know," she whispered, voice trembling and cutting out. "Chris has only been out of town for three days, but they know and they're coming for me."

"Who knows, Mo?" I shot up, heart racing as I stuffed my feet into shoes and grabbed my keys. I pulled the nearest pair of cargos off the floor and pulled them on amid a small cloud of dust. Winnie rolled off the bed, and I clipped her leash on. "Where are you? Did you call 9-1-1? Who's there?"

"I'm at home. What are the cops going to do?" She hissed. "No. Please, go away!"

The line went dead, and I ran down the stairs, Winnie on my heels as we hit the door full speed ahead and jumped into the Jeep with practiced ease. Turning the key, I fired up the engine and peeled out of the alley on two wheels. Winnie was in full combat mode, ears up and keeping watch through the windshield.

Mo lived outside of town, just off the main highway. Her house was completely overgrown with plants, the front door obscured in the daylight by foliage from creeping vines and dense shrubbery. Rows of trees lined both sides and while it was easy to park your car, it was nearly impossible to find the car when you were ready to leave.

We arrived in seven minutes, the lit windows offering a dim glowing beacon of our destination. Stuffing the knife I kept in the glove compartment into my cargo pants, I let Winnie lead the way while I held onto her leash and tried to keep up. Her superior nose was more useful than my pathetic human senses at night hunting, and we still didn't know what we were hunting for. Pausing at the door, I pulled my knife and listened.

Inside, something crashed to the floor and Mo cried out, "Stop it!"

It was all the confirmation we needed to breach the door without knocking.

Gripping the handle, I checked in with my partner and then burst through the door, knife drawn. The immediate entryway was clear. A small doorway led into the kitchen, but the movement was coming from the right. Winnie and I turned, rushing in, ready to fight and defend my best friend.

"Cyn!" Mo whipped around; panic written all over her face. "Thank goodness you're here!"

"Mo! What is it? Did the intruder leave?" I quickly checked her kitchen, bedroom and bathroom before finishing my loop and ending up facing her again. The house was in order, the kitchen a wreck of baking supplies, but not out of place for a visit to Mo's. The only thing that wasn't normal was clutched in her hand, thrashing around.

"Why do you have a kitten?" She looked down at the orange ball of fluff in her hands and burst into tears.

"Because my life is over! The cat distribution system has chosen me, and Chris is never coming back!"

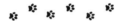

"Alright," I said, wrapping Mo's hands around the mug of tea with a splash of brandy. It had taken tremendous effort, but I'd gotten her settled and wrapped in a blanket on the couch. Tea in hand, I sat across from her and waited for her to take a sip. "Now... like a sane person, tell me what's going on."

"Chris left for an out-of-town trip and he's been gone for three days, but I had a bad feeling he wasn't going to want to come back. It made me too anxious to sleep, so I stayed up, baking. Then I heard this sound when I went to take my apple cores out to the compost. I came back inside to get a flashlight, searching the ground for an injured animal or something, and that's when I saw them." She pointed at the two kittens snuggled up against Winnie in the center of the room. The all black kitten had appeared once Mo had stopped crying, and they'd immediately taken to Winnie. Though my partner had never birthed a litter, the dog seemed surprisingly at ease having two kittens kneading at her underbelly.

The little orange male cat and all black female appeared to be the same age, but I had no idea if they were siblings. Neither looked old enough to have been weaned off their mother, but my ability to estimate the age of newborns I hadn't helped bring into this world was neither accurate nor precise. Four feline eyes blinked at me, coming to life by pouncing on Winnie and then rolling off her.

It was adorable, and I felt a tug in my chest at the sight.

"OK... so... you called me up and dragged me out of bed at 2 AM because... you think the cat distribution system has decreed you are a spinster?"

She nodded, blowing on the steam coming off the tea in her mug.

"And you think this because... Chris is out of town for... a week?" I asked, trying to remember what she'd told me about her boyfriend's trip. He was a nurse, but also one of the volunteer firefighters in the Sweet Pea Fire Department, usually serving as an EMT. They'd met when I shot off a man's hand in her kitchen and she'd needed help to get home "because of the shock".

None of that helped me remember why he was out of town.

"It's not going to be a week! It's going to be forever! He's going to fall in love with one of the bridesmaids at his cousin's wedding and move to Albuquerque forever!"

Right, he'd gone to a wedding in New Mexico that Mo couldn't attend because she owned and operated her own business. Though she'd hired help, the woman was worse at letting go and delegating than I was.

Not that I was ever invited anywhere or had a reason to go... Or had anyone to delegate to.

"Mo... did you call Chris and talk to him about your feelings?" I tried for gentle and reasonable, but I wanted to look in her kitchen and see if what she was baking contained crazy pills. Or marijuana butter, because her paranoia could not be naturally occurring.

"No! Because I don't want him to think I'm insecure," she spoke into her teacup and took a long drink. Admitting defeat, I walked into her kitchen to see apple turnovers with a perfectly brown puff-pastry crust and artfully placed sugar crystals. On the counter was a stick of normal butter and I opened her fridge to see... more normal butter. I peeked in the trashcan and saw the wrappers for more regular butter.

What does a marijuana butter wrapper even look like?

"What are you looking for?" Mo asked, walking into the kitchen wearing her blanket like a cape. She'd tucked the corners under her arms so she could continue to drink the spiked tea gripped between both her palms.

"Drugs. Do you cook with marijuana butter? Are these turnovers really edibles?"

"What? No! Why would you-"

"Because Chris loves you, Mo. He did a weird ass commitment ceremony to tell everyone you were together. He puts up with me and Winnie and our many injuries, though I'm still a little bitter he wouldn't stitch my ass. The fact he even looked was a testament to your love and not our friendship, because he and I are not friends. Also, those kittens are adorable and even if you don't want to give them a home, they are not one of the signs of the apocalypse. Why are you really freaking out?"

"Because Larry loved you for half his life and he blew it. Chris and I don't have your longevity, so if you two can't make it work, what hope do the rest of us have?"

My heart started pounding in my chest and I walked over, wrapping my friend in a side hug.

"Mo... Larry and I have always had a lot of problems to overcome. His mom getting between us is just the adult version of the same crap he pulled in elementary school, high school, and college. No matter what he says, he's always going to choose his own self-preservation over me. We had fun, and I love him, but there's only so many times a woman can let it go before it's just another form of self-harm." I rubbed my hand up and down her arm, looking at the turnovers and then down at Mo. She was nodding, absorbing my words. "I didn't know you were so affected by our breakup."

"I wasn't at first. It was those damn kittens. When I was doing Teach for America overseas, there were so many homeless animals. Everyone was starving, the people and the animals. The only meals some of them got were the ones I made them. When I saw them out there, hungry and scared, and then they wandered in, I wanted to call Larry for help, but then..."

"You can still call him, Mo. You guys are friends... maybe he and I can be friends again one day, too. But he's the only vet in town and he should look over those kittens. Also, he's allergic to cats, so making him do it will also be an act of petty vengeance on my behalf, and you know I love those."

She seemed to settle, moving gingerly across the room to blow snot from her nose. Mo had been a baker in town since I returned and I often forgot she'd had a whole life abroad while I was gone. It had been a long time since she'd mentioned anything about her time overseas, and this was the first she'd said about the challenges I'd assumed she would face.

"Can I ask you something about your time with Teach?"

I let her toss the tissue and grab another while I started cleaning her kitchen. My brain was on exhaustion overdrive, fighting back the anger I felt at having been pulled from bed for a dramatic freak out that was uncomfortably similar to the ones I'd been having recently. Mixed in with the anger was shame, regret and something a lot like love for my best friend.

Emotions are weird and suck... Closing the seal on the flour container, I put it back in her pantry with the sugars and cinnamon. There wasn't a good way to ask about her time over there, and even less awesome ways to mention that a teacher *in* America was hurting kids with her narrow-minded stupidity.

"Yeah. What do you need to know?" She moved into the kitchen and dropped her blanket on a wooden chair. Moving me out of her way, she re-wrapped the butter in a way that suggested I was doing it wrong. "You're doing that wrong."

So much for suggesting.

"Did you ever encounter... bad teachers? Ones you thought did more harm than good?" I sat in one of the kitchen chairs and steeped my tea, bouncing it in and out of the cup. Now that she had started cleaning, I would just be in the way. Instead, I watched her take everything I put away back out and return it to the cabinet in a minutely different position.

My friends are all nuts.

"Yeah, there were some people out there teaching because they just wanted to have their loans forgiven. The kids they taught didn't really benefit much until the other teachers slowly took over their care. We called it 'adopting' students from a bad teacher's class. Making sure they got food, education and whatever else we could do to help." She was wiping out a measuring cup that looked like it had water in it but smelled like ethanol, not appearing to realize she was in this room and not back over there. "I heard rumors that sometime back when the program first started out in the early nineties, there was this teacher who'd gone over there and told the kids who struggled that it was because God hated their hedonistic culture. She was the only person to get kicked out of the program where I was stationed that anyone knew of. I think she was from this area, which is why I heard about it. Like a 'we're watching you' warning."

I stared into my tea. "Do you know how they were able to finally get rid of her? Someone at the school Stella teaches at is doing that to the special ed kids..."

"Seriously?" Mo went from pensive to pissed in a split second. "Hell no. I think she got caught committing a crime. Or maybe she got set up for one, though don't hold me to that. Let me ask Drew. He's still over there and has access to the records."

She pulled out her phone and sent off a message.

"Is that what you're looking into?"

"Not exclusively. There's also a missing stripper, his missing wife, a dead guy murdered in their house and a developer whose buildings never actually get developed... except the one that might be poisoning people. Also, Mrs. Margot has a bi twin who has the hots for Leonard's wife, and even though I think there were a few group activities, the woman wasn't into it and Mrs.

Margot the Second, is pining. Also, they're both Mrs. Margot because they married fraternal Margot twins."

Mo's stood there with her mouth hanging open and I realized it had been a while since I'd been able to visit with her.

"Also, I started dating again, kind of. It's weird, because I think either he's hiding something, or I don't know how normal relationships happen. His name is Levi, hot and nerdy, which is feeling like my type. Works with Seth but since we've met, he's had dinner at my house, seen my mom in leather, woken up hungover in my apartment, learned his aunt and uncle are missing, found a huge ass blood stain in their house and had to go look at a dead body. He's kissed me and asked me out, and I don't know why. None of this is stuff that a normal person would be like 'yeah, baby, gotta date me that' and I think maybe he's..." I paused when her phone dinged, but she just kept staring at me.

"You know that Chris and I got together after he walked me home, covered in blood, because you shot off a man's hand in my kitchen. It's not like we weren't building a relationship on lust and shared trauma."

Her phone dinged again.

"You're a catch, Cyn. Hot, confident, you have cool stories and Winnie..."

"Mo, phone," I said.

"But..."

It dinged a third time.

"Lady harming kids psychologically, Mo. Phone! My confused dating life can wait."

That shook her from the stupor, and she checked the phone.

"Looks like what got her fired was refusing to allow the kids to get vaccines. They couldn't really fire her for using free speech, since I guess the constitution applies over there to people from here, but the denial of medical care was the clincher. She's quoted as... geez, she's quoted as saying disease is nature's divining rod, leading the weak home to the lord. Geez, this Bolton lady is a piece of work."

"Wait, what? The lady? What's her name?"

I took Mo's phone and read it again.

Mrs. Jessica Bolton from... Fairborn, Ohio.

"It's the same person!" I snarled, setting Mo's phone down. "How the hell did she get hired here? Do you think she faked a reference check?"

Mo's wide eyes clouded over.

"Not sure... but I have an idea. Grab that apron. We're cooking up some revenge while you tell me about Levi and all the unfinished construction projects."

Chapter Twenty: Teacher's Present

Red is dead, pink to party... Red is dead, pink to party.

I kept the chant going the entire drive from Sweet Pea to Pads Elementary School in Fairborn. On the seat beside me were two plates of turnovers. The one wrapped in pink plastic was the normal batch of apple turnovers she'd made before I arrived. Full of buttery sugar goodness, they were the perfect bribe to offer as an exchange to the front desk for entry into the school, and the dozens of bite-sized versions were perfect for distributing to verbally abused children who deserved a treat.

A weird turn of events since I used to use pastries to sneak *out* of school, but I guess everyone grows up, eventually.

Plate number two was covered in red plastic and had exactly one turnover on it.

While it wasn't actually going to kill her, it would probably make her wish that she was dead. Mo had prepared a chocolate apple turnover laced with laxatives, and while she swore it would taste every bit as good as the regular turnovers, I had my doubts.

Though I wasn't doubtful enough to try them.

Red is dead, pink to party…

The color was unimportant when the pink plate was three times the size, filled with bite sized turnovers and technically a platter, but the mantra kept my brain occupied.

Underneath the plate of pink turnovers was a file from Drew, emailed and printed in the middle of the night, of Mrs. Bolton's behavior overseas. When Mo told him she was still teaching, he'd immediately given us all the information he had from her personnel file. Then Drew contacted the main office and asked them for any publicly available data. I had two copies, one to convince the school to do the right thing, and one to provide the media if they didn't.

Or maybe even if they did.

My phone rang in the middle of my chant, and I picked up without looking.

"Hello?" I answered with the hands-free button while still monitoring the road. The grassy farmland wasn't that interesting, but deer and cows occasionally wandered into the roadway, and I was not getting in an accident with a laxative turnover. With my luck, a cute firefighter would eat it and I'd be brought up on charges of assault on a first responder.

"Hey..." Larry spoke over the line, and I flinched.

Should have checked caller ID.

"What's up?" I asked, trying to sound casual. Normally Winnie would be there to provide a performance review, but she was kitten-sitting at Mo's.

"I was going to ask if you wanted me to bring Winnie over? Mo brought in the kittens, who came with their own canine cat sitter. I checked them over under her watchful eye and I have to say she's worse than you about making her feelings known regarding the care of her babies. They aren't quite ready to live on their own yet, but without their mother, I'm not sure staying here is any better than anywhere else. We gave them formula, drew some blood, and they're doing well, but Winnie is..."

I heard a long howl in the background and swallowed hard at the lump in my throat.

"She was told to kitten sit. I'm out in Fairborn... any chance you can just let her sit with the kittens? Maybe on that dog bed in your office? I won't be back for an hour or two... Normally I'd drop everything for her, but this is important."

"Hot date?" he asked, resigned that it would happen eventually. For the first time, he sounded more passive than outraged, but it was definitely a step in the right direction.

"No. I guess if I get caught, I'll have a hot court-date, but hopefully it will be handled quietly. I'd hate to find out I no longer know any lawyers." I yawned over the line, Larry moving around his practice on the other end filling the cab of my Jeep. I heard a metal cage open and whisper instructions to someone else in the office. Footsteps replaced the sound of metallic cages, and Winnie's howl cut off mid-serenade.

"I don't know why I'm surprised that worked. You and this dog are freakishly connected... she might also have adopted those kittens, so I hope you have..."

"Caramel Coffee," I interrupted with another yawn.

"Are you ordering at a drive thru?"

"No. Those are their names. Orange is Caramel, black is Coffee. It's unclear if they'll be living with me or Mo. You going to be OK with cats in your office for a few hours, or should I ask my mom to come over and grab them? I'm not trying to kill you," I said, trying to be considerate of his allergies to cat hair. As a commercial vet, he claimed his allergy to felines wasn't an issue since he'd never have to treat them.

But here he was, treating cats because the domestic vet had moved away.

The irony of his chosen profession completely lost on him.

"Caramel and Coffee can't leave the practice for at least a few more hours while I figure out their age, check for a microchip, and run the bloodwork. I'll send Brianne in here to check on them, but they're all fine in here as long as I keep the treats in another room. I can work in the break room. It's not a big deal."

"Thanks, Larry." I turned into the school parking lot with gratitude that he was going to take care of the babies while I took care of Mrs. Trunchbull, but worse. "I just got to the school where the mean lady is abusing children. Let me know if anything happens with the kittens, please?"

"Yeah, sure. Let me know if you need me to get you a lawyer or bail you out of jail. Hey, Cyn?" he asked, and I held my breath. "I miss you."

I hung up without answering him, whispering quietly to myself, "Miss you too."

Pads Elementary School looked virtually indistinguishable from other schools in tornado country. A low, single-story red brick building expanded outward from a central entryway with chain-link fences on the outside edge to keep the community safe from the kids when they played outside. It had a surprisingly large parking lot for a school no student would ever drive to, but the sidewalk bordering it was covered in hopscotch patterns and childish art that did not include bloody caricatures.

Clutching my turnovers and the folder underneath, I stepped over a butterfly drawing and slipped on a piece of abandoned chalk. My foot slid away from me, and I felt a loud popping from my hip before I landed hard on my knee and a rip from the seat of my pants.

"Ow!" I squeaked, flopping over to the side and oscillating between grabbing my knee or my hip. Since both hands were occupied by turnovers, my only options were to suffer in silence or throw away the plan.

"Damn it, Carlie!" A woman's voice joined the burst of AC from the general direction of my feet. "Are you OK? I'm so sorry. I tell Carlie to put the damn chalk away every day and... are those turnovers?"

Relieving my hands of their plates and folder, a pair of sensible flats joined the at-home manicure floating in my line of sight. I clutched my knee, hoping the pressure would distract my synapses from the agonizing pain and stop the moisture leaking out of my eyes.

"Yes," my wheezing voice was barely audible to my own ears. "Ms. Bolton's class. Thought... treat. Elvis."

"Oh..." Her surprise spoke volumes. "Mrs. Bolton's class. Why don't I escort you there?"

Phase one of Operation Trunchbull complete... and I needed to celebrate with anti-inflammatories.

"Sure, thanks..." I pushed off the ground and made it to standing. Sharp stabbing pain radiated from my left hip, my right knee taking on a throbbing pulse of its own. "Uugh... standing..."

I took a minute to look around, eyeing a work truck on the other side of a chain-link fence amid a sea of SUVs and sedans that were old but serviceable. The parking lot behind me had two cars aside from my Jeep. Both cars sporting stick figure families and windows that hadn't been washed since a baby spat up on the surface. It was clear I was looking at the distinction between employee parking and room mom parking.

"You gonna make it?"

I turned to see a woman in green trousers and a striped short-sleeve button down. Her charcoal hair held back in a wide green headband.

"Most likely. I'd give my left boob for some naproxen, though."

"You might want to pull off your hoodie and tie it around your waist," she suggested, and I looked over my shoulder at the torn pants and rainbow undies.

"Damn." I removed the hoodie and tied it in place. Checking all the angles, my undies were no longer visible, and I gave the woman a thumbs up.

Ambling toward the door, I relieved my helper of the turnover plates. Peeling back the wrap, I offered her one of the turnover bites from the platter. After a moment of hesitation, she took one triangle and popped it into her mouth.

"This is amazing. Did you make these?"

I followed her through the door into the air conditioning. A curved counter sat beside the door with an efficient middle-aged woman manning the phone while two children occupied plastic chairs beside her. Their heads hung low toward their shoes, scraped knees and elbows lending evidence to a fight.

"No, my friend Mo made them. She owns Mary's Muffins and More out in Sweet Pea." I tried to peek into the principal's office to see if the occupant looked as terrifying as the sullen children alluded to, but there was no one behind the desk.

"I've been there. Which explains why these are so good. I don't think that woman makes a bad pastry." She was walking, talking, and eating without spitting crumbs, like a damn boss. We'd exited the administrative section into a hallway that dead ended at a large cafeteria, rolling tables being cleaned and returned to their place along the wall.

Three hallways led off, like the spokes on a wheel, with one to the right, one diagonally across and one to the left on the far side of the hot food line. Without breaking stride, the woman led us diagonally across to the spoke opposite the admin entrance. Though I hadn't taken back the folder, she wasn't looking through it yet. Her hands held the folder like it was an extension of her arm, and I suspected she forgot she was holding it.

"Third and fourth grades are down here. K through second to the right and fifth and sixth to the left. There is no separation for the special ed classes, but that doesn't seem to stop the kids from talking." She let out an annoyed breath. "Sometimes I wish we could just..."

Her frustration ended with a wordless desperation to defy human nature and get everyone to look at each other as equals. We walked past classroom doors with paper cutouts of rainforest animals, a teacher's name taped diagonally across, or photos of either the teacher or student's pets. Though the doors themselves were a shade of beige that made me want to cry, each teacher had decorated it and made it look welcoming from the outside. Children's voices drifted out, the occasional laugh or song amid the sound of pencils and computer keys clicking.

"What's your name? I'm sorry, I forgot to ask," her question, thrown over one shoulder.

"Cyn. Cyn Sharp, nice to meet you Ms...." I extended my hand as we arrived at a completely undecorated door with silence on the other side.

"Dr. Patel, I'm the school's principal," she said, turning the knob and opening the door. "Mrs. Bolton!"

A blonde woman, thin with a pinched face and spray tan, had her manicured nails impaling a child's arm. Tears streaked down the little girl's cheeks, her pink pants wet. Two desks were knocked over and a smaller boy was still trying to extricate himself from the carnage.

"Let go of that student!" Dr. Patel shouted, moving between the teacher and the small girl. Though Mrs. Bolton towered over the principal on spiked heels, she took a step back from the doctor. Not turning her back on the blonde, Dr. Patel angled herself toward the student and checked her arm. There were deep grooves in her skin and a bruise was already forming.

"That filthy little brat pissed her pants on purpose! These disgusting little..."

"Enough! Get out of this room, now!" the principal barked, and Mrs. Bolton took another step backwards. "Do not worry about your belongings. They will be joining you shortly. Wait in the hall."

Fierce protector eyes glowered at the soon to be former teacher until she was out of the room. As soon as she was on the other side of the door, Dr. Patel helped the trapped boy free himself from the wooden death trap. In a fluid motion, she had the desk back upright and was speaking quietly to the little girl, directing her to the bathroom attached to the room.

"OK, class. Your... the former... This is Ms. Sharp, today's guest lecturer. She'll be sitting with you for the morning while I attend to some... pressing principal things."

"Cyn!" Elvis popped up from his desk. He started walking toward me, caught sight of the principal watching him, and sat back down awkwardly. "Where's Winnie?"

"She's kitten-sitting. Where's Stella?"

"Ms. Lane has an exam and wasn't scheduled to arrive until this afternoon. I will see about having her arrive earlier. However, education is our top priority. Are you able to be here?" Dr. Patel asked, and I looked at the kids, eyeing me hopefully.

Damn...

"S-s-sure," I stammered, noting that at least two of them were sticky and one was oozing from the nose. "But... I'm not really"

"Perfect. Class! Ms. Sharp has brought treats! Line up to wash your hands while she hands them out!" Dr. Patel announced, and the kids moved as one to the sink in the room's corner. The doctor lowered her voice so only I could hear. "You have terrified bunny face. Clear that off before you turn around or they'll eat you alive. Show no fear, soldier."

And she strutted out of the room to address the woman in the hallway.

Glancing around the room, I noted a complete lack of color or anything remotely interesting on the walls. It was a wonder everyone didn't just take a nap from the lack of stimulation.

"I can do this..." I tried to pep talk myself as the first students returned to their desks with clean hands. Grabbing a stack of paper towels, I walked up the aisles and placed a napkin with a turnover bite on each desk. At the end, there were two bites leftover, and I breathed a sigh of relief that there was enough.

"Aren't you going to eat yours?" Elvis asked, pointing to the large one on the red plate.

"Oh, I'm not... this one isn't for eating."

"Can I have it?" Another kid asked, and I panicked.

"No! It's not for eating."

"It looks like it's food," a little boy said, inching closer. "Maybe I should try it?"

"No!"

Oh, my dog... I peeled back the red plastic and took a tiny bite of the corner. The kid's face fell slightly, and I wondered if hurting his feelings was better or worse than potentially giving him diarrhea.

"Yum! Let's grab the construction paper and bring this classroom to life!" I advised, and the kids just looked confused.

"Do you have construction paper?" I asked and thirty heads shook. "Crayons? Computer paper? Markers?"

More head shaking.

"Alright, one second," I said and poked my head out of the classroom door. Across the way was an exciting door covered in paper parrots. I creeped across the hall and knocked. A spectacled man peeked through the window beside the door and opened it a fraction of an inch. "Hi. Can I borrow construction paper? I'm... uh... subbing."

He looked between me and the open door behind me, straightening his glasses.

"Where is Mrs. Bolton?"

"She's... no longer with us. I just wanted to..." His head disappeared back inside the room and I stared at my boots, wondering if I should have sent a student. A few seconds later, the teacher reappeared with a plastic tub filled with art supplies.

"Stella stored these over here for when Jessica would take 'heathen breaks'," he whispered, eyes darting around. "Is she gone... for real?"

"The principal saw her man-handling a student." He smiled at my words and opened the door a little wider. "I have a few minutes before my kids get back from the library. Let me help you set up. I'm Mr. Martin."

"Cyn," I said, leading him back into the room and offering him a turnover bite. He accepted and started having the kids rearrange their desks from neat rows into pods, each one with a different art supply. While he worked, I used the computer at the front of the room to google diagrams on how to make animals out of construction paper, nibbling on the turnover as I searched for the different animals kids were shouting out.

"OK... what are we thinking?" Mr. Martin asked, and I looked between him and the kids.

"Should we make this place Fall-O-Ween themed chaos? Maybe pumpkins, dinos, leaves... whatever you want, as long as it's wearing a costume or a scarf?"

"Mrs. Bolton said Halloween was the devil's holiday. She wouldn't like it if we put stuff like that up in her room," one kid whispered and I smiled.

"Even better. Let's make this place look like something she would hate."

Everyone shared a nervous laugh, and Mr. Martin nodded his permission to those who looked his way. Nerves faded into genuine excitement and I felt like a queen at bringing them joy.

"OMG!"

"Awesome!"

While the kids got to work, I picked up the turnover and took another, larger bite without thinking. Sending off a text to Stella and Larry, I let them know what was going on. Larry responded with a picture of Winnie serving as a cat bed for Caramel and Coffee. Mr. Martin waved his departure and I smiled at the transformation that began in the room.

The kids laughed, joking around while I found some age-appropriate music to stream through the computer's speakers. Dinosaurs joined the fall themed cutouts, also cats, dogs, snakes, and something that I was going to call a peach and dispose of before a responsible adult showed up.

I was helping the girl in once pink shorts, but she'd changed into blue. We were trying to make the safety scissors turn purple paper into a cupcake, but they just kept folding the paper without cutting.

"These are the worst..." My stomach burbled. Immediately, my eyes went to the red wrapped plate.

Except the plate was empty, and my stomach rumbled again.

"Oh, crap."

Chapter Twenty-One: Leaving the Lookout

"I'm dying," I groaned from behind the door in the staff bathroom.

It had been about an hour since Stella arrived to take my place, right in the nick of time. I'd barely made it down the hall, cheeks clenched, before all hell broke loose. Though I'd managed to keep the mess out of my pants, there was no stopping the train that had left the station once it got moving.

And it was moving...

"You're not dying. Why did you consume so many laxatives?" Stella asked from the other side of the stall, passing me a package of wipes. This was not the first time we'd been in each other's company where I'd had poop-apocalyptic cleaning needs. "You are aware that their function is to induce gastric motility in the colon, right?"

"Yes," I groaned while my phone chimed from outside the stall. "I wasn't supposed to eat it."

Stella passed me my phone from under the door.

"Who was supposed to eat it?" she asked, somehow missing the obvious retribution on behalf of those innocent children. It would have been a sign of apathy from anyone else, but Stella wasn't the vengeance-seeking type. She knew Mrs. Duncan was trash, and Stella would do anything to protect those kids, but it would never occur to her to take out the bad guy. Her acts of rebellion skewed toward little things like hiding art supplies in a neighboring classroom.

Not weaponized turnovers and colon-bombs.

Stella had clearly not been desensitized to violence by rock music and video games.

"Ms. Trunchbull," I heaved as a long string of flatulence echoed around the tiled chamber.

"I believe that character is fictional," she said, not in the least put off by my impersonation of a trombone. "Or were you using that to avoid confessing a planned crime against Mrs. Bolton?"

"The second one."

While I fought to get my breathing under control alongside my abdominal contractions, I checked my phone. There were a few promotional emails, a couple of pictures from Larry and a missed call from Levi that he followed up with a text message requesting a phone call.

"I saw the school superintendent in the parking lot. I believe your untimely arrival and Dr. Patel's witness to Bolton's behavior were sufficient to end her employment. Why did you need to eat the laxatives?"

I filed my bathroom paperwork and exited the stall, still clutching my contracting abdomen.

"To deter the children from wanting it initially... and then I forgot it was poison and kept eating. Has she already been escorted off the property?" I asked, wondering if I could tail her to her residence and see if poisoning her was still an option.

"I'm not sure, but I don't recommend loitering in the school." She accepted the key I took from my pocket after washing my hands. "Recess is almost over; I need to get back. Thank you. For helping the children... though it doesn't resolve their potential illness, it does alleviate some of the stress and I can only hope their joy continues."

Nodding, I looked down at my shoes and took a deep breath through the pain, retying my hoodie to keep it over my backside.

"I went to the apartments last night," I told her, leading the way out of the bathroom. "I overheard some... details. I think you're right. Any estimate on the results?"

"Not that I'm aware of." She shifted awkwardly, and I nodded toward the door for her to go first. "Is that why you have a cut on your hand?"

I blinked at the scrape I hadn't noticed for hours.

"Maybe?" We were out in the hall, and I waved her toward the classrooms while I ambled back toward the main office. The lady at the desk gestured for me to hold in front of her while she completed a call. She reiterated to the caller that it was not within school policy to allow a child to come in with head lice, even wearing a swim cap, and Mindy would have to stay home.

I felt my scalp crawling while my stomach churned.

I reflexively started scratching under my ponytail and rubbing my belly.

"Dr. Patel wanted me to ask you about the folder you were carrying," she began, shouts seeping through the shut door of her office. "Did you come here intending to provide that information to the school?"

"Uh..." Something shattered on the industrial carpet, but the receptionist remained nonplussed.

Woman has nerves of steel.

"Ms. Sharp?" She didn't need to repeat her question.

"Yes. I met Elvis yesterday and what he'd said about her... I happened on the information and if it turned out he was right, I thought I might need something more to sell the case." The doorknob jiggled, and I felt my pulse jump in my throat. "I didn't want to get her in trouble, but I also wasn't willing to do nothing if kids were being harmed."

I trembled slightly, still scratching my scalp and the soft blonde fuzz on my arms.

"You scare easy," she remarked. "Weren't you in the military?"

"Yes. But explosions and armed snipers are far less dangerous than children and deranged, entitled white ladies," I whispered, inching closer to the door when the principal's office handle shivered again. "If she doesn't want the folder, shred it, but I need to..." I gestured out to the lot.

With a slight nod, she dismissed me, and I bolted into the parking lot. My aching guts were relieved when I could sit down on the sun-faded cloth seats. Plugging my phone into the charger, I turned on the car and took a deep breath.

The phone rang almost immediately.

"Hello?"

"Cyn! It's Levi," his voice filled the car, and I confirmed his identity on the phone screen. "What are you doing right now?"

"I uh... Why?"

The school's front doors flew open, and Jessica stormed out, toothpick heels eating up the pavement. Two geriatric security guards wobbled behind her, carrying banker's boxes filled with what little memorabilia the woman had accumulated in her time at the school. Checking my folder, I saw she'd been there for ten years.

Two banker's boxes for ten years?

Most teachers I knew needed a cargo container and ten highly trained professionals to move after one year. It was another indicator she didn't care about her students or her job.

Passing through the chain-link gate, she walked purposefully to the work truck. Pulling the boxes from each guard, she tossed them into the back. The men barely had the chance to stand clear before she gunned the engine, rattling the metal rails over the truck. The truck lurched forward, pulling up to the vehicle gate and waiting for it to rattle open with a testy rap against the steering wheel. With a view of the side, I saw an abstract diamond pattern in blue with hooked lines dipping into the white vehicle's body paint.

"Cyn?" Levi's voice brought me back to our active call.

"Yeah, what?"

"I was asking you what you're doing right now?" His voice was far away, and I blinked at my phone. Our thread was still open, and he'd been insistent on getting me on the phone for a date there as well.

It felt wrong.

"Not sure. I'll talk to you later."

I hung up before he could offer a followup question about how I didn't know what I was doing if I was doing it. His behavior wasn't sitting well, but I couldn't figure out why.

My stomach started rumbling, and I breathed through the next abdominal contraction while my phone spasmed on the dashboard. I reached for the device, intending to send Levi to voicemail. Pushing the display button on my Jeep, I saw a new text message from Crystalline instead of another clumsy dinner invitation.

CR: *He's here...*

It took five minutes to get to the county planning office.

Sitting in the parking lot were at least two dozen vehicles. Work trucks, pickup trucks and a cement encrusted vehicle that may have slept with the fishes. I cruised the lot, eyeing the logos, plates and various states of uncleanliness. Though I'd been here at opening yesterday, I hadn't thought it ever got busier.

Clearly, I was wrong.

Pulling on a plain hat, I walked in through the main doors and toward the planning office. Around the first corner, I came up short at the stationary mob before me.

It was like every nightmare of the zombie apocalypse I'd ever had.

There was a line to enter the office space, extending all the way to Sharon's counter. Everyone in suits, dress shoes, or jeans and work boots combo. All of them were shifting uncomfortably, checking phones, watches and waistbands, anything to keep their circulation moving in a bureaucratic freeze-frame. None of them matched the imperious developer I'd seen on the internet, but it was unlikely my contact would have seen him if he was still in line. Just past the doorway were the groupings of chairs, half of them occupied, but I couldn't see the occupants facing away.

Approaching the front of the line was a women's bathroom, and I shuffled my way over. Quickly popping in and then deciding to actually use it, I exited while on my phone and pretended not to see the line as I wandered into the planning office and took a seat in one of the blue chairs facing the doorway on the far side of the room.

Among the occupants in my quad set of chairs was Jay Gitt. *Dumb luck*.

He was using his phone on speaker, shouting to someone about a delivery and meeting the window.

"You'll arrive at ten or you'll lose the space. Do you understand?"

"Then I'll be refunded and let everyone know what you've got going-"

"Don't threaten me, Charlie. Ely's in the morgue. You could join him," Jay snapped into the phone and hung up. I was still working the phone in my hand, pretending to be deeply engrossed in my home screen while eyeing everyone else in the lobby.

Either no one heard this man threaten someone with a trip to the morgue, or no one believed it was more than a threat. The nearest person was about twice my distance away, a person speaking into a headset behind the counter opposite the one I'd met Crystalline at. I compared his voice to the two I heard last night, but it was impossible to tell without the echo and threat of raccoon dismemberment and infection.

The neighboring pods were all engrossed in their own aggravated phone conversations, both the customers and those forced to talk to them. No one looked happy, or mentally stable, and I wondered if everyone who worked here needed a Valium.

Or some edibles.

"What did you say?" Jay asked, startling me into looking away from my phone. My gaze darted to the side, worried some of my thoughts had slipped out as words. But he was back on his phone. "How did that happen?"

"Jay?" Crystalline called out, summoning my pod mate to the counter. In her hand was a semi-transparent roll of paper with blue lines slicing the surface. It was larger than a computer printout, about the width of brown package wrapping paper, held together with a single paperclip on the top and the bottom.

"We'll deal with this later." Disconnecting the call, Jay's huge snakeskin shoes slithered over, somehow menacing *and* absurd.

"What's all this about, Crystalline?" He took on a different tone than the one he'd used on the phone. Instead of loud antagonism, he adopted counterfeit professionalism that made my teeth tingle. Chancing a look at the counter, Crystalline looked bored and unaffected by either side of the man's vocal coin.

"You didn't sign the mylar you brought over last week." She held back a yawn and unrolled the paper. Pointing to a lower corner, she tapped the paper against the counter.

His lip went up in a grotesque sneer.

"That's not my subdivision, girl. Can't you read Jamie Galliger?"

She blinked, looking from him to the paper and back.

"Huh... guess I made a mistake. You have quite similar names. Have a nice day then." She shrugged it off and started to move back into the bowels of the department. Her gaze caught mine, and she gave me a saucy wink before vanishing into the maze of cubes. Jay stood at the unmanned counter clenching and unclenching his fists while his molars worked overtime beneath the wrinkled skin of his jaw. Pounding his fist on the counter, the developer took a step back and rubbed his own hand.

"Dumb bitch," he murmured, cursing under his breath as he moved toward the door. I followed behind him, pulling my hat low and trying to look casual in my khakis and T-shirt smeared with dried glitter glue. Sharon eyed me from behind her fortress and I instinctively pressed a finger to my lips like some secret agent.

She rolled her eyes and waved me off without interrupting the woman in front of her, demanding to speak to the manager.

New life goal, I want to be her when I grow up.

I waited until Jay exited the building and gave him a ten second lead before walking out into the sun, grateful for my decision to hide my face with a hat. It took my eyes a moment to adjust, and my body slammed full force into an object paused on the sidewalk. I stumbled back, managing not to fall, and met the annoyed eyes of Jay Gitt.

"Watch it, Big Foot!" He snapped, finishing his call and sticking his phone back into the pocket of his windbreaker. Putting on sunglasses, he strode toward the parking lot and meandered the opposite direction of where I'd parked my Jeep.

"Hey! Are you... Do you know about building stuff?" I bluffed the question. "I want to build an accessory thing on my house."

He came up short, eyeing me up and down the same way Winnie assesses a new sucker who might give her treats. With great effort, I tried to adopt the face and body language of a sucker.

"You mean an ADU?" His contempt stained the words. If he had children, they were probably scared to speak with him and counting down the seconds until he died.

Or maybe the second part was just me projecting.

"Sure? I don't know what... Is that what an accessory thing is?" I tried to look like someone who'd never heard of accessory dwelling units and was also a sucker.

Which wasn't too hard, because before yesterday I hadn't.

But my acting skills wouldn't be winning me any awards.

"I don't usually work with small-time, but what kind of residence are you looking to add to? Is there already a structure there? A foundation?"

His ingratiating smile was at odds with the calculating look in his eyes.

"A uhh?" Cocking my head to the side, I tried to come up with an answer while his look transformed to condescension. I was letting down all of womankind by letting this man believe he had stymied me with basic questions. None of it sat well, and I went for broke.

"Leonard and Ferrah referred me to you. Said you were the one who got their accessory deal up and running. When I heard you get called up inside, it seemed like kismet. Do you have a card or something?"

I watched his face flash through emotions like a toddler swiping through emojis. When he stopped, the dice had landed on anger.

"You're that psychopath from Sweet Pea! The demolitions expert with the dog!" He advanced on me, but came up short when he realized he was, in fact, *short*. Craning his neck up ruined the tough guy routine, so he backed up and crossed his arms. "I read about you blowing that idiot's house sky-high, though he was supposed to go with it. You know if they're selling it?"

"I wouldn't call us experts... but we do OK. Psychopath is a little strong." I shifted from foot to foot, a reminder that nonchalance wasn't in my repertoire. I pretended not to notice his disappointment that the man was still alive. "I'm guessing you aren't talking about Roger's trailer since he *did* die... just not from the explosion. Brad's trailer is still standing... just in police custody. Why are you so interested in it?"

"Property out that way is worth a lot, girlie. A nut job blowing himself sky high is just the right catastrophe to get it available for cheap. Does he have any next of kin?"

"No idea. He's in jail if you want to go ask him," I shrugged, watching disappointment war with annoyance that set my teeth on edge. His guilt in this wasn't subtle.

And neither was I.

"So, did you kill Leonard and Ferrah along with Ely and trying to take out the nut job? Or did you outsource some of them? Seems like a lot of effort to go through to build some cheap ass apartments that poison people."

His anger erupted with the enthusiasm of a baking soda volcano. Foaming at the mouth, he sputtered out curses that failed to become words.

Once again, he tried to get in my face.

And once again, he couldn't reach.

"Come on, little man, I don't have all day to wait for an answer," I taunted him, but he didn't take the bait. Stomping in his boots, he stormed through the parking lot, but didn't go very far. He climbed into an all-white work truck, illegally parked diagonally across two accessible spaces. Cranking over the engine, he floored it out of the lot, flipping me the bird as he went.

"That wasn't really a no, but your line of questioning lacked finesse," Crystalline graded my interrogation skills from my left side and slightly to the rear.

At the corner, Jay took a right turn on two wheels and I studied the blue logo on his truck, complimenting the red paint splattered on the tailgate. He was already back on his phone, shouting at someone whose voice carried slightly from the cab of the truck, but not enough to make out any words.

"Could you remind me what the complaints were that you received on his projects yesterday?" I asked, thinking about the giant hole and the storage unit. None of it looked noisy, but if he was murdering people...

"Failure to comply with site noise requirements and construction after hours. I assured them no work had been approved to begin, so there was no construction happening." She studiously took in my body language. "Have you been out there?"

"Yeah... There're deep holes in the ground at two of the project sites you gave me. What's the penalty for doing work that hasn't been approved yet?" I didn't mention the man with the gun or the one in the suit, but I wasn't sure why. She seemed trustworthy, but I didn't want her out there alone with armed security and no Winnie to back her up. There was also the chance more visitors could contaminate the scene, and I didn't want to lose any evidence that might be lying around.

At least not until I knew what it was the scene of.

"Code compliance goes out. If they're in violation, they have to pay a fine. There isn't much threat to someone who has more money than time."

Nodding, I scanned the lot for any other familiar vehicles.

"Do you think he'll ever talk to me again?"

I checked a message from Levi.

LL: *9-1-1, meet us at Gertie's.*

LL: *Hurry!*

"Not unless you are very skilled at make-up... or invisibility."

I nodded and sent Levi the OMW message.

"That always happens when I accuse someone of murder."

***

There were no cars parked in front of the Margot / Hollbrook residence.

I wasn't sure if it was a good thing or a bad thing, but it sent my hackles on edge. Normally, I would consult Winnie's superior canine senses, but she was kitten sitting. Without her, I had no one to bounce ideas off... or teeth to bite the bad guys.

The only instinct I had to rely on was my own, and that had proven useless.

Case in point, I ate a laxative filled turnover to avoid telling children they couldn't eat it.

Levi's vehicle wasn't parked at the curb, nor in the driveway. Mrs. Margot's martini glass looked dry and forlorn where it perched in the center of the lawn. Crime scene tape was still in place across the front door, the residual fingerprint powder still coating a small section of the un-covered front porch. Each side of the door had a planter filled with leafy green shrubs I don't remember seeing before, but must have been there.

Across the street, Gertie's neighbors had taken refuge indoors. Though I thought the sixty-degree weather was delightful, I got the impression seniors found it uncomfortable. Heavy drapes covered most of the neighboring windows, drawn tightly shut against a sunny day with no nude performances.

"Cyn?"

I jumped and flung a fist toward the male voice. Levi fumbled back, avoiding my fist but landing flat on his ass in the grass. His face held surprise, confusion, and a few more lines than I remember seeing the other day.

We stared at each other in silence until he broke it.

"Is it... instinct for you to punch first and ask questions later?"

Instead of answering, I offered him a hand up. Taking it, he dragged my arm forward, catching me off guard and off balance, so that I landed on top of him on the lawn. Long arms snaked around my waist, and he pulled me in for a quick kiss that curled my toes and sent butterflies dancing in my belly.

"Hi," he whispered. Genuine affection sparkled in his eyes. It felt like he was moving fast, a little too attached a little too quickly, but I didn't have a gauge of what was normal. All I knew how to do was hook-ups and relationships with... well, Ian and Larry.

Maybe this is normal?

"Hey..." I rolled off him, uncomfortable with the squishy feelings floating around. Rocking back and rolling up to standing, I offered him my hand again.

"You OK?" He asked, standing up without my assistance. Then he took my hand and laced our fingers together, swinging it slightly like an excited kid.

He's adorable.

You're going to ruin his life.

"Yup. Just... stomach problems." On cue, my abdomen rumbled and supported my claim. It wasn't the source of my current discomfort, but it wasn't a lie, either. "I ate a lot of laxatives."

"Why?" he asked, leading me down the driveway toward Gerti's ADU in the rear. The long driveway seemed longer when I wasn't muddy or rushing to stop the shouting that carried down the block.

"Karma."

It was most certainly not a cat purring in my lap at the moment. Whether or not she deserved it, and she definitely did, the whole law of two-fold return was no joke. If you were going to cause harm to defend harm, then all you'd get back is righteous pain and suffering.

I had a completely empty colon and stomach cramps to prove it.

Behind the house, I saw Levi's SUV parked in front of Gertie's mini house. I stopped and really looked at it. There was no lawn behind the house, just a desolate dirt field with scraggly weeds and tree bark. Gertie's front door was book ended by empty planters, wood chips sitting beneath planter boxes of fake flowers. Despite the beautiful front yard, the rear of the house was a messy desert.

Levi paused and followed my line of sight.

"Yeah, the yard took a hit after the ADU was put in. At least that's what Aunt Ferrah said." He shrugged, but there was something else behind it. I tried to scent the air, but all I got was a whiff of a clean male that went straight to my lady parts.

"I thought you said there was an emergency... why aren't you more hurried?" I asked, looking down at our joined hands.

"Before we go in, I need to prepare you for..."

No noise was coming from inside the house. Before there was music or shouting, and the omnipresent hum of the dryer. A face appeared in the window and then quickly vanished again with a sweep of olive and orange floral curtains.

"Who else is here?" I asked, taking my hand back from Levi and checking my pockets for potential weapons. One thigh only had cheese crackers and the other contained cookies and dog treats. I turned back to Levi, who was shuffling uncomfortably, gesturing for me to go inside... with the blade of a knife.

Chapter Twenty-Two: Nabbed and Stabbed

"I'm really sorry, Cyn. But you need to go inside," he sighed, his limp wrist no real threat with or without the blade. His pinched expression showed genuine regret, though I wasn't inclined to care about his feelings.

Karma better give him a zit the size of Pluto on his ass.

Puffing out a breath, I stomped into Gertie's home and slammed the door on Levi's face.

Locking it shut.

"Cyn!" He banged against the door, but I left it bolted and squared off against the people inside, prepared for an armed assassin or a firing squad of ink-filled octopi.

Or a single, very attractive and unarmed person, because that's what was standing there.

The pictures hadn't really done Leonard justice.

His squared jaw and Mediterranean complexion beneath an artfully messy head of shaggy salt and pepper black hair gave Hallmark movie lead vibes. All around us, the small home showed signs of disturbance, a shattered vase and overturned end table. The man, on the other hand, wore clothing that was rumpled and stained in patches at the underarms and side pockets. Unlike the room, there wasn't much out of place about his appearance. There was no bruising, cuts, or urine streaming down his leg.

Just an average man who needed to do laundry.

Except his eyes.

They held none of the warmth I'd seen in pictures. In its place was fear and something darker, a contained violence that coiled beneath the surface, searching for an outlet. As he wasn't sporting any injuries and I was still potentially at risk of pooping my pants, that outlet would not be me.

"Why did you shut the door on Levi?" He asked and I raised an eyebrow.

"Why did you tell him to direct me inside with a knife?"

"I didn't tell him to threaten you with a knife... damn kids and their improvisation..." he trailed off, muttering something about millennials and everyone being a director.

Leonard's head dropped to his chest, shoulders wilting forward when his spine lost some of its steel. It was like watching a balloon slowly deflate, depressing but not unexpected. A racking sob shook his body before he rallied and faced off with me once more. His arm rose, holding a black semi-auto pistol pointed in my general direction.

I'd be scared if there was even a chance he could hit me, but right now, he'd take out a lamp two feet to my left.

Between Leonard and Levi, I was in the middle of a tragic comedy where the loser was whoever I disarmed first by breaking their wrist... then their nose.

And maybe their testicles, if it was possible to break those.

Maybe they popped?

"Open the door, poppet."

"What the hell is a poppet?"

"Now, love. Open the door," I went from poppet to love, but his aim was getting farther and farther away from my person.

"No," I crossed my arms over my chest and stared him down. Even if he had been fully upright, his head wouldn't have reached my chin. Normally, being tall wasn't something I held over people's heads, but in this instance, he deserved to feel small. "If you want to let him in, do it yourself. You have hands."

"I have a gun?" His voice went up at the end, like he was asking me for confirmation. "Listen to me."

"I don't care. You don't look like you could hit the broad side of a barn. Put it down before I break your face and tell me what stupid thing you did that needs fixing."

"Who said I..." The front door opened, and Levi walked in, his spare key still in the deadbolt. Both his hands were raised in surrender, an invitation to confirm he was unarmed.

Laying on the porch behind him was the knife he'd pointed at me, his cell phone and maybe his wallet. From this angle, the blade looked more matte than shiny, and I wondered whether it was even real.

Why he needed to leave his wallet on the porch was a mystery. I'd never once taken anyone's lunch money.

''I told you this was a bad idea," Levi said to Leonard. The older man sighed and tossed the gun across the room. It bounced off the couch cushion and clattered to the floor, butt first, slamming the hammer into the rear of the gun.

My whole body tensed, waiting for the gun to discharge while my airway closed.

A second passed, then another, the firearm resting on its side.

"Don't throw guns, you idiot! It could have gone off!" I shouted, still staring at the gun in fear that a round would pop out and impale me. The physics said it was impossible, but the rumble in my gut said anything was possible if you were dumb.

"It's not real," Leonard responded, sliding his fingertips up his cheeks to rub at his eyes. The callouses on his palms scraped along the stubble at his jaw while working his eyeballs in their sockets. "None of this is real. It can't be."

Levi slung his arm around the older man's shoulder and angled him toward the muscular chest I'd ogled minutes ago. Their easy affection felt foreign to me, like the far side of the moon. I knew families showed care toward one another, but I'd never seen it.

My family skewed more toward the aggressive compliment, deconstructive criticism you shouldn't take personally and fierce allusions to violence against those who crossed us.

We didn't hug unless someone died... or we thought they were going to.

"Why do you look more likely to run away watching two people hugging than you did when you had a gun pointed at you?" Leonard asked, righting himself and studying me with the same diligence I'd devoted to looking anywhere but at the pair before me.

"Why are you attempting to analyze my psyche instead of telling me why you pointed a fake gun at me?" I deflected like a semi-pro. "Let's start with an easy question: where are Gertie and Ferrah?"

My brother's coworker led the older man to one of the white couches and helped him sit. In a matter of moments, he'd aged two decades. Prominent creases bracketed his down-turned mouth, but I couldn't tell if he was being genuine or acting.

One downside of knowing the man was a stripper—he'd definitely have acting skills.

Levi, on the other hand, looked authentically distressed, but I hardly knew him any better.

Flopping into the armchair opposite the couch, I steepled my fingers and attempted to look formidable. Dry grass stuck to my forearms, and my left elbow was sporting a smear of mud where it perched on the armrest, ruining the illusion that I was anything but an amateur with good intuition and a dog.

"They took Gertie, to lure Ferrah and I out of hiding. I wasn't willing to risk coming out, and Gertie is a tough old lady, but Ferrah... she wouldn't let anyone pay for what she did. She snuck out while I was asleep to meet up with them and trade herself for Gertie. But instead of letting her go, now they're holding both of them until I give them what they want." He heaved out a sigh that reminded me of the ocean tide.

"Who are they? You and the Margots suck at storytelling with this aversion to proper nouns," I criticized while tapping my index fingers together in thought.

"I don't know who they are," Leonard lied through his perfect teeth. Not only did he know, but he'd just confirmed he had zero acting skills. It was aggravating and reassuring at the same time.

"Hmm?" I prompted, leaning forward so that the coffee table was the only barrier between our noses. "Try again, Leonard."

"They said they'd kill me!" His eyes darted around, like speaking on its own would somehow summon the monsters from under the bed to off him.

"Fine. Tell me or *I'll* kill you," I lied. Killing people wasn't really my thing, but I was banking on the fact he didn't know that.

"No, you won't," he called my bluff, eyes popping out of their sockets in alarm. Despite having deduced the truth, he was still scared of me. Scared people were more likely to lie. It was one reason torturing captives rarely worked in situations when information was more valuable than power.

"No, I won't. But tell me anyway. Is it Jay Gitt?"

His fingers trembled. Another dead giveaway.

"But not just him. Who else is involved?"

Leonard's upper lip joined the quivering in his fingers. Levi was staring at his uncle, face unreadable beneath drawn eyebrows.

"Levi?" I switched to the younger man. Despite the clear misery written in his expression, there was a subtle fear beneath the surface. "You know too, don't you?"

"I... have some suspicions," he scratched the back of his head, arm forming a triangle that framed Gertie's empty kitchen and took me back to yesterday morning in my apartment. My brain started screaming that he hadn't belonged there. It was all a set-up.

But was it?

"I don't have all day. Did you know that email was fake? That we'd find blood in your uncle's house?" I demanded, and he shook his head.

"No! I... I really thought they were fine until you showed me the email weirdness. Then I was convinced they might be dead until he turned up this morning. I... the date... Originally, I was trying to ask you out, but then I needed you to come over and help and then he said we should threaten you and I don't know why it seemed like a good idea but it did and then I saw you and I just wanted to kiss you but you tried to run and I thought you were going to send my uncle to prison..."

"Why would I send your uncle to prison?" I interrupted, his rambling a little too endearing for my comfort. When neither of them answered, I upped the ante. "One of you start talking or I'm calling Carla to report an attempted abduction."

"I killed that man whose blood was in the kitchen," Leonard cried out and I jolted backward. "It wasn't supposed to happen. Ely showed up, saying he needed to talk to me about a project I'd submitted a proposal for. Your brother's company was doing the proposal for the build-out of the design and they needed numbers to figure out the cost. But he came in shouting, threatening me into keeping the secrets I'd seen while working at Pickles."

"Pickles? You mean Eggplants? What does the strip club have to do with any of this?"

"I saw them trying to make deals with the contractor on the property when renovations started, but the new owner came out and shut it down hard. Dhalia wasn't interested in old arrangements, but the next day she ripped out the parking lot and the club was shut down Monday through Thursday a few weeks ago." Leonard paused. His pink tongue poking out to swipe at his upper lip reminded me of a snake, tasting the air to see if it was safe. I knew he was lying. Jake had told me the club was closed just this past week, but I wanted to see where his story veered back into the truth. "I went into the club after hours, parking a few blocks away, because... well, that's not important. There was a plastic lining in the ground, and they were unloading stuff from the hole. I thought it was a police operation, there was an unmarked vehicle there, but when I saw Ely..."

"OK, so he came to your house to shake you down. You got scared and stabbed him. Why didn't you call the police instead of dumping the body?" My head was in my palms, rubbing my temples. I wanted to be like Will Trent and walk myself through the crime into a voice recorder, or Harry Bosch always taking notes, but I was a bit too accustomed to flying by the seat of my pants to get organized now.

"I did call the police!"

My hands fell back to my knees, and I gaped at him. Levi looked as confused as his uncle, but for two entirely different reasons.

"This detective came, told me to clear out so the techs could work when they arrived and took the knife. Ferrah and I packed up our stuff and ran. We never heard from him, so we thought... well, I assumed I would be arrested at some point. Tried for manslaughter or something where I'd need to claim self-defense." His hands trembled as he wrang them in the V of his legs. One foot bounced up and down while his line of sight wandered around the room.

He'd just lied to me again, since he took off long before Ferrah did and the blood wasn't that old.

"Was it self-defense?" I asked, and he swallowed hard without facing me.

"He threatened my wife, my business..."

"But was it self-defense?" Needing to ask again was a pretty obvious answer on its own, but I needed him to say it. Admit to what he'd done before we moved forward so I could see if he could tell the truth. Levi scooted away from his uncle, forcing the older man to support himself, his eyes showing the same revelations about Leonard's story.

The older man didn't notice, he just kept going.

"He really would have killed us, I knew it. We'd seen too much between the club and digging the holes that were too deep for foundation. I would be implicated, sentenced. I needed to get out from under him and then the detective could find out how terrible he was, but the detective didn't call..."

Leonard shook with dry sobs, arms wrapped around his torso. Rocking back and forth, he reminded me of Erich when he was overstimulated. Just trying to self-soothe and hold himself together.

"So, where did you dump the body?" I asked, looking at Levi. He shook his head, not buying this routine but trying to prompt his uncle into answering with a reassuring back pat.

"I never moved the body, I swear! It was laying in my kitchen when I ran!"

My lie-dar was all over the place and I couldn't seem to get a direct answer. Frustrated with the hysterics, I pulled out my phone and called Carla.

"Hey, I was just going to call you," she said in lieu of an answer.

"Me first. Where was Ely Mollusk, the dead guy whose blood was in the Hollbrook house, found?"

In the background, I heard the chatter of a police radio and the barking laugh of Barney. I could picture her fingers tapping the keyboard keys while the cell phone was cradled between her shoulder and ear. Since the Village of Sweet Pea Police Department was separate from the County, I wasn't sure how much access she'd have, but I kept my fingers crossed she could see enough.

"Why does it sound like someone is sobbing?" She asked, and I looked at Leonard. His cheeks were slightly damp with the tears

I'd missed seeing him shed, but how and when was a mystery. My brain weighed the pros and cons of telling her the truth, knowing that if I said Ferrah and Gertie were missing, she'd launch into full cop mode. I wasn't sure if Leonard's cop was really a cop or just a hired actor.

I wasn't sure if I could trust the man in front of me when he said they were gone.

And I really needed some more damn coffee.

"Radio," I lied, while she sipped something on the other end.

"Got it. Looks like Ely was found... near a college frat house. The body was discovered during a party, police responded to a noise complaint and... someone tripped over it running away," she concluded, but I could hear the underlying implication. The body had been dumped where it would be found, and it needed to be somewhere that wouldn't tie back to this house.

"Interesting, thanks. Why were you going to call me?"

The silence stretched for a moment. I could hear more keys tapping while she took another drink.

"Carla?"

"Hmm?"

"Why were you going to call me?"

"Oh, the explosives! Brad finally sobered up and said he found them. Someone had left them at the edge of his property, like a gift. I had an old friend from the feds do an analysis, and the C4 matches the composition commonly used by construction companies. I searched for the number on the side of the wrapper and the C4 was purchased by a Jayam, LLC for..." She consulted her notes. "A construction project here in town out by the school."

"What are they building?" I asked and waited as she worked on the computer keyboard.

"A car dealership, applicant was Jay Gitt. Also, full disclosure—it sounds like the judge is going to grant Brad bail soon, so if you have more questions, I'd recommend coming in sooner rather than later."

"Great... just great," I muttered, hanging up on my sister-in-law. I stared between the two men on the couch in front of me and decided I didn't need to be in this house with either one of them anymore.

"I'm gonna go. Text me if you learn when the meetup is to exchange... what were they demanding in exchange for Ferrah and Gertie?" I stood up and felt my vertebrae pop one at a time. Leonard shifted in his seat and Levi looked down at his shoes. "What?"

"They want you."

Chapter Twenty-Three: Human Sitting

M y jeep felt crowded.

Leonard and Levi seemed to be hogging all the air with words unspoken. They needed me, not to help them, but to trade for two other women. I still don't know if Leonard was secretly a serial killer, or Levi was only trying to get me on a date so his uncle could take me hostage. But when I tried to leave the accessory unit without them, they begged me not to.

Neither of them would say why, but I'd seen enough crying today, and I didn't have any solutions for their current predicament. The only things I knew for certain would help were to head back into Sweet Pea, get Winnie, drink coffee and maybe eat some cheese.

Coffee, cheese and Winnie were the hat trick I needed to put together my thoughts and maybe a plan that didn't turn me into the sacrificial lamb. In a showdown between an entitled developer, mysterious associated parties, and me with the two men in my backseat, my money wasn't on us.

Those two were soft.

"Where are we going?" Levi asked from the passenger seat. Since we'd been driving for twenty minutes and neither of them had bothered asking before we got in the car, it felt like a *day late and a dollar short* situation. Which, much like everything else they'd told me today, was not surprising.

"Shouldn't you have asked that before you begged to come with me? Or tried to take me hostage to trade for other women?" I countered, once again tightening my two-handed grip on the steering wheel. He'd tried to take my hand twice when it was just resting on the center console, and now I had to keep them out of his reach.

"I trust you. And I trusted you to know what to do to get everyone out safely," he said, shrugging a stiff shoulder. "The knife wasn't real."

"The feeling isn't mutual. And you know what's better than assuming I'd help everyone and solve the problem your uncle created by becoming a construction working stripper with a snooping problem? Asking, you dumbass!"

His lips flattened with a single nod, an acknowledgement of the tension he'd created by pointing a knife at me and being over-eager to jump into my dating pool. If it hadn't been for the morning in my apartment, I'd have handed him his ass and told them both to solve this themselves. But Seth knew and trusted him. Mrs. Margot the second, deserved to be rescued, and unlike her husband, Ferrah came across as a worthwhile human to save.

Basically, the only one that really belonged on my hit list was Leonard.

"We're going to get Winnie."

I answered his original question, the squishy feelings of affection still simmering in my belly. I didn't know if he'd really been interested in me, but I had definitely been into him, and that was unacceptable.

"Cyn, I... We-" Levi stammered, interrupted when Leonard poked his head between our seats and sniffled.

"Who's Winnie?"

Levi switched to staring out the window, lost in thought, and didn't answer. I glided the Jeep into the dirt lot in front of Kirby's Critter Care. His practice had been named by Amber and I'd learned during our tenure as lovers that she'd wanted to start all three words with the letter K, but he'd somehow convinced her not to do that.

Amber had apparently never heard of the concepts of less is more with body spray or racism and inappropriate acronyms.

"You'll find out soon enough," I answered, and considered his face briefly. Brianne appeared in the doorway and held up a finger at me to wait. I'd texted her when I left that I was on my way, and she promised to bring me my bestie with no awkward encounters.

Opening my door, I climbed out and circled to the back passenger side door. Lifting slightly, I popped the janky handle and looked in at Leonard. He was wearing the lap belt in the center, legs spread to have one in each foot well. If he'd been the same size as Levi, it might have made sense. But at five and a half feet, he didn't need both.

He barely needed one.

"Pick a side, dude," I demanded, and he raised a brow at me. "I'm serious. Slide over or..."

The stampede of thundering paws kicked up a cloud of dust. Her jingling collar tags performing the theme song to the man's imminent demise. I stood back and let nature take its course.

"Ah!" He shouted, fumbling with the belt as my dog took a flying leap into the car. She landed squarely in his lap where her nose immediately shoved into his junk, furiously inhaling his scent. Behind her, Brianne approached with the carrier containing Caramel and Coffee.

"I thought they couldn't leave yet?" I asked, and she shook her head. I took the carrier and placed it on the floorboard behind Levi. Winnie abandoned Leonard's junk to check on her kittens.

"Their blood work and other tests came back clear, and the office was giving them kitten anxiety. You have to bottle feed them this formula." She slung a canvas tote off her shoulder and passed it to me. "There are also some toys, collars, treats, litter, litter box and the number to a vet who isn't allergic to cats, but we both know Dr. Kirby would treat them in a second if you asked. Are they going with you or back to Mo's?"

I shrugged as I hefted the bag around the rear and put it into the shoebox-sized cargo area.

"I don't have a plan, but for now I think they're bunking with Winnie."

She glanced into the Jeep and motioned me down to her microscopic five-foot height. Once I was closer to the ground, my back threatening to spasm, she whispered into my ear.

"Who are those guys?"

I studied the front of her scrubs while I tried to think of an answer. At this point, they were equal parts suspects, victims and major inconveniences.

"Just... friends." I sighed. The answer was accurate, technically, and that annoyed me. "Technically, one of them is a murderer, maybe. I'll talk to you later?"

Brianne looked unconvinced, but a chorus of barking from the building summoned her indoors. With a last look at both men, she offered me a two-finger salute and sauntered off toward the clinic. The sounds inside grew louder when she opened the door and then dimmed as it closed, her voice taking charge of the animals within.

A warm wet piece of sandpaper attacked my face, and I pulled Winnie closer, grounding myself in her soft floof. She nuzzled my neck, and I ruffled her ears before shutting the passenger side door and walking back around the car. Leonard was pressed against his window, Winnie's paws pushing against his thigh to eject him from her car.

Whether her opposition was to him personally or the prospect of sharing her seat didn't matter. He was getting enough help from me. Winnie was one battle he could handle on his own if personal space was important to him.

Back in the driver's seat, I rested my forehead on the steering wheel and tried to come up with a plan. Tried to piece together several seemingly unrelated problems and identify the common thread.

Winnie nudged me behind the ear, and I shuddered at the cold, wet nose. I raked my nails up her nose in response.

"Right, coffee," I agreed with her, though I wasn't certain that was what she was suggesting. Backing out, I pointed the car toward town, tapping my fingers against the steering wheel as I went, talking myself through the facts.

Jay Gitt owned poisonous subdivisions and liked to dig holes. Something had been buried beneath Eggplants and the new owner wanted it gone. Leonard had stabbed Jay's right-hand man, claimed to have called the police, but the body had been dumped by someone else and no one knew about it. Brad the Separatist had nearly blown himself up with explosives technically owned by Jay. Ferrah and Gertie were missing-ish. Whoever had them wanted me, and I still didn't have a complete picture of who or why.

I pulled up in front of Mo's and climbed out. The door behind me opened, and I startled when two men got out, accompanied by a Winnie. She let out a soft whimper, and I nodded, opening the rear door and picking up the kitten carrier, not wanting to leave them in the car. Levi had paused in his exit, reaching for the carrier. His body language was weary but hopeful, another shot of cute to counteract my annoyance and I allowed him to take the felines. Then I went into the back of the Jeep again and grabbed their bag of cat supplies in case Mo needed them.

Like a really lame parade, we trooped into Mary's Muffins and More while the bells on the door announced our arrival. Many of the tables were completely bare, including the day old section, the pumpkin spice section, and the turnovers. All that remained were a few slightly squished sourdough bread bowls, and I had a feeling they wouldn't be here much longer. My best human friend had her head angled down over an ancient laptop she was cursing.

"Stupid piece of..." Winnie popped up, licked her cheek and took one of the pet cupcakes from the tray on the counter. My friend patted my furry other half and waved in the direction of the door without looking up. "Coffee's fresh, syrups and sauces are..."

She glanced up and took a step back.

"Ooh! Hi!" She wiped her palms down her apron and eyed the two men I brought in with me. Since I'd seen them both, I went to the coffee machine and filled my cup while Winnie pilfered another puppy cupcake. I walked behind the counter and moved the tray out of her reach, confident Brianne had given her more than enough treats at the vet center.

"Mo, this is Levi and his uncle Leonard. They tried to abduct me and trade me for Leonard's wife and Mrs. Margot's twin. Now they want me to help them instead, even though Uncle Lenny is a murderer. Stupid males, this is Mary O' Connor, aka Mo, and she owns a lot of knives. Do not let the short one near any of said knives and monitor his hands." I drank several gulps of coffee and pointed to Levi. "Pay her for my coffee and I'll consider forgiving you."

Levi pulled out a twenty and handed it over.

"It was his idea. I was just going to ask her nicely."

They both looked at Leonard and his ears turned pink.

"While we're on the subject of you asking her nicely, did you really like her or were you just trying to get her to keep your uncle out of prison?" That was Mo, always asking the important questions. Doesn't matter that Uncle Leonard is a murderer or that two women might be in peril. Nope, she needed to make sure the man she spent the entire night trying to talk me into giving a shot wasn't just using me.

"I really like her," he answered, his ears also going pink. "Not many people I know are that loyal, honest, and fierce. Also, she knows how to pour coffee, has awesome stories, loves her crazy family and has a mean right hook."

I smiled at the last part and refilled my coffee. Twenty dollars at Mo's was more than two cups, but I was willing to let him over-tip her.

Especially since it was all tip, Mo never charged me for coffee.

"She's had a lot of practice. So, what're you going to do next?" She asked. I wasn't sure if she was asking me about my plan or Levi about his intentions, but I took the lead and pointed to the kittens.

"Could you watch Caramel and Coffee? Possibly also Leonard and Levi... I need to go down to the police station." Leonard and Levi started at once.

"You can't leave me!"

"Are you going to turn me in? What about the gals?"

"Woah, both of you, simmer down. I need to talk to an arrestee before he gets out of jail. Leonard, I'm not turning you in until you're unlikely to end up dead. Levi, dude, codependency is unattractive." I was already moving to the door as I talked, Winnie shadowing me while the men made hooked fish faces. "Be back later. Remember what I said about the knives!"

Mo waved goodbye, and I slipped out the door with my extra-large coffee.

Winnie jumped into the driver's door before me and proceeded between the seats to the rear while I started the car. We backed out, and I took the ten-minute drive to the Sweet Pea Police department, a series of three portable trailers and a partially underground brick building that housed prisoners.

When I'd first come home, I'd learned the front building was administration and the one behind and to the left was interrogation and the break room. I had no idea what was in the third trailer, but all three town law enforcement vehicles were parked in front of it. Originally, the town had had one cruiser and a marked bicycle, but Carla had bought an old Crown Vic and got the wraps updated, so Barney and Daniel didn't fight over the AC in the summer.

Ascending the ramp, I followed the click clack of Winnie's paws to the door of the administration building. The route was in front of several large windows, but I knocked on the brown metal door before turning the handle, anyway.

Inside, a cadet manned the front desk while our town's dispatcher, Jenny, popped her gum at the desk beside him. While the cadets rotated regularly, Jenny had been our town's one call taker since she graduated high school. The woman was the worst gossip and the absolute last person you wanted hearing about your most horrifying life moments, but no one else wanted the job.

So, she answered the calls, and the mayor crossed out the confidentiality section of the contract.

Carla poked her head out from the doorway facing them and shook her head.

"You're about five minutes too late." She gestured to the empty wooden bench with handcuff loops bolted into it. "Judge granted bail, and it was paid almost immediately. He's back out in the world."

"What? How? He didn't have a job, and his one asset is in evidence. Who'd underwrite a bond for him? Did they know he doesn't pay taxes?" I stared at the empty bench and the clipboard hanging above it. Brad Bosley's name was scribbled as "in" by Daniel Kirby. On the next line, he was marked as out with a ten-thousand-dollar payment made to the front desk.

"Did you accept the payment?" I asked the kid standing behind the desk. He nodded, looking between me and Winnie with a giant smile.

"Oh man! You know you two are famous?"

Sighing loudly, I just shook my head and looked at the desk. Carla came up beside me and filled in my question.

"I need to see the receipt, Mario."

He pulled out a spiral bound receipt book and showed us the last entry. A ten-thousand-dollar receipt to J. G. for one B. Bosley. In the memo line by the signature, he'd left a note.

You have two hours, or I finish what I started.

"Whoa! Who wrote that?" Mario asked, and I rolled my eyes. Wherever Carla got her cadets from, they were definitely not on a trajectory toward MENSA.

"I need the credit card receipt... or the check... how do people pay ten grand?" Carla shrugged, and I took a picture of the receipt book.

Mario opened the drawer and pulled out a credit card receipt and I looked at the name.

J. Gitt

"Damnit."

Chapter
Twenty-Four: UTL

We had a list of all the properties with active projects in Jay Gitt's portfolio. Only the proposed car dealership was in Carla's jurisdiction, with the "Old Huffleweiss" place straddling the line. The school wasn't technically anywhere near the police station, but the whole town was about 8 square miles, so proximity was relative.

In under ten minutes, we were staring at a freshly paved pad of asphalt.

"Was this like this yesterday?" I asked, and Carla just shook her head.

"No idea. I haven't been out this way," she responded. Pulling out her phone, she worked the keys, and I heard Daniel's voice through the line. "When were you last out by the school?"

She listened, staring at her shoes while Winnie and I walked on the new pavement. Dirt boot prints traversed the surface and the outer edge, mingling with tire tracks that hadn't quite stayed off the asphalt. One side had more traffic than all the others, and we gravitated that direction.

Besides a greater variety in tire widths in the dirt, there were also more shoe styles. In addition to the diamond cross pattern of work boots, there were running shoe treads, smooth stacked heel and what looked like either high heels or very uncomfortable loafers with no heel. Few of them went toward the newly poured surface, instead getting redirected to a far corner. I followed a grouping of prints and ended at a flattened-out piece of dirt at the very edge. Two squares sat about twenty feet apart, with an oval imprint in the center. There was a gap and then a crossbeam indent. Every foot along the rectangle, another indent went across, ending about forty feet later in another pair of squares.

I closed my eyes and tried to picture a huge, heavy rectangle.

Carla's voice drifted over with the sound of a passing truck.

"All that was out here yesterday was a deep hole and a cargo container?"

My eyes snapped open, and I eyed the area again. Superimposing over what is the image of two would-be subdivisions with a giant hole and a cargo shipping container.

"How did they move a cargo container and pave the lot in under twenty-four hours without anyone noticing?" I wondered aloud. The driveway was incomplete, and if this was to be an auto lot, there should be a building for the workers to make deals that weren't really deals at all. "What was so important that they needed car parking in place before everything else?"

All the expensive, plate-less cars came to mind, and I tried to reconcile that with this lot.

Except...

"Except I didn't see any when I went to Mo's..." I looked around again, like the cars could be hiding behind the scrub brush and tumbleweeds. I closed my eyes and tried to remember if I'd seen them leaving my apartment this morning... My stomach burbled and Winnie lifted her head, wiggling her eyebrows at me in alarm. "I was at Mo's this morning... Were they there last night?"

I couldn't remember.

Carla ended her call and came up beside me.

"What are you thinking?" She asked, and I scrunched my nose, sniffing the air for the first time. I took a long deep inhale and held it in my nose and throat like someone sampling wine. It was metallic, but sweet, like gasoline and gun oil with an undercurrent of...

"What do you smell?"

Carla's nostrils flared, her pupils sliding back and forth like a typewriter.

"What is that?" She looked from me back to the fresh asphalt.

"I think..." I swallowed and tried to put the idea into words. "I think Jay is dumping hazardous waste in his developments, paving over it and then putting in businesses. Could you demo this?"

"I could if I had a warrant, but I'd need more than your hunch to get one."

I walked across the asphalt and jumped up and down, stomping my boots and driving my heel into the surface.

Nothing happened.

"Did you think that would work?" Carla asked, and I shook my head. "We're down to an hour and forty-five. What do you want to do?"

I scrubbed my hands over my face and looked out across the farms and into downtown. The sun was slowly starting its descent, and I was pretty sure night would fall after our bomb builder detonated. There wasn't time to check all the properties, not when he had projects in so many of the surrounding communities that weren't complete but were also no longer in the planning stage.

Where would he go... where would you keep someone you tried to blow up?

The answer was Florida, obviously, but it was unlikely the developer would spring for airfare just to off someone. I scrolled back in my brain to my conversation with Jay and the moments before sitting in the planning office... he'd wanted it to look like an accident. The man would have to accidentally blow himself up, *but he'd left a warning in a police station?*

My temples throbbed, and I caught Carla checking her watch.

Watch, clock, *ten or you lose the space.*

"I think I know how to get the evidence you need. But... you'd be on your own to find Mr. Bosley and..." I hesitated to make my next comment. *What if I'm wrong?*

Ely's already in the morgue.

But Jay hadn't put him there.

"Check the Huffleweiss place and if he's not there, check the bars. Jay is a douche canoe, but he isn't stupid. He left a warning on an official police document. I think it's a distraction and the only place he could plant our prepper without rousing suspicion is with the boozehounds." My stomach flip-flopped, and I tried to quell the rising bile. If I was wrong... *I'm not wrong.* "Call in Mrs. Zuber and the rest of the good time geriatrics to help you look. Most of them are probably already in the bars anyway."

I whistled for Winnie and made fresh dust tracks on the asphalt to my car. My sister-in-law hadn't moved yet, and I shouted at her.

"Hey! What are you waiting for?"

She blinked at me and then pondered the ground for a moment. I continued walking to my car, backward with small running skips that scraped against the smooth surface. Finally, Chief Sharp raised her head and pulled out her phone.

"I'm getting too old for this crap." She started scrolling through her contacts, presumably to the letter Z, while I opened the car door for Winnie. "Turn on your damn GPS location sharing."

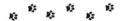

Tapping my fingers on the steering wheel, I stared out my windshield at the development where I encountered armed security. Instead of parking to the front, my car was on the far side of the six-business shopping center. Winnie and I had circled it twice, triple checking the two still in-business store fronts were locked down for the night before getting back in and waiting.

There was no way to know if we were right.

"What if it's the other one?" I asked Winnie. She wagged her tail and nudged me with her snout. "You're right. This is where the activity was. This is where..."

A hum filled the air and bright light poured from both sides of the building. We were completely sheltered in the shadows, but whatever was happening on the far side of the building needed light.

Lots of light.

My phone was still sharing my location with Carla, and I pulled it off the charger to stick in my pocket. Reaching under my passenger seat, I pulled out an orange ball and a collapsible baton. Stuffing them into my pants pockets, I got out as quietly as possible and Winnie clicked down into the parking lot with her nails. It was barely audible under the heavy buzzing coming from the generators that powered the lights, and I could only hope no one else could hear them.

The rear of the business park was a maze of dumpsters and loading docks. Most of the service entrances had been vandalized with graffiti or blunt instruments. We approached cautiously, using each indentation as cover to creep our way closer to the tarp clad fence. Step by step, we inched our way to the neighboring property, trying in vain not to inhale the scent of sun-cooked urine and stale beer.

At the last loading dock, we were about twenty feet from the fence and I stared at it. A shadow cast off the bottom, a long oval with a pole shaped hat... that started gliding sideways. More light filled the business park as the section of fence in front of us lurched into motion along a metal track, opening first to the width of a person and stopping at the width of a car.

A silhouette filled the space, its long shadow covering the distance between the fence opening and my hiding spot. Winnie's nose worked, her ears fully erect, and I tried my best to make up the sensory difference with my eyes. While her vision was lacking, mine was useless around corners.

If I poked my head out, it would be a target in a shooting gallery.

Staying here, however, meant I couldn't gather evidence.

Winnie's body rumbled beside me with a growl that shook our metal dumpster shield. Before I could ask her what the problem was, a shotgun ratcheted behind me and jammed into the base of my spine.

"Get that animal under control or say goodbye," a heavy masculine voice bellowed from behind me, and I gave Winnie a look.

"Leave it."

She sneezed at me and lifted her lip.

"Leave it."

The gun barrel jabbed harder into my lumbar spine and a vaguely familiar voice ordered us forward.

"Move, now!"

Taking hold of Winnie's collar, I walked out from the loading dock and into the blinding light of the generator powered lamps. Behind us, the gunman shuffled forward while we got closer and closer to the figure at the gate.

"Hurry it up!" She snapped, and the gunman tried to jab me in the back with the gun, but my vertebrae had had enough. I dodged left, taking Winnie into his path so he'd trip over her body.

Detective Duncan fumbled over my best friend and landed on top of a 12-gauge shotgun, fingers crushed against the trigger, and the gun exploded into the brick wall behind us. I let go of Winnie's collar, leapt over Duncan's form, and tried to grab the barrel.

The hot metal singed my palm, and I stifled a scream as I tried to tug it out from under the too-heavy man.

"Stop, or you can say goodbye to your dog."

The female shadow had hold of Winnie's collar. Dropping the gun barrel, I shielded my eyes with one hand and held up the other in surrender. It took several seconds for the bursts of light to clear before I could finally make out the person threatening my best friend.

Jessica Bolton was holding a semi-automatic, and she had it trained on Winnie.

I blinked again, and Leonard stepped out from behind her, his gun pointed at me.

Chapter Twenty-Five: Lucy in the Sky

"You rat bastard!" I snapped, preparing to launch forward until I remembered I wasn't the only one with a gun trained on me. Winnie whimpered slightly, and I checked my anger. "Where is Mo?"

"Ms. O'Connor's male friend returned early. When I left her, she was doing the dance with no pants." For the first time I noticed the accent, subtly lurking beneath his self-assured veneer of masculinity. "Levi stepped out to take a call, and I just... walked away."

He'd been the man arguing in the parking structure.

"Can I have Winnie back now?" I asked, my hands still raised awkwardly. Behind me, I heard Duncan getting to his feet. If he jammed the gun in my spine again, I was going to take the shotgun and shove it somewhere incredibly uncomfortable.

For him.

"You can have her back once you have these on," Mrs. Bolton held out a pair of flexicuffs. I took several brisk steps toward her, sliding my hands into the plastic and using my teeth to tighten the pull tabs. I stared up at the stars, tracing the diamond twinkles and looking for dinosaur skeletons, biting down on the plastic and tugging.

Just enough to look like I can't get out.

When I couldn't find any dinosaurs, I remembered that Lucy was a human skeleton named after a Beatles song played on repeat when she was found.

I stopped looking up then. If I wanted to see people, there were plenty right here.

"What were you doing at the school today, Cynthia?" Jessica asked conversationally, looping the leather leash over my upright thumbs and pulling them backward to over-tax the tendons. Sharp licks of pain ran up my arms, but I kept my face neutral and tried to yawn at the attempted violence. "Trying to out me?"

Duncan came up behind me and slammed the butt of his shotgun into my face. Crunching cartilage in my nose was the soundtrack of my mouth, filling with blood that dripped from the corners of my mouth.

I spat it out onto his shoes.

"You hit like a bitch," my nasally, fluid filled voice was unintelligible. Leonard took hold of my flexicuffs and dragged me across the prepped land. We skirted the edge of the excavated ditch, Leonard's leather sandals at odds with Duncan's dress shoes and Bolton's FMPs.

Winnie's paw prints barely left an impression, and neither did my sneakers, as we were marched to the metal cargo container. The hinge creaked, metal latches screeching against one another as Duncan heaved against the lever. Another wail accompanied the door swing, then I was hit with the smell.

Human feces and urine mixed with BO, the light shining in on a pissed off Gertie and a filthy woman with hollowed cheeks and matted hair.

"Get in," Duncan growled, and I raised an eyebrow at him. "No."

It wasn't my best play, but I got the impression that once someone went into the container, they didn't come out again. Winnie and I would not go down in a metal prison. It was unacceptable. We did not survive Florida to be suffocated to death in a shipping container.

"You can't tell me no!" Duncan whined, an overgrown child in grown-ups clothing. "I have a gun!"

"Ask me if I care?" I got in his face, my belly pressing into his while I towered above him. Using my bound hands, I pushed the shotgun rounds out of the elastic sling that held them against the stock. Each one that slid out, I allowed to glide into the sleeve of my shirt. Duncan's face was turning purple and red, toxic masculinity keeping him from backing up while I stared down at him.

"Get in the damn container!" He cross-checked me in the chest, Winnie letting out a low snarl that earned her the barrel of Leonard's revolver aimed at her chest. Duncan slammed the stock into my sternum and stole my air while my fingers gripped the hem of my long-sleeve top to hold the shells in.

We won't get out unless we go in.

"OK! Geeze!" I raised my bound hands and walked into the container with the other women. Using the massive flood lighting, I took stock of the container's contents and felt my chest constrict. Ferrah, it had to be her, had been in here a long time. The overflowing hardware store bucket filled with waste was only the tip of the inhumane conditions.

I regretted not shooting Leonard when I had the chance.

Toward the back were construction supplies. Miscellaneous left-over materials and a handful of tools were all I could catalog before the door slammed shut and the metal brace screeched into place. It was immediately dark, nothing penetrating the foul space around us.

"Ferrah?" I whispered, and a small whimper was all that emerged from her hunched form.

"What's your plan, Cynthia? I didn't live this long to die like this." Gertie's voice barely penetrated the rush of blood pounding in my ears as I discovered I might be claustrophobic.

"I need a second..." I gasped as slowly as possible and tried to keep my inhale a mouth-only deal. Moving slowly, I felt into the nothing until my fingers touched metal. I pressed my palm flat on the wall, and then my back, until I could sit on the floor. Winnie was immediately beside me, licking my face.

Stroking along her cheek, I dropped the shells out of my sleeve and arranged them by feeling in front of me. Winnie sniffed each one and then nudged my left my left pocket.

I ignored her while I tried to picture the inside of a shotgun shell.

Winnie head-butted my leg again and I nudged her to the side, grabbing the keys still looped to my pants. Beneath them, my cellphone warmed my leg, and I pulled it out, the light from the screen glaringly bright in the dark space.

"Call for help?" Gertie asked, but I shook my head, showing her the display.

"No bars. But I'll send a message and hope it gets enough service to send at some point," I spoke while typing out a quick plea for help to Carla, summarizing the criminals present and hoping that if I died, she'd avenge me hard.

Winnie head-butted my leg more forcefully and I let out a frustrated sigh.

"You want the ball?" I stuffed my hand in my pocket and grabbed a small brick the size of a pack of gum. She nudged it again, and it fell into the light.

C4... I'd spent the whole day with C4 in my pocket.

I took C4 to a school.

Nausea rose, but I pushed it back while I grabbed her ball from my other pocket along with the detonator. I stared at the pieces in front of me, the beginnings of an idea starting to take shape.

I shined my light around the rest of the container, careful not to point it at Ferrah or her bucket as a common courtesy.

Climbing through the construction debris, I found bits of wood, nails, drywall, housing insulation and cans of varnish. Prying off the lids, the cans were mostly empty, but there was still a little liquid. I dragged those over to my collection of supplies, along with the nails and the wall insulation.

"What are you doing?" Gertie whispered, but her voice echoed off the interior of the container.

"Wishing I smoked, so I'd have a lighter," I mumbled. A metallic click bounced around and then a stream of bright blue and orange flame was floating beside me. "How?"

"Might have noticed, they don't frisk us," she scoffed, and I accepted the lighter. Stuffing the insulation into the can, I used it to soak up the varnish and flipped it varnish side up, stuffing it back into the can. The pocketknife on my keys wasn't very sharp, but it cut through the plastic surrounding the little ball-bearing pellets in the shotgun round. Careful not to cut below the wad, I dumped all the scattershot onto the varnished insulation along with the nails.

Then I did it with two more rounds and sealed the can. Opening another can, I soaked another piece of insulation in varnish. Taking two wood planks, I made a stand for my can and circled the can with the gunpowder, placing the soaked insulation on one end of the plank. Reassembling the landmine, I sacrificed my ponytail holder to wrap it around Winnie's ball and place it in the pocket with the C4. A last resort idea I wasn't inclined to use.

"Ferrah, I need to move you," I whispered, carefully cradling her diminished form and carrying it halfway down the enclosed chamber. Using the other cans, I stacked them up with the drywall and a few pieces of particleboard.

Praying the wall was enough, I got Gertie behind the wall and walked up to my makeshift giant shotgun shell filled with nails. Crouching beside it, I tried to re-confirm the physics, but there was no way to know if this would work.

Outside, an oversized vehicle backed up, the steady beeping unnerving in the giant metal tuning fork. Inhaling slowly, I flicked open the lighter and lowered it to the cellulose fill insulation, grateful these guys were cheap.

It took a second to catch, but I flicked the lighter closed and ran back to our shelter. The insulation reached the gunpowder with a sizzle, and the room heated. Sizzling gunpowder turned into brighter flames, the wood planks catching next, heating the can further and more steadily.

Steam started coming from the can and I grabbed the two other women, hunkering down to stay low to the ground, covering Winnie with my body when the first shot slammed into the side of the can.

Then another.

The first round to shoot from the side pinged off the metal wall, followed by another, until the lid exploded off the can and metal shots were bouncing off every wall with the occasional impaling nail. Outside, someone screamed. The container door lurched, heavy footsteps and vehicles stampeding around. Taking Ferrah under the arm, I hauled her up, hand on Winnie's collar. I gripped the drywall and looked at Mrs. Margot, who did the same.

Using the drywall as a shield, we charged forward at first light.

A wet slap, a male screech, and we charged out over the fallen conspirator. My can continued spewing rounds, and I kept us running away toward the back wall when burning pain ripped through the back of my pants, warm blood dripped down my leg.

I lost my grip on the wall, stumbling forward and taking the other women with me. We crashed into the ground at the feet of a pair of dress shoes.

"Do you have any idea what you did?" Jay asked, kicking out a shoe that connected with my jaw. Head snapping back, his kick was the tipping point to send me flat backed onto the drywall, my sticky blood soaking into the surface through my sweatshirt skirt. Winnie snarled, her teeth snapping his direction.

"Winnie, no!" I called to her, trying to drag her back and cover her with my body where I landed facedown. A gun hammer pulled back, and a shot exploded into the sudden silence.

Chapter Twenty-Six: Unhappy Marriages

J ay's chest jerked back, red pools blossoming beyond the edges of my vision in his shoulder. The casual suit over a blue button down turned a deep burgundy while his mouth moved soundlessly. Eyes wide, his body crumbled in slow motion to land beside me with an O of surprise forever on his lips.

A scream cut through the night, bouncing off the solid boundaries surrounding us.

"What did you do?!"

To my left, Ferrah and Gertie huddled, both appearing free of blood.

Small favors.

Stilettos briskly crunched the gravel beside me. I turned my head to look at Mrs. Bolton, her arm held out, leveling the black gun at the man choking on his own blood. Gurgling gulps of air struggled through his lips, the least arrogant the man had ever looked.

"Why?" He wheezed and Jessica just shook her head. "I did everything you asked."

Construction equipment continued to fill the air with diesel fumes and engine rumbles. Jay's words strangled in the continuing work behind us. Pushing up onto my elbows, I flopped to the side like a beached whale, carefully avoiding the reassembled landmine in my left pocket. Three dump trucks sat backed up to the hole, slowly pouring concrete and a thick black sludge that reminded me of recycled tires into the cavernous rectangle. A half-dozen people in high-vis vests and hard hats circled the trucks, adjusting the spouts for even distribution.

Looking anywhere but at us.

The irony that they were concerned with workplace safety attire after watching people break out of a freight container, then a man getting shot, escaped them... Or they always wore reflective, neon clothing while committing crimes.

Duncan remained on the ground in front of the container, potentially bleeding, Ferrah and Gertie joining me to stare at Mrs. Jessica Bolton and her gun.

Waiting to hear why she shot the developer.

"I did the Lord's work. Do you think He thought you were worthy to run this operation?"

"But..."

"You were a lousy husband. I told you to line the holes, but you cut as many corners in business as you did in the bedroom. I've been solely responsible for my own orgasms for a decade, serving penance for the kids you poisoned because you can't listen!" She fired a round into his other shoulder. "I told you to leave the drunk alone and instead you gave him explosives linked to OUR business because you wanted it. You always want more but you never think of the consequences of your actions. Never think what God would want, and now! Now you've made me a sinner. I told you. Leonard told you. Now the cops are interested, do-gooders like this bitch are sniffing around, and all because you didn't pay attention in fourth grade earth science! Couldn't learn to play with the toys you have. Now I have to beg forgiveness from the Lord for allowing you to carry on as you have. For not acting sooner. For seeking comfort in the arms of another."

Jessica shot him in the leg, an ethereal howl bouncing off the brick wall. The gun woman remained unmoved, gliding forward to stand over him, his pride pulling him up off the ground with what little strength he had left. His dark hair caked in dirt and blood clung to his neck, his eyes pleading with the woman in front of him for a second chance.

"But the worst part, the very worst offense you committed, was being too damn stupid to see that you'd get way more money blackmailing the companies you sold chemical dump space to after they dumped it. These corporations saved millions circumventing the EPA, getting tax cuts and tax breaks for being green, but you didn't have the balls to cash in. You think too small, like your dick," she concluded and put a bullet in his head at point blank range, the sound carrying for what felt like miles in the expanding quiet. Machines shut off behind us, my vantage showing the workers stepping away but still not looking over here. "The Lord giveth, but it was time I taketh away."

Ferrah dry heaved beside me, Gertie holding back her hair, while I watched the wall behind Jay get painted by the contents of his skull.

Mrs. Bolton was panting, sweat beading on her face as she spun around without seeing. A manic satisfaction warred with personal horror until Leonard sauntered over. His hand slid around her waist and pulled her in for a sloppy kiss with too much tongue.

"I love it when you let out your inner wild woman," he purred. Ferrah dry heaved again, calling attention in our direction. Both murderers looked over at the group and the detective's unmoving body. "I think we'll need to buy another cop, babe. But you have avenged the pious by removing the sin."

"Plenty more where he came from!" Her voice was too high, a braying call that carried uncertainty and fear. "We need to get this cleaned up before the deliveries arrive."

Leonard nodded and looked at his wife while I still tried to work through the made-up bible babble.

"Sorry, babe, guess you weren't the forever type." He winked, and I slid my hand into the pocket on my thigh, gripping the orange dog ball and sliding a finger under the hair tie to wrap it around the palm sized chunk of explosives. Far off in the distance, I thought I could hear sirens, but Leonard was in possession of Jessica's gun, hand steady as he pointed it toward the older women.

Gripping Winnie's collar, I stood up on shaky legs with the ball in my hand, along with my baton. Two guns swung my way, confused when I turned toward the mixing trucks and chucked it as hard as I could, following through to whip out the asp.

Leonard was close enough that the same flick that telescoped out the baton brought it down on his arm. The gun fell, and I swung it up toward his face. He angled back, exposing his neck, at the first plastic thunk of the ball bouncing off hard-packed dirt.

Damn-it physics, I thought the weighted side always landed down...

I swung again, catching him in the chest and dropping to the ground to deliver a hit to his knee. My legs wobbled, but I kept my feet.

Another howl cut through the night and the ball cast a shadow as it arced downward again. Jessica seemed to come to, stumbling in her impractical shoes, when the ball landed with a clink against the side of a truck.

"Grab her!" I said to Gertie and pulled Winnie over, taking Ferrah's other arm and hauling her up between us. The pressure switch pinged off, releasing the charge. A fireball erupted at the base of the truck, catching the petroleum in the mix to set the whole excavation site ablaze.

Heat clawed at my back as a secondary explosion rained small pieces of truck onto the ground. Gertie was stumbling and Ferrah's feet could no longer hold her. I tried to angle us toward the shelter of the container while fighting the sharp stabs of dirt violating my open gunshot wound.

"Take Winnie!" I ordered, passing the leash to Gertie and pulling Ferrah onto my back like a monkey. Without the added weight, Gertie picked up the pace, and I glanced back to see flames crawling up the pour spout of the second truck.

"Faster!" I shouted, limping more quickly and knowing that we couldn't outrun it if the third truck went. "Use the shipping container as a shield!"

"Cyn!" A voice cut through the smoke, and I tried to go that direction, but my leg collapsed and I took the impact on my chest to spare my passenger. "Cyn!"

Ferrah moved above me. Winnie licked my face but I couldn't get back up. Gertie's face floated in my periphery, bathed in red and flames.

"Try to get Ferrah and Winnie out!" I told her, crawling along the dirt and knowing it wasn't fast enough. "You need to tell the—"

Carla appeared with Officer Stead and people in alphabet soup suits—black and government approved. As soon as Gertie and Ferrah were with them, I closed my eyes and gave into the pain, letting my body float away on a river of agony.

Chapter Twenty-Seven: Staycation

"**C**an I go home now?" I asked an orderly who just smirked at me while he continued his rounds. His name escaped me, but I was pretty sure he'd unglued my feet from this very floor... or another one. All the VA Hospital floors looked the same, and I'd experienced some level of embarrassment on all of them.

"You need to stop begging people to let you out," Seth muttered, and I glared at him. "First of all, it's Sunday and your ass would be here anyway. Second, your ass has a bullet hole in it and your pants have a hole, so at least wait until you get new pants."

"No, Sethany, it has a bullet indent. They sewed the hole closed," I stuck my tongue out at my brother, and he chuckled. He had a point about the pants, but no way would I tell him. "This place sucks. There are no dogs. The coffee tastes like they made two pots with a single bean, and the nurses keep laughing at me!"

On cue, a set of green scrubs in rubber shoes looked in the window at me and snickered. It wasn't obvious what exactly happened in the past 30 hours to warrant this level of amusement, but I had been heavily drugged. The snippets of video no one would show me indicated I might have mooned people and asked them to kiss my booboo.

There were also grippy hospital socks taped over my hands.

You are apparently not supposed to scratch gun wounds, stitches, your face or the face of your loved ones on hospital property.

"You always said you wanted a hospital vacation. People bring you food, let you stay in bed all day, and you never have to take off your PJs. Sit back and enjoy it!"

"I can't sit back!" I gestured to my barely covered butt in the rear-opening hospital gown. It was facing the wall, but occasionally I was flipped to the other side to prevent bedsores and it faced the window for all passersby to see. There was laying, there was standing, but there was no sitting. "You know they have cushioned ramps that blockade the other half of my bed so that I don't roll onto my back?"

"Well... you carried a person who hadn't bathed in a week on your back over an open wound. Now you know that causes infections, don't you?" My brother just kept smiling and then tapped his index finger on my nose. "Boop!"

"I hate you."

"Is that any way to talk to your favorite brother, who arranged a surprise for you?" He was using a quasi-baby voice I would punch him for if I wasn't mooning the wall with socks on my hands. Since he was my only brother, it wasn't hard for him to get the title of favorite. I, on the other hand, was the youngest of his three sisters and it didn't take a mathematician to project the odds were not in favor of the ranking being returned.

"If the surprise is Sylvia covered in vomit because she was cleaning it up for being a bully who tormented a kid into drawing her death, fine. If It's Sylvia in any other capacity, I would rather take another bullet to the butt."

"Scattershot," he corrected.

"I know what it was! I put it in the can!" I tried to roll over in annoyance to stop looking at him, but my cushioned prison prevented it. The clock on the wall said it had been fifteen minutes since I'd been turned like a pig on a spit. I wouldn't be rotated again for another 45 minutes. "Why are you deriving so much joy from my suffering?"

"Yeah, what's up with that?" Carla asked, walking into the room holding Winnie's leash. The dog was freshly groomed, and her tail knocked excitedly into the metal tray beside my bed. With a graceful leap, she was on the bed in front of me, wedging all ninety pounds of herself in the six inches of space between my chest and the bed's guardrail. Burying my nose into her fur, I slung my arm around the tan body of my best friend and held tight.

"Hi girl," I whispered, wiping a tear onto her neck. "I was worried about you."

Seth and Carla bickered, but I tuned them out to listen to Winnie's steady heartbeat. It eased my mind, like the soft rhythm of a metronome. My eyes drooped.

"You can't sleep yet," Carla interrupted, and I looked at her. Standing beside her was a woman with purple streaked hair and a nose ring, her curves and tattoos on full display in leggings and a Three Days Grace tank top. "Sorry, I got the basics from Ferrah and Mrs. Margot, but there are a few questions I need answers to, and Dhalia wants to talk to you."

She gestured to the woman beside her.

"Hi, nice to finally meet you. Dhalia Margot, though I think you know me as Aunt Glen's niece?"

"You're the cracker?" I asked, peeling my eyes wide. "And the whole Eggplant thing?"

She chuckled softly and answered, "Yeah. Though I hear you find my art skills lacking. I'd be offended, but I got the same feedback from all the others. I wanted to give you this."

She held out a laminated card to me, and I took it in my sock-covered hands.

"You know I'll never use this, right?" I asked her, staring at the lifetime pass into the male strip club.

"It comes with free drinks and as many guests as you want? Say... a bachelorette party?"

"OK, I... might use this. Is Chris..." She interrupted me with a finger to her lips and leaned in closer.

"His browser history says yes."

I smiled.

"K," I said, looking at the clear plastic card poking out of my taped-on socks. I knew it was connected to the IV in the back of my hand, but I wondered if it was actually spraying skin cells in there because I'd lost my hand and the VA had figured out how to regrow them. "I'm going to miss these drugs."

"I bet. I brought you another couple of guests, but they don't seem to want cats in here," she gestured over her shoulder, and I peeked around her to see Elvis and Elisa, each clutching one of the kittens. Caramel and Coffee were contentedly sleeping in their arms and I smiled. "Stella thought since their new place allowed pets and Elvis is super into cats, they could adopt them. Mo agreed, but they wanted to say goodbye. You're welcome to visit."

"I think that's the perfect place for them," I smiled, waving at the little orange kitten whose paw was moving under Elvis's direction. Elise checked her watch and looked pained. I gestured for them to go on and did the universal one thumb typing gesture to signify my intention to text. She smiled and waggled her phone back with the little black kitten in her other hand, moving away from the room. "Where is the new place? What about the other kids?"

"They'll all be moving into my building," Dhalia answered, and I blinked at her.

"You can't let kids sleep in a strip club!" I hissed, and she laughed.

"No, I own a few parcels and the one they're all moving to just finished being built. Everyone will move in today and the old complex is being quarantined. The EPA will do a full scale environmental hazard clean-up."

I nodded and patted my hand.

"I'll let Carla take over so you can get some rest. Hope to see you at the club soon." She winked and disappeared. My sister-in-law looked after Mrs. Margot's niece and just shook her head.

"So... what questions have you got for me?" I asked, letting my eyes slide closed. Carla set my member card on the metal tray and I heard her notebook flip open.

"We got the warrant to dig up the parking lot, and it was filled with corporate marked toxic waste. As was the New Classic Apartment complex, where so many of Stella's students live, which you know from Dhalia. They are in treatment with poison control experienced doctors and it's likely they'll recover. The clean-up for the old site will take decades, but eventually the soil should be clean."

"So far none of that's a question," I yawned, and Winnie joined me, her throat squeaking at the end.

"How did the cement trucks full of rubber fill blow up?"

"Remember that 5th bomb?" I answered her question with a question. My eyes were closed again so I couldn't see her face, but I hoped it was remembering. "I found it in my pocket. Great for the emergency, but pretty sure I shouldn't have had it at Stella's school. Do you know what Dhalia found under her parking lot?"

It seemed important to move on from my destruction of evidence as quickly as possible.

"It was drugs. They were in Duncan's garage. Not that we can charge him, he didn't make it." Her notebook pages ruffled, but I didn't detect a single trace of regret.

"Thanks for bringing me Winnie," I said into the silence, and I heard her smile.

"We didn't expect it would be so hard to get Winnie in. She's here all the damn time, but you look ten percent better just because she's here. Anyway, Leonard confessed to murdering Ely Mollusk. I guess Ely was trying to back out of their arrangement after seeing the drugs and Leonard was already planning his new life with Jay's wife. Ferrah filed for divorce, not that she needed to. Gertie's daughter took care to make it look like their marriage was never official and everything is in the name Ferrah Lovelace... I'll pretend I don't know that if you share your Eggplants pass."

Nodding, I wondered if she'd ever be the same. If Ferrah and Gertie could live in that house, or close their eyes without seeing Jay's lifeless body. Gertie seemed tough, but I didn't know about Ferrah. I didn't know if she had the strength, but if she could survive being in the container, I might be underestimating her. Despite what I'd been through, I wasn't sure if I could've survived what she did.

I was barely making it in the hospital.

"Brad Bosley was drunk as a skunk in a bar, you were right," her words came with more rustling of paper. I was getting a notebook summary of the events I'd experienced. It was nice to know how things shook out, but now that I had Winnie, I just wanted to sleep.

"And you have one more visitor." She cleared her throat, and I peeked out of one eye at a very large rainbow unicorn plushie. It was pressed under the plaid-sleeved arm of a man clutching two cold brews with an orange tint, a coffee mug slung on his pinkie.

"Coffee?" I squealed and the cold brew came closer. Thanks to the grippers on my sock hands, I took the cup and started gulping from the straw like my life depended on it. Plaid arms deposited the second cup onto my hospital desk with the new mug, and the unicorn on the far side of my bed.

"Levi?" I asked around the plastic straw. Dark circles rimmed his eyes, the whites streaked with red and bloodshot. He had minor bruising on his cheek and a cut lip, but his expression was pure guilt and a touch of affection.

I glanced at the mug he'd brought me. It had a German Shepherd with a unicorn horn and rainbow mane that said *Dog Hair and Coffee are Fluffing Magical.*

"I'm sorry," he whispered. "I... I wanted to believe."

I patted his hand with my stockinged IV arm. His apology wasn't necessary, but I knew how he felt. It was like when he saw my mom wearing leather whipping my dad: technically not my fault, but when it's your family... You'll always feel responsible for the damage caused by people you're related to.

"What happened to your face? Leonard said you and Mo were distracted so he was able to sneak away? Though, now that I say that out loud, I'm not sure why I believed it." My attempt at a topic change put another shadow on his features, and I cursed my inability to talk with this man. One day, I would figure out what my mouth tasted like without my foot in it.

"Mo's... boyfriend? Chris walked in while she had us in her home. He freaked, thinking I had broken in while she was in the shower... because she was in the shower. And I was standing in her kitchen with a knife cutting up veggies for minestrone." I stifled a laugh, but it slipped out as a snort, and he cracked a small smile. "She came out in a towel and started jumping on him to stop hitting me. He got distracted when she lost her towel and I don't know if she needed to explain, but they got busy and I lowered the soup to simmer, added the rest of the ingredients and left."

"I'm sorry about them. They're... just sorry." My face was stretched in a wide smile, and I don't think I looked sorry at all. Levi crouched next to the bed, bringing a chair over with his foot to sit at my eye level. Our faces were very close together again, the body of my best friend the only thing preventing our faces from touching. "Hi."

It came out a little breathy.

"Hi. We got off to a weird start."

"I'm a weird start," I answered and then drank more coffee.

"I like you, but I didn't handle it well. Do you think... could we start over?"

I shook my head and put the empty cup down, taking up the second one.

"No do-overs. Own the weirdness or be normal somewhere else." I started drinking, and he smiled, leaning in to kiss me even though I had a straw in my mouth. "But before we can date, I have to ask you a very important question."

His eyebrows raised, hand gesturing for me to bring it.

"Now that you've demonstrated that you know the importance of unicorns, dog hair, and coffee... How do you feel about paintball and margaritas?"

About the Author

E. N. Crane is a fiction author writing humorous mysteries with plus-sized female leads and their furry friends. She is one of two authors under the Perry Dog Publishing Imprint, a one woman, two dog operation in Idaho... for now. My dogs are Perry and Padfoot, the furry beasts shown above. They are well-loved character inspiration in all things written and business.

If you are interested in joining my newsletter, please subscribe here: https://e-n-crane_perrydogpublishing.ck.page/578ed9ab 37or on my website, PerryDogPublishing.com

You will receive A Bite in Afghanistan, the prequel to the Sharp Investigations Series, as a thank-you for joining. I only have one newsletter for mental health reasons, so both romance and mystery are on there! If you only want one in your inbox, follow

Perry Dog Publishing on all socials to stay on top of the latest news... and pet pics.

Made in the USA
Las Vegas, NV
10 December 2024

13817121R00179